The Fifth Stage

BLUE FEATHER BOOKS, LTD.

The Fifth Stage

A BLUE FEATHER BOOK

by

Margaret A. Helms

THE FIFTH STAGE

Cover design by Ann Phillips

A Blue Feather Book
Published by Blue Feather Books, Ltd.
P.O. Box 5867
Atlanta, GA 31107-5967

www.bluefeatherbooks.com

ISBN: 0-9770318-7-X

First edition: 2003
Second printing: 2003
Second edition: March, 2007

Printed in the United States of America and in the United Kingdom.

CHAPTER 1

I was born two months before my eighteenth birthday. Sounds silly, but that's how it felt at the time.

On a rainy October afternoon, what seemed like an innocent conversation twisted into an incident that shattered my hazy existence and blinded me with the truth—a painful truth at the time, and a sometimes infuriating fact even now.

Until that day I had lived a textbook childhood, but what else would you expect from a girl delivered in the sixties who grew up in a sleepy mid-South town that barely managed its own ZIP code? Franklin was the kind of place where people left their car windows rolled down at night, and most folks didn't lock their front door because they couldn't remember where they hid the key.

Franklinites were in a self-induced trance, perhaps a time warp. They were happy to have one movie theater, two red lights, and four town cops. Life seemed simpler that way. In a time when disco sucked and kids in far-off places like Seattle and New York were piercing their ears with safety pins and snorting cocaine, the most incorrigible teenagers in Franklin were still smoking homegrown weed and hurling rotten eggs at the high school principal's house.

My family was placid, even by Franklin standards. Our house was like any other in town, no better, no worse—red brick with white painted eaves and shutters. Like most homes of that time, the family room centered around a nineteen-inch color TV. Our set had vertical control problems and a glitch in the picture tube that made *Bonanza's* Lorne Greene look nine feet tall as he rode his trusty steed across an eggplant-colored prairie.

My dad used to say he didn't get his first remote control television until 1985, but if he were alive today, I'd beg to differ. In our house, I was the remote. From the time I was big enough to reach the dial, I'd stand for what seemed like hours, turning the big silver channel changer to one station, then the next while Dad reclined in his easy chair, directing me with "Okay, go on, next, go back." If we'd had more than

1

four channels, I would've been in prison for murder by my twelfth birthday.

Other than the occasional channel conflict, we got along pretty well. A fine, upstanding family, the folks around town called us. Mom's full-time job was keeping house and raising my brother, Robert, and me. Dad went to work every morning in a coat and tie and came home each evening to a warm dinner. Four more kids and a live-in maid and we would have been a regular Brady Bunch.

Robert was the ultimate example of a Brady boy: considerate and compassionate, but likely to break a vase once in a while. I didn't feel like a Brady girl though—not perfect like Marsha, a bit more unsettled than Jan, and never a cute, lispy cherub like Cindy.

With barely two years between us, my brother and I shared our mother's steel-gray eyes and abundant blonde hair, the only remaining and slightly-diluted traits of a Swedish ancestor long buried beneath our mongrelized family tree.

"I'd swear them two was twins," the waitress at Woolworth's lunch counter would whine between gum-pops. "Why, they're the spittin' image of you, Maureen."

Mom would pay for our milkshakes and thank her for the compliment, but Robert saw red at the comparison. He couldn't stand that I was nearly as tall as him and could win two of three falls in our daily wrestling contests. After a while, he started calling the waitress Babbling Betty, but I liked her. Her friendly eyes reminded me of Miss Ann, our Sunday School teacher—a trashy, trailer-park version with a half-smoked Lucky dangling from her lips, but Miss Ann nonetheless.

In our earliest years, Robert and I were constant companions. We would run barefoot through dew-covered grass, chase lightning bugs to the point of exhaustion, and tumble into Dad's ratty old hammock. We'd giggle and tickle each other breathless and finally succumb to weariness and the muggy summer heat and allow the man in the moon to lull us to sleep.

Eventually, Mom's voice would come booming out the back door. "Robert! Claire! You can't sleep out there all night. Go brush your teeth and get ready for bed." We'd stumble to the bathroom, and Mom would stand over us like a vulture over roadkill as we washed behind our ears. "My children won't go around nasty," she'd say, making certain we did a proper job. "People will think I don't take care of you."

Then she'd march us to our rooms and tuck us in with a kiss. Even now I can't go to bed without washing behind my ears and brushing my teeth.

In later years, Mom often found us in Robert's room with Fleetwood Mac, Kiss, or Foreigner albums blaring as my brother filled me in on the intricacies of being a teenager. We'd sit by his stereo while he shared a gold mine of adolescent wisdom, deftly guiding me through the roughest parts of life. He cautioned me about Mrs. Johnson, the worst algebra teacher to ever touch a chalkboard, warned me to never eat pinto beans in the high school cafeteria, and told me to always stay clear of the kids who hung out in the smoking zone.

But days like those have a way of sneaking past you, and before you know it, the mystical years are gone. By that October afternoon, Robert had been away at college for two years. There was no one for me to turn to, no one to confide in, but I'm not sure even my brother could've helped me with my quandary.

It wasn't like I didn't suspect something. I was innocent and sheltered maybe, but not stupid. Actually, by the time I turned seventeen, I was beginning to wonder about myself. Something didn't seem right. I was preparing for my senior year in high school and, to my chagrin, hadn't developed the desire to date boys. I hadn't experienced the white-hot flash of hormones my girlfriends so vividly described and couldn't work up a giggle-fit about the captain of the football team if my life depended on it. I never sneaked out for a late-night cruise to lovers' lane with a guy from Lit class and had refused at least five invitations to join the gang for a skinny-dip in Johnson's pond. For some reason, I didn't have the desire to wallow around with some guy like a couple of night crawlers in a bait bucket.

That afternoon in October, I found out why.

CHAPTER 2

I'm on the verge of forty now, and memories of my youth are starting to haunt me. Long-discarded events tiptoe around my brain, reminding me of where I've been and what I've done, but those recollections don't feel like warm sentiments to cherish in my approaching middle age. They are too vivid, too real.

It's as though I'm going through the maze of discovery again and finding the second time around more difficult than the first. This time I'm staring middle age right in the face, single for the first time in two decades, and more apprehensive about my future than I was at seventeen. It's only a thirty-minute drive to my hometown, but the person I used to be seems a million miles away.

To anyone who doesn't know my story, I might appear to be the picture of success. I have a closet full of designer labels, there's plenty of cash in my wallet, and my investment portfolio befits someone twenty years my senior. But when I'm alone at night and I look into my bathroom mirror, the eyes staring back at me seem jaded, the blonde hair falling around my shoulders is showing signs of gray, and the lines around my lips look deeper every day. What happened to the sneaker-clad kid with the sparkly eyes and fair skin, the girl who didn't have two cents to rub together? That kid had guts. I'm not sure I do.

It seems my life has degenerated into a series of rituals. I get up. I go to work. I go home. At first the pattern kept me grounded, it made those first days alone easier to get through. But the days turned to weeks, the weeks to months, and so on, till there was so little variation that I could operate blindfolded. But over the past few months, I've made a slight modification to my routine. I've taken to dining at a local restaurant three or four nights a week.

Choppy's is one of those middle-of-the-road eateries—not fancy, but above average. You can get a huge salad, a burger, or a decent steak and won't feel like you've been robbed afterwards. The restaurant is pretty common in appearance. There's an elevated bar area tucked into the far corner, flanked on two sides by rugged brick walls and on the third by a row of high-backed booths. Someone did put some original thought into the placement of the main dining tables. They're far enough apart to afford private conversation, but close enough together to maximize seating. All in all, I could go to any of a dozen restaurants in town and get the same atmosphere and the same food, but something else draws me here.

You see, I have a crush on the manager, Rebecca Greenway. I don't know much about her, only that she's the owner's daughter. She runs the place now that her father has remarried and spends his time traveling with his new wife. Most of the time Rebecca works in her office, hidden behind a plain door with her name engraved on a brass plaque. No one would know she was in the building if she didn't make an obligatory appearance during the lunch and dinner rushes. But when she does emerge, she makes quite an impression. Her makeup is applied with a master's subtle touch, her expensive skirt is fresh from the cleaners, and her modest gold earrings bobble about the curve of her cheek. She meanders from one table to the next, flashing genuine smiles and making sure her customers are happy.

It's hard to explain this infatuation. Rebecca is at least ten years younger than me and probably not into women, but somehow, she seems to know what goes on inside my head, how my heart starts to pound when she looks at me. She has to see it on my face, hear it in my stuttering. Maybe it's my imagination, or just wishful thinking, but sometimes she seems to straighten her hair and make sure her blouse is open just right.

You'd think that at my age, I'd be too mature for this adolescent ogling. But you'd probably also think that after being single for nearly three years, my loneliness would've faded and the remorse would've withdrawn into the distant recesses of my memory. You'd think that by now I wouldn't miss my lover so much. But when I leave the office and head for home, I get a gnawing in my stomach and my head starts to feel like it's in a vise. The closer I get to my mostly-unused, too-expensive house, the tighter the vise gets.

Somehow, that feeling eases up when I wheel into Choppy's parking lot. As I touch the door's brass handle and see my cloudy reflection in the etched glass, the knots in my guts loosen. The sickness is almost bearable when I catch a sniff of fried onions and searing meat from the kitchen and hear grumbling voices around the bar. But when I see Rebecca, it goes away. For the first time in three long years, I am peaceful.

I have to see Rebecca—for health reasons, of course. I have to latch on to the instant when that little dimple burrows into her right cheek, have to watch her saunter up to my table and say, "Hi, Claire. How's it going today?" and see the wink she gives me when she walks away. I record these things in my memory and replay them when the walls of home start to close in.

Is there something wrong with me? I eat at a restaurant I'm not that fond of almost every day so I can look at a woman I'll never have. Maybe I'm a stalker. Will something snap and cause me to crawl through her bedroom window and force myself upon her? Will my inner mass murderer spring to the surface and disembowel her on Valentine's Day?

Nah, not my style. I don't want anything from her that she can't give. I like to be in the same room, that's all; nothing sinister about that. There's nothing wrong with stealing a lingering glance and watching her eyes do that little embarrassed waltz when she catches me.

What's the harm in an innocent crush if it keeps depression from driving me insane? Rebecca's safe. She'll stay at arm's length, never offering more than her services as a polite hostess. She'll never feed me all of her, and that's the way I want it. I won't feast and grow fat, only to have my sustenance snatched away.

It's kind of funny how someone like me, who's made a living talking to all kinds of people, can go so blank around this young, sexy woman. Everything I say comes out like a cement-covered marshmallow. Sometimes I wish she wouldn't get too close. With Rebecca Greenway, I'm much more charming from a distance.

Tonight I've finished half of a club sandwich and am waiting on my check when Rebecca approaches my table. She's holding a cup of soup in one hand and a fountain soda in the other. "Claire, I know this is rude, but every table in the place is full. It's about five hundred degrees in the kitchen, and I haven't had a bite all day. Mind if I join you for a minute?" Her eyes lock on mine and a playful smile turns up one corner of her lips.

I gulp down a drink of Sprite and choke out, "Sure," but I've gotten pretty stretched out sitting here alone and can't get my ankles out of her way fast enough. She kicks my leg as she sits down, and I feel an inch-wide snag run up my stockings.

"Oh, God, I'm sorry." Soup sloshes out of the cup, and she nearly spills her drink. She looks under the table, but now I've got my legs tucked on my side of the booth. "I know I ripped a hole the size of the Grand Canyon. I'll buy you a new pair, promise."

For once, I'm the one with a little presence of mind. "Don't worry about it. I've got a spare in the car, and besides, I'm going straight home."

"I'll make it up to you. No argument." She wipes up the spill and then watches me as she blows on a spoonful of yesterday's ham-and-bean soup. "How's the salad?" She points her spoon toward my plate.

"Very good, but these sandwiches are so big. Sandy's bringing me a to-go box."

"Size does matter in the restaurant business. Seems like we have to keep serving bigger and bigger portions just to keep up with demand."

She's wearing that green dress with the wide belt that makes her waist look tiny and her eyes resemble the big shiny marbles my brother and I used to fight over in the backyard—the ones with green and gray streaks swirling around all the way to the middle.

I'm swimming somewhere between those eyes when I realize she's waiting for me to say something. So much for my presence of mind. "Size matters, yeah. Guess that's why Americans have gotten so fat."

"You said it. I'm just trying to keep up with the competition." After another spoonful of soup, she adds, "We're using a new recipe for the honey mustard dressing. You should try it next time."

Rebecca looks at me too hard, and I dodge her stare. Any other woman, any client, I can dead-eye all day, but not her. This lady makes me want to crawl under the table and hide. Or crawl under the table and lift her dress up over those shapely thighs. Either way, she wouldn't be eyeballing me. Either way, I could get some relief.

"How's business?" she asks, dabbing her lip with a cotton napkin.

"Not too bad for this time of year. Now that the Christmas bustle has worn off, customers are ready to talk to me again." I adjust my collar and take a sip of Sprite. When did it get so hot in here?

"I don't see how you keep up with your product line. It must be huge." She puts down her spoon and glances toward the bar where Patti, a waitress in tight khaki pants, is waiting for a drink order.

"How many items are on your menu?" I steal a glimpse of her profile. Her features are an interesting mix of hard and soft: straight-line nose and strong cheekbones hiding under an angel's delicate skin. She's no supermodel, but I've noticed that I'm not her only not-so-secret admirer. Some of the other regulars practically salivate when she walks by.

"Hmm... how many items are on my menu?" She calculates in her head, keeping track by tapping her thumb against her forefinger, then the middle finger, and so on. When she runs out of digits on her right hand she stops. "Not counting the bar, about forty, maybe forty-five items. Why?"

"Your product line is larger than mine. From the smallest home-filing cabinet to the biggest track-rolling system, I've got thirteen basic units. It's the way we configure them that makes it seem like more. We can tailor a complex system from three or four units."

"I see." Rebecca shoots a concerned look at Patti, who still hasn't gotten her order from the bartender. "But slinging hash for less than twenty bucks a plate is a little different than making thousand-dollar deals over the phone."

"Maybe so." It's not really different, but I concede her point. For one thing, I don't want to come off like a know-it-all. For another, it's kind of nice having her think I'm smart. A boring stiff maybe, but smart.

When Rebecca returns her focus to me, a frisky grin prances across her lips. "Maybe you could give me some lessons in business management. This place is driving me crazy."

"Seems like you're running things smoothly."

"Appearances can be deceiving." She winks at me before looking back at the unassisted waitress. "Oh, well, duty calls." She slides out of the booth and grabs her half-eaten cup of soup and empty glass as she stands. I see her weary smile before she turns away. "Thanks again for letting me join you. Looks like I've got a lot to do before I can go home."

"Any time."

When she walks away, I wonder where home is and who's waiting there for her.

I wonder if she loves him.

CHAPTER 3

To understand the way I am now, you have to know how I got here. I guess most stories like mine start with a girl. My girl was Lora Tyler.

Lora used to say she'd seen up more skirts than a Peeping Tom with mirrored shoes. It wasn't her choice, though. As the tallest and strongest of Franklin High's all-girl cheerleading squad, she was planted at the bottom of every human pyramid the coach could think up. But she carried her responsibility like the trouper she was, grimacing slightly as an anorexic sophomore dug blue and white sneakers into her shoulders.

Lora wasn't the prettiest girl in school. As a matter of fact, none of her features alone were anything special. Her large brown eyes slanted a little, her nose was a snip too long, and her full mouth seemed a little crooked. But when those elements came together with her high cheekbones, they formed a timeless beauty—a captivating radiance that kept her phone ringing off the hook even after she'd started wearing Jock Richardson's class ring.

She'd been blessed with an infectious, upbeat attitude that made her an integral part of the student council and allowed her to carry on conversations with anyone, from Principal Jarvis right on down to Rainbow Griggs, the worst of the bad girls around campus. Whether it was an aspiring suitor, out to connect with her lean body, or a girl in gym class, Lora kept everyone on a string.

I had known her in a distant way all my life. It was hard not to know almost everyone when your school had a graduating class of one hundred and ninety-five. Lora and I had started kindergarten at the same time, had attended the same elementary and junior high schools, and had plodded our way to high school together. We had never shared classes, recesses, or lunch breaks, so we never had a chance to be good friends. To me, Lora was a nice girl with a pretty face, not much else. Senior year, all that changed.

It was the first day of school, and I had found a seat near the back of my fourth-period advanced composition class. I was probably the only kid in school to be glad for classes to start. Summer was over, and I wouldn't have to spend another day picking corn, beans, or tomatoes at my uncle's farm. I didn't have a particular aversion to hard work or to vegetables, but the snakes put me into a panic every time I got close to the fields. Anything longer than my five-foot-six height shouldn't be slithering around beneath the thick green leaves of bean plants. At least, that's the way I saw it.

Now, sitting alone in the classroom, I relished the musty aroma of ancient encyclopedias and chalk dust and appreciated the sturdy feel of the wooden seat beneath me. Franklin High had its share of snakes, but they were the two-legged variety, and I wasn't afraid. I could manage them, keep them in their place and me in mine.

Lora was second to show up for class. She breezed into the room, a picture of preppy fashion wearing khaki chinos, a pale-blue button-down shirt, and no socks with her Top-Siders. She plopped down at the desk beside me and shoved a lock of dark hair away from her eyes.

"Hey, Claire. I didn't know you decided to take this class," she said, breathless.

"I'd rather get it over with. It transfers to State as freshman comp."

"You've already decided to go to State?" She dropped her books onto the worn tile floor. "I haven't decided where I'm going to college, but this class is a good idea, even if I end up going somewhere else and the credit doesn't transfer."

"Still with Jock?" I asked, eyeing the huge gold class ring secured to her index finger with a rubber band.

"Yeah, two years this spring." She polished the ring on her pants and inspected the aquamarine stone before opening a brand-new spiral notebook to the first page.

"I bet you two will be the first to get married after graduation."

"I want to get my college degree before I get married, but Jock doesn't see much point. He's bound and determined he'll make the minor leagues next year and play pro baseball in two years."

"He's pretty sure of himself." I watched Donnie LaForce, a freckle-faced loner, wander in and take a seat near the door.

"Jock never doubts anything." Lora nodded at Gina Blessing as the rotund girl took the seat in front of me.

Gina dropped her books on the desktop and twirled around to face us, quite agile for her size. "Let's get this show on the road, girls. I'm ready to get this year over with and get out of this hell hole."

"Be careful, Gina," Lora said with a smirk. "College may not be what you expect."

"I don't care if I end up digging ditches as long as I don't have to come back here."

We broke into laughter and chatted about the upcoming football season as other students milled in. That year, little Franklin High had been blessed with two seriously talented athletes. Lora's boyfriend, Johnny "Jock" Richardson, was not only being scouted as a baseball pitcher, but had also been recruited by three major universities for his talent as a wide receiver. With him teamed up with Matthew Carter, a quarterback with realistic plans to play professional ball, there was little doubt we'd win the district title and possibly land our third state championship.

The conversation rambled from football to my new position as starting point guard for the girl's basketball team, pulling Lora from her sappy trance and giving me a chance to boast about how well we'd do in the upcoming season. Although I'd made the varsity team the past three years and posted respectable stats off the bench, I'd lived in the shadow of Lacy Mays, the best darn guard, male or female, ever to grace the floor of Franklin High's gym. But this year would be different. Lacy had graduated, and my time had come. I was ready to step into the limelight—such as it was for girls' sports—and relish my own fifteen minutes of fame.

We talked about Lora's dream of becoming a social worker and Gina's goal to be a college professor. When I announced that I hadn't made a career choice yet, it was like I'd confessed to murder.

"Oh, Claire, you have to have a plan if you want to be successful," Lora said. "It's never too early."

She began to quiz me about my likes and dislikes, how I wanted to live, and what I expected my income to be. I babbled "I'm not sure" and "I don't know," but she measured my answers and did a few computations in her head. She then pitched career options and studied my reactions with more interest than Miss Fielder, the school's lone guidance counselor. I had to laugh. We barely knew each other, and Lora was more concerned about my future than I was.

Yet from the safety of the room, graduation seemed an eternity away. Chalkboards and chemistry labs would be our world for one last go-around in the public education system. We had nine whole months to rule the school before setting foot in the real world.

Eventually, our teacher showed up in his trademark plaid shirt and knit tie and brought the group to order. Mr. Burns stood in front of his desk, hands folded behind him, staring at a spot on the wall above our heads. "To communicate facts and opinions in a concise manner, you must do two things. First, you must read. Second, you must think." He paused and cast a dramatic glance at each student's face before continuing. "In this class, you will be expected to do both."

On legs too short for his long body, he then paced the front of the room, tracing a stubby index finger along the chalk tray and then wiping his nose. By the time he'd outlined the rigors and uncompromising demands of the course, he had a line of white powder streaked from his nose to his chin.

Looking intimidated, Lora leaned toward me and whispered, "Want to be my study partner?"

I nodded. Lora made it easy to believe we'd been friends forever.

* * *

"Hey, Claire! Wait up."

I was heading into the cafeteria when I turned and saw Lora sauntering toward me. As usual, she was hand in hand with Jock Richardson, a long-legged, muscular boy with a mischievous grin and wide brown eyes surrounded by the longest lashes I'd ever seen. They stopped a few yards away. Jock whispered something in Lora's ear and gave her a lingering kiss on the cheek. He nodded in my direction, turned, and headed back down the hall.

Lora didn't watch him walk away, but I did. Jock stole up behind Evelyn Blanchard and draped his arm around her shoulder. Evelyn, with her straight blonde hair and perfect white teeth, was the undisputed beauty queen of Franklin High. From behind, I could only half-see Jock's profile as he looked at Evelyn, but his glassy-eyed gaze seemed to indicate a more than friendly greeting.

As I watched Lora shift a pile of books from one arm to the other, I whisked away the tingle of suspicion lingering in my head. She'd turned her back on Jock and hadn't glanced over her shoulder to check on him. If she trusted her boyfriend, why should I doubt him? After all, it didn't affect me one way or the other.

Lora snorted as she joined me at the cafeteria door. "I thought senior year was supposed to be a breeze, but it doesn't look like it so far."

"It's the first day of school. They're just trying to scare us."

"It's working."

A boy with greasy hair and round, wire-rimmed glasses stopped beside us. He glanced at the schedule card in his hand, then down the hall. Even in a school as small as Franklin, freshmen got lost on the first day of classes. As seniors, it was our duty to ignore lower classmen, but Lora tapped the boy on the shoulder.

"Lost?"

"Uh, yeah. Where's the library?" He gazed at my friend in amazement. He was a small, weak-looking kid who'd not yet crossed the threshold from little boy to young man. I felt sorry for him. He was a prime target for the bad boys.

Lora gave him a kind smile and pointed toward the end of the hall. "Up the stairs, first door on your left."

"Thanks." He beamed, revealing a mouth full of tin. "Aren't you a cheerleader?"

"Yeah," Lora replied, and, as the boy turned away she touched his arm. "You like football?"

He looked back, eyes wide. "Sure."

"I've got a couple of free passes to the scrimmage this Friday. My locker number is three-ninety-four. Stop by about seven-thirty in the morning, and I'll give them to you."

"Gosh! Really?"

"Yeah. But don't be late."

"No way! I'll be there." He blushed and hurried away.

Now everyone in town, regardless of their year in school, knew that scrimmage tickets were only two bucks each. But to a squirt with tin teeth and oily hair, free passes from a varsity cheerleader were worth their weight in gold. Just being seen at Lora Tyler's locker might save him a couple of days of teasing.

After the kid disappeared up the steps, Lora and I walked into the cafeteria. We passed four rows of lunch tables and dropped our books on an empty square one by the windows. Sunlight poured through the glass, its heat enhancing a putrid aroma that could only be coming from the kitchen—cooked cabbage. What teenagers in their right mind liked cooked cabbage? We wanted burgers and fries, or tacos with crunchy corn tortilla shells. Even frozen pizza with a cardboard crust would've been better than cooked cabbage, but the cafeteria manager didn't see it that way, so we endured the smell as best we could.

"Are you going to eat?" I plopped down in the metal folding chair farthest from the smell.

Lora crinkled her nose. "Nah. I have to go home and check on Grandpa after school. I'll grab a sandwich before work."

"Don't blame you. Smells like a sewer in here."

"Gross." Lora glanced at the kids waiting in line to be served green septic-tank mush. Most of them were wet-behind-the-ears freshmen. One trip through that line on cabbage day would teach them a lesson they'd not soon forget.

"Know any of the new kids?" I indicated the lunch queue.

"My cousin Darcy, but I haven't seen her yet." She scanned the lunchroom. "Still don't see her. Maybe she's got another lunch period."

"I think this is the first time you and I have had lunch break at the same time."

"I've always had third lunch because of cheerleading practice. Mrs. Van Houser wants us to eat late. Says it gives us more energy."

"I've had second lunch every year before this one." I pulled my schedule card from my purse and double-checked. "Yeah, I'm in the right place. Says so right here."

Lora winked at me. "Guess that means we were meant to get together this year."

I tucked the card back into my purse. "We'll need each other to survive advanced comp class."

"Hey, why don't you give me your phone number? I don't have to work tomorrow afternoon. Maybe we can go to the bookstore and get those books for class."

As I grabbed my spiral notebook and yanked a piece of paper from the wire, a strange excitement prickled at me. Maybe this year would hold new things—new friends, new experiences. Not that my old friends were bad, but they were tired, or maybe I was tired of them. It was time for a change, time for Claire to do something different. Even that first day, I sensed that Lora Tyler was the key to my new life.

CHAPTER 4

I'm still thinking of Rebecca as I steer into the driveway and wave at my neighbor, Elizabeth, with her bleached hair and Jackie Kennedy style. She's unloading her kids' sports gear from the beige Caravan, and she waves back.

There are always so many people next door—other Junior League wives like Elizabeth, milling around, trying to out-smile one another with their collagen-plumped lips. They all look pretty much alike, and so do their kids, preteens with too-expensive clothes and monogrammed Eddie Bauer backpacks slung over one shoulder.

I don't care much for the country club set in general, but my neighbors are different. Both Elizabeth and Jared Kingsley come from working-class backgrounds, so they recognize their superficial acquaintances for what they are—self-absorbed big fish bumping around in a small pond.

Jared's never let his status in the community give him a big head. He's a thoughtful neighbor and always offers to clean my sidewalk when it snows. He's proud of his Craftsman snow blower and doesn't have that many chances to use it. I let him, more for the entertainment value than from necessity. Despite his well-toned physique, Jared is not the most macho guy in town, so the blower drives him instead of the other way around.

I love their lives. I love them. They are so simple and clean.

I pull into the garage and punch the button on the visor to lower the door. For an instant, I consider leaving the car running. How simple it would be to put a melancholy end to my story, to fall asleep and escape the cold bitterness that has me clamped in its grasp. Death could be the key to freedom. I might laugh again, love again, be me instead of the broken-hearted bitch I've become. Then I think of them finding me, days later in my own excrement, my face blue and lips turned wrong side out. I can't stand the thought. And besides, I'm afraid of what might lurk on the other side, so I cut the ignition and grab my briefcase from the back seat.

I should move. I loved this house when we bought it, but it was never really my style. It's too modern, too beige and white on the outside, and has too much crown molding and recessed lighting on the inside. And it has too many windows. Whatever happened to the old-fashioned houses where you could close one curtain and sleep all day, never knowing whether it was sunny or cloudy outside? And what do I need with four bedrooms? I haven't even been upstairs since my brother was in town at Christmas. If the cleaning lady didn't come once a week, there'd be at least three inches of dust up there. I've even got a formal living room and dining room. That makes about as much sense as a hat on a dog.

On the way to the kitchen door, I placate myself with frail reassurances that life will go on, that my ordeal will one day seem like last-week's nightmare: fuzzy and unreal, and not nearly as frightening as it seems today. I think how lucky I am to have a nice home in an upscale section of town, how fortunate I am to have good health, and how successful I've been with my career. Yet when I throw open the kitchen door, the house caves in on me. I ward away the panic with a feeble shake of my head and catch a breath. I slide the Choppy's leftovers into the refrigerator and open the freezer to let the cold air hit my face.

Yes, I should get away from here. I should leave all the memories, leave her dust behind for someone else to clean up. But I won't. I'll live in this house till I die. And she will be here, teasing me with images of what might have been. She'll linger in the rooms like an apparition, shadowy and untouchable. She'll lie with me at night as I struggle for sleep and berate myself for not doing the right things. She'll remind me that she's never coming back.

I put my purse on the kitchen table, step out of my pumps, and walk toward our room, opening the door to the guestroom as I pass. Like a hairy tornado, Jitterbug invades the hallway with her hippity-hop routine of sideways cartwheels and barks at my briefcase.

I don't scold the dog when she scratches at my legs and tears my pantyhose. Rebecca already ruined this pair. I smile, relishing the shared experience. A run in my stockings is a small price for a tiny connection. Probably nothing more than an uncomfortable incident to her, but a weapon for me. I'll wield the memory against my black-eyed demons, slice them down to manageable size, and deal them a deathblow with the one ounce of pride I've been granted. I am empowered for the evening.

Jitterbug follows me to our room and waits for her after-work scratch behind the ears before curling up at the foot of my bed. Every time I look at the little buff-colored cocker, I thank God for the company. The first time I saw her, though, I wasn't so sure about the arrangement. To be frank, I didn't want a dog in our new house, didn't want to deal with pee on the carpet and poop in my shoes. But with two sets of big brown eyes begging to let her stay, I never stood a chance and Jitterbug has been here ever since. If only I could say the same about her benefactor.

I flip on the overhead light and survey the room, just in case. I keep hoping that one night I'll saunter in and find her waiting for me. Not tonight. The sleigh bed is empty, the plaid comforter still askew from last night. The pine dresser and chest of drawers still hold only my clothes, and that one silly snapshot of us is still missing from the wall beside the bathroom door. Now there's just a lonely nail.

I pick up the picture frame from the bedside table. From behind the glass, the pressed four-leaf clover looks almost as green as the day she discovered it, over twenty years ago. She said it was our good-luck charm, and as long as we kept it, we'd be together. The clover's magic worked in our first dinky apartment and in our first house. For a while it worked here, but then the spell withered.

I put the frame back and glance into the mirror over the dresser. The years fall in on me all at once. I sailed along, never realizing how quickly time was passing. Then, before I had a chance to enjoy them, my twenties were gone. I'm too thick-headed to learn from experience, so my thirties will soon be gone as well, and I'll have little to show for either decade. Nothing important, anyway. I spent all that time, all that energy, to end up alone in a big house with a cocker spaniel and a large-screen TV. Even my own gray eyes look at me too sternly, and I turn away.

CHAPTER 5

It was the fifth day of school during my senior year, and Franklin High's Lady Warrior basketball team was preparing to take on Cross City's Lady Devils. The usual crowd of parents and friends filled only half of the bleachers lining both sides of the court, but the faint odor of my own sweat and the need to prove myself pumped me up tighter than the practice ball I'd been dribbling for the last twenty minutes.

I smelled the fresh wax on the court, saw how it made the hardwood shimmer. I knew each board by name. They were mine now. This time, I was going to hang the championship pennant in the rafters. It would be me who hopped up on the stage at the head of the court and led the pep band in our fight song during Friday morning's pep rally. We were going to win, and I would get us there. It was my turn at last, and I wasn't about to miss a minute of it.

In pre-game warm-up, I'd shot my umpteenth lay-up and was rounding the court to join the rebound line, when I noticed Lora sitting in the bleachers. I was surprised to see her. In my four years on the team, she'd never come to a game, probably because Coach Larson had recruited her like a mad dog. Lora had turned him down flat, citing the conflict between the girls' basketball schedule and the football schedule as her main reason for not playing. Sure, she had the size and natural ability to be a star forward, but with all her other extracurricular activities as well as a part-time job at Pizza Oven, she had enough on her plate.

"Hey, Study Buddy," she shouted, hands cupped around her mouth. "Go get 'em!"

I grinned and waved. Lora and I had met after school for a Coke a couple of times and gone to the bookstore once, but I didn't know she considered me a friend. Her presence at the game told me she did, and although Lora Tyler was friendly to everyone, she had only a select few cronies. I was flattered to be one of them, and a drop of pride pushed my adrenaline a little higher. I couldn't be beaten, not tonight, and not with my own personal cheerleader in the stands.

I took my place in the rebound line behind my best friend, Jill McMurray, a lanky kid with somber blue eyes and short-cropped brown hair that was feathered away from her long face. Her claim to fame was wearing a size eleven sneaker, the biggest of any girl in our class.

Jill glanced toward Lora and wrinkled her freckled nose. "What's she doing here? I thought she didn't have time for basketball."

Most people didn't know how to take Jill. Roaring mad or deliriously happy, she always kept the same even expression, the same level manner, but I caught a note of resentment in her voice. As starting forward, Jill could be great. She could also be lousy, and it was no secret that my best friend would've lost her position if Lora had decided to play ball. That irked Jill plenty.

So instead of expressing delight at my new friend's presence, I shrugged. "Maybe she's waiting for Jock. The guys are practicing late."

Jill started to say something, but the scoreboard buzzer sounded, signaling the start of the game.

* * *

"I might as well have been throwing bricks at the basket," Jill moaned as we filed into the dressing room, which was already humid from the running showers.

I gave her a pat on the back. "Don't worry about it. We won, didn't we?"

"No thanks to me." Jill collapsed on the bench in front of her locker and wiped her forehead with a towel. She'd been off her game, making the first competition of the season a hideous testament to her ball-handling skills.

"Don't worry about it," I said in a firmer tone. "You had a bad night, that's all. We'll shoot some extra baskets this week and work on it, okay?"

Jill nodded, but tears welled in her eyes.

I wanted to help my friend, but I was riding high from my own performance and not yet ready to come down. I had run the offense like a seasoned pro, feeding one perfect pass after another to our best shooters and hitting five out of six jump shots from the floor. After each successful basket, I had glanced toward Lora, and her enthusiastic applause propelled me to the other end of the court where I'd managed to force five turnovers.

I had been invincible, empowered by the unmitigated energy radiating from the bleachers. Not only from Lora, but from all those she'd infected with her team spirit. Everyone had stood and clapped, spurred on by a single off-duty cheerleader. By the end of the first half, I had been convinced that Lora Tyler could single-handedly propel the girl's basketball team to the state championship without ever setting foot on the court.

Not everyone shared my sentiment. Jill smirked when she saw Lora peeking around the far end of the lockers.

"Well, if it ain't the mouth of the south," she quipped, at a volume only I could hear.

Lora bounced toward us. "Excellent game, girls."

"Thanks," I said, gushing. "It was your cheering that got us fired up."

"Gave me a headache," Jill mumbled. "Couldn't hear myself think." She opened her locker and tossed her court shoes onto its floor. They hit the metal with a cold slap.

Lora straddled the bench between the rows of lockers and looked toward Jill. "I'm sorry. I'll keep it down next time, okay?"

"It's okay." Jill looked away, blushing.

Lora fished her car keys from her purse. "Let's go down to Pizza Oven. My treat. It's the least I can do to make up for my big mouth. I'll be waiting at the south doors." She loped away, not giving us a chance to refuse.

I snapped my towel toward Jill's ankles. "Hear that? Free pizza. Can't beat that, can you?"

"She works there. It's not like she's paying for it out of her own pocket." She stood up, peeling her sweaty jersey over her head. "I'm not going."

"Why? You can't have homework this early in the year."

"I don't want to go."

"Why not?"

"I just don't."

My mood deflated as I opened my locker and untied my sneakers. "Then I won't go, either."

Jill glared at me, clutching a towel to her chest. "Go. Have fun."

I kicked off my shoes and mopped the back of my neck with a towel. "I can't have fun while you're still pissed about the game."

"I'm not pissed. It's early. I'll get my rhythm." She tugged her sweat socks off and grimaced. "Really, go on and don't worry about me. I'm fine."

"You're sure?"

"Sure."

With that I raced toward the showers, leaving my best friend alone in a stinky locker room after the worst basketball game she'd ever played. I should have been there for her, but I didn't understand. I didn't realize that one friendship was about to blossom while another was about to fade.

CHAPTER 6

"Claire. Are you awake?"

"Huh?" I barely recognize Tonya's voice over the static of her mobile phone. I roll over to check the time—3:00 a.m. I've known Tonya since college, and it still startles me when she calls at this time of night.

My friend belongs in Vegas, where time is an insignificant notion, a mere regulator for unfocused and weak-minded drones who live by the clock's steady hands. But my inconsiderate friend doesn't fall into the drone category. For over three years, the clock on her DVD player has been sixteen hours slow.

"I'm losing you, hang on," Tonya says.

I close my eyes and pray the connection is gone. After going to bed with a blinding migraine and a handful of pills, I do well to remember my own name, much less absorb one of the famous Tonya Knight escapade stories.

"Still there?"

The link is clearer, but it still sounds like she's calling from the bottom of a whiskey barrel, which might be the case. Jack Daniels was her best friend in college, and she still likes to cut loose once in a while.

In younger days, her passion for partying and loose women earned her the nickname of Fly By. And she still wears it like a diamond-studded tiara, even naming her business *Fly By Knight Interiors*. But my friend isn't the wild child she once was. She'll never settle down with one woman, but she's got her little black book trimmed to a short list of about five regular sex buddies. Most are married women with husbands who either don't know what their wives are up to, or do know, and choose to look the other way. That's the way Tonya likes it—no strings, no bother.

I look at the clock again. "Do you realize what time it is?"

"No, but I've been thinking about you and thought I'd better check in."

"Check in tomorrow. I have to get up in two hours. I'm hanging up now."

"I'll call right back."

I wipe my eyes on the heel of my hand and try to sound awake. "Okay, okay, what's so important?"

Tonya breathes into the phone, sending a loud crackle of static into my ear. "You need to go out clubbing with me this weekend. You know, mingle, meet the new girls on the block."

"You woke me up for that?" I imagine myself in the smoky limelight at one of the local lesbian hangouts, lined up with dozens of other single women like tin cans on a split-rail fence. One by one, the infamous womanizers about town shoot their best pick-up lines at us till we swoon and topple into their waiting arms.

Right. That'll happen. A chuckle rises in my throat. "You know I haven't been to a bar since... well... since..." The laugh turns into a lump that almost cuts off my air, hanging in my neck like a chicken bone. If it were a bone, I could cough it out and be rid of it. Instead, I have to wait for it to melt and then wonder when it'll show up again.

She huffs another crackle into my ear. "Come on, girl. Get back into the swing of things."

"I'm swinging fine, thank you."

"How long has it been since you've had sex?"

"Kiss my ass!" I give the handset three hard whacks against the nightstand before putting it back to my ear.

"Okay, that hurt. And you know I'd love to kiss your sweet ass, but you won't let me."

"I don't fuck my friends."

"If you can't fuck your friends, who can you fuck?" When I don't reply, she adds, "Anyway, don't even try to tell me you wouldn't do a number on that sexy neighbor of yours if she gave you the go-ahead."

I groan and roll over. Jitterbug slurps at my nose. Her Alpo breath isn't doing my headache any good. "We're not going to rehash my friendship with Elizabeth, are we?"

"Guess not." Tonya softens. "I just thought a night out on the town might be fun."

"I don't know, Fly. I just can't seem to get my shit together, you know?"

"Listen, girl, I don't blame you for being scared. Hell, I've been in the game since high school, and I still get scared sometimes."

This is the side of Tonya that few people know: the gentle lady who hides beneath the armor of catty comments and one-night conquests. To most of the world, my crony flings a fuck-it-before-it-fucks-you attitude. She may be an obnoxious, inconsiderate slut at times, but she's a good friend if she likes you—and she loves me.

"I'm too old to learn the game." I know she's right. But I've been bitten, had a hunk the size of Texas chewed out of my ass to be precise, and I don't think I have another try in me.

"You're too damn young to mope around the house all the time," Tonya says. "Come on, go out with me this weekend. Get your feet wet, see how it goes."

"Maybe I will." I know full well I'll back out by Saturday afternoon.

Tonya knows it, too. "No more chicken shit. I'm holding you to it. We'll go out for a few drinks, see some new people. It'll do wonders for you."

"Maybe." My chest begins to tighten.

The phone goes quiet, then crackles again. "I'm heading toward a no-service zone," Tonya says. "Call you tomorrow."

I drop the phone and punch my pillow. I'll probably fall asleep ten minutes before the alarm goes off.

* * *

I get up at 5:30. It's been my ritual for years, but now I have to make my own coffee and toast my own bagel. I hate that, not because I want someone to cater to my needs, but because I miss her doing those little things once in a while.

As every morning, I take a shower and put on my makeup, feed Jitterbug, and take her for a quick walk in the vacant lot across the street before putting her in the guestroom for the day. It's nice to be needed, even if it's only by a dog.

I back out of the garage at seven and see Jared Kingsley plodding up his front walk. He has the morning paper tucked under his arm, and his tan overcoat flaps in the breeze. Jared eyes my Lexus again.

I roll down the window and shout over the whistling wind. "Why don't you just break down and buy one?"

"Still thinking about it. We might go for the GS 430."

"That'll set you back an extra ten grand."

Jared shrugs and finger-combs his tousled hair. "Can't decide on a color, anyway."

I wonder why it's so tough for a doctor who makes life-and-death decisions every day to decide on a car color. He's on the ER staff at

Mercy Hospital, so rushing into critical decisions is his job. Maybe it makes sense for him to take his time on the mundane things in life. I roll up my window, wave again, and back out of the driveway. After a short trip through town, I arrive at work by 7:15. The manufacturing plant is a long, gray, high-roofed building with the words *Office Solutions, Inc.,* in big blue letters across the front. I wave to Pete Archer, the plant supervisor, and let myself in the back door. I lock it, switch on the break room lights, and turn on the coffeepot. Mary, the office manager, is a bear before she gets her morning caffeine fix, and I'm not in the mood to be growled at this early.

I go to my office and drop my briefcase in the visitor's chair. Tracing my finger along the top of the cherry desk, I circle around and plop into my chair. I notice that I left the computer on again last night. I should be more careful.

"Why do you have to be so damn efficient?" I snarl, slapping the top of my CRT. "Whoever invented you is making it harder and harder for me to earn a living."

I glance at the picture sitting on my desk. That old sour feeling creeps up into my throat. Swallowing hard, I allow myself a lingering look at her big eyes and lopsided smile.

"We had more good times than bad, didn't we, honey?" I wonder if she ever misses me.

Reggie, my boss, stumbles into my office and leans against the wall with his arms crossed. He's a pretty good guy and usually leaves me to myself, but this morning he's got those three deep wrinkles on his forehead that mean trouble.

"Claire, you've got about sixteen weeks of vacation time piled up. Why don't you let me call the travel agent and book you on one of those cruises? My treat."

"Thanks, Reg, but I can't see myself frolicking around the Bahamas with a bunch of honeymooners."

"So take someone with you. Go out and find a tall-dark-and-whatever." He glances away. After a long pause, he goes on, "I thought a few days in the sun might kick up that old spark in you."

"I'm not sparky?" I pick up a folder, open it, and pretend to read.

"Don't be a smart-ass." He rubs his face with long slender fingers. "I miss that go-getter who barged into my office—what is it now, sixteen years ago?—and told me she'd put me on the map. What happened to her?"

"Come on, Reg, you're still on the map. I won't let you go back to peddling manila folders and rubber stamps from that hole in the wall on

Main Street." I try to give him a playful smile, but he quit buying that routine a long time ago.

"Listen, kid, you came to me with nothing but a few drawings and a full head of steam, and look where it got you." He catches my eye. "How many people do you know who've gone from nothing to a six figure salary in less than ten years?"

"It wasn't all me. My designs were pitiful. I practically asked Harold to build a three bedroom house with paperclips and chewing gum."

"He did it, though, didn't he?" My boss chuckles and shakes his head. "Those were the days, huh? Remember all those nights, the three of us swilling coffee to beat the band and cussing each other till the sun came up?"

"Yep, I remember all right."

Reggie shakes his head. "If I'd known then what I know now…"

My palms get damp and I snatch a tissue from the desk drawer to dry them. "Reg, do you ever think maybe we went too far? Maybe we spent so much time building this business that we missed out on the good things in life? You know, the important stuff?"

"It's possible." He hooks his thumbs through his leather suspenders and, for an instant, gets a far away look in his eye. He gives his suspenders a tug and lets go of them with a snap. "No going back now, and I've got the divorce papers to prove it."

"Guess you're right." I rock back in my chair and fold my hands across my middle. "Don't worry about me. I'll get my momentum again. Besides, you need to do more than sit in your office and play electronic poker all day."

He grins. "I can't do this without you, Claire. You know that."

"You won't have to."

"The Healthmark proposal is due. Ready for it?"

"Ready and able, boss."

He nods and saunters away. I throw a salute as he disappears down the hall.

I check my schedule and see I have a conference call at 10:00 that should take about an hour. It hits me that I've been scheduling my appointments and meetings around lunch at Choppy's. I'm altering my life to look at a woman who doesn't care if I exist. That's pathetic.

I spend the rest of the morning returning phone messages and going over a proposal to provide filing systems for a chain of hospitals. If the sales rep can land the account, it'll mean a hefty bonus for both him and me.

I start to get daydreamy about 9:30 and go to the break room for a cup of coffee to whisk away the cobwebs.

I find Mary pouring what must be her fifth cup and leaving the pot empty. I've always been jealous of her ability to drink up all that sugar and never gain a pound, but I'm not jealous of her ability to apply eye shadow. Some mornings she looks like she spent the night duking it out with George Foreman. Pity, she's got skin like a baby doll and great bone structure. She dresses like Liz Taylor—a little over the top for a business office, but we don't mention it.

Mary doesn't look at me as she dumps sugar into her mug. "Haven't seen you this morning. Busy?"

"Not too bad." I put a clean filter into the coffee maker. "I'm almost finished with the Healthmark proposal. Can you type it up this afternoon?"

"Gotcha covered." She twirls away, her flowing skirt sending a breeze against my legs.

When the coffee is ready, I pour a cup and go back to my office to find the phone ringing. Rounding my desk, I grab the receiver and sit down.

"Claire Blevins," I say.

"Hey, girl." It's Tonya.

"Hey."

"Got any good leads for me?"

Always got to find new leads. Leads for me, leads for Tonya, leads for the sales reps. In Tonya's case, it's the least I can do. She's as much a part of my success team as anyone.

I flip through the stack of folders on my desk and pick one from the group. "I gave your card to Dr. Wolford. He's thinking of updating his waiting area."

"Shit, Claire, I don't want to decorate offices. They expect me to create the Taj Mahal on a ten-dollar budget. Houses, that's where the money is. Get little wifey to sign the checks."

"It's a foot in the door, Fly. That's all I can do."

She giggles. "I know, and I appreciate it. Besides, some of those doctors' offices are prime prowling ground."

"Geez, are you out to bed every woman you meet?" I toss Dr. Wolford's folder aside and glance at the clock.

"Only the pretty ones." After a pause, she says, "We're still on for Saturday, right?"

No need to reply. I sip my coffee and clamp the phone against my shoulder as I think about the sales proposal on my CRT.

"I thought we'd go to Sister Moon. That okay with you?"

"Fine."

"Then I thought we'd go to Platters and make love in a bathtub full of Jell-O in front of half the town." Can't fool good old Fly By.

"Whatever. I don't want to be out too late, okay?"

"Afterwards, you'll wise up and admit you love me."

That got my attention. "Fly, we agreed not to go there."

"Smell the coffee, girl. You know you've been the love of my life ever since we met."

"So that's why you've bedded every woman in the tri-county area over the past fifteen years?" This conversation is so old I can recite it like the poem about Abraham Lincoln I learned in fifth grade.

"Got to do something while I'm waiting. You know, keep in practice for when you wise up. I wouldn't want to disappoint you."

"I'm sure you could teach me a thing or two, Fly, but you'd get bored and I'd get hurt. Then what would I do? You're the only best friend I've got."

"Have it your way. We'll always be together, one way or another."

"I know, sweetie."

A light flashes on my phone telling me the conference call is waiting. "I'll talk to you later. Okay, buddy?"

"Catch you later."

I punch the conference line. "Good morning, all."

The meeting drags on as usual, and after forty-five minutes of a jumble of voices droning through the speaker, I'm ready to bounce off the walls.

After all, Rebecca is waiting.

CHAPTER 7

Senior year had moved into late September, and the summer's haze still clung to the sky like a humid blanket, saturating the region with wet heat. Jill and I had spent two hours after school in the gym's office to finish up a fund-raising project for the girls' basketball team. Silently, we walked toward the student parking lot.

Jill had never been a big talker, but since the beginning of the school year, she'd hardly strung together a dozen words at a time. Whenever she did utter more than one complete sentence, she was talking to someone else.

Jill either loved or hated someone, without much middle ground, and it wasn't always clear how a person ended up out of favor. One day she'd like them and the next, for no apparent reason, she'd cross them off. If you asked her why, she'd say, "He gets on my nerves," or "She thinks she's so cool." And just like that, she was finished with them.

Lately, she'd been acting as though she was moving me to the hate category. I didn't know what I'd done to alienate her, but a showdown was coming and I wasn't looking forward to it.

"Want to shoot some baskets later?" I asked, shading my eyes against the afternoon sun.

"Maybe." Jill didn't look at me, but focused in front of her as if fixing on an unseen target. "I figured you had plans with your new buddy."

I didn't understand her disdain for Lora Tyler. Lora was smart, funny, and made sure I had a good time, no matter what we were doing. Sure, I'd spent a lot of time with Lora. Almost every day we'd cruise by Pizza Oven after school, and on Sundays we'd get together and watch campy horror flicks on channel six.

Okay, so Jill wasn't around, but it wasn't my fault she didn't like scary movies. And every time Lora and I went to Pizza Oven, we invited Jill, but she always had something more important to do, like go grocery shopping for her mom or clean her room. Fat chance. I'd been in Jill's bedroom a hundred times and knew the excuse was totally lame. She hadn't cleaned her room since eighth grade.

"Have you ever met Lora's mom?" I asked.

"No, why?"

"God, she's a hateful old woman. That house is like a concentration camp."

The senior citizen I described couldn't have been over forty, but to my teenage eyes, she seemed ancient. She was the source of Lora's dark good looks, with thick undisciplined hair and penetrating brown eyes, but that was the extent of their likeness. Mrs. Tyler had the personality of a drill instructor. The first time I met her, she let me know my place with only a scorching look. I was to mind my manners in her presence, and I did so in military style.

It didn't take a psychoanalyst to find the source of Mrs. Tyler's sour disposition. Lora's maternal grandfather spent his days at their house and his nights at the veterans' home across town. He was a dried-up old man who sat in a lawn chair on the front porch in his undershirt and blue mechanic's pants, smoking unfiltered Camels and drinking malt liquor from a can. In all the time I'd spent at their house, he'd never said a word to me, never looked in my direction, and didn't treat the members of the Tyler family any better.

"He was at Normandy," Lora had explained. "Mom says he was shell-shocked. Hasn't been himself since."

But I'd been desensitized to violence by too many Jamie Lee Curtis movies. Real gore and death didn't register, so Mr. Kane looked like just another old geezer with an attitude problem.

Jill glanced at me. "For someone who hates it so bad, you sure do spend a lot of time at her house." Her fixed look lasted an instant but fired a bullet into my chest.

"We've got a lot of studying to do." I followed her to her yellow Volkswagen Beetle and leaned against its front fender as she fumbled through her purse for the keys.

"Hey, Claire! Jill! Wait up." Lora rushed up to the car, nearly dropping her armload of books. "Where are you guys going?"

"Home." The flare in Jill's nostrils revealed her thoughts to me if not to Lora.

"Jock and Matthew are waiting at Pizza Oven. Let's all go, okay?" Lora grinned, but as usual, her attempt to crack Jill's defenses fell flat.

"I'm up for it," I said, but I knew Jill's response even before she shot Lora a hateful smirk.

"I have to pick up my little brother at piano lessons."

I laughed and bumped Lora's shoulder. "I've heard him play. Trust me, he can use an extra hour of practice."

Unfazed by Jill's cantankerous mood, Lora giggled and started toward her car. "Okay, I'll see you two there in a minute."

"I told you, Claire. I'm not going," Jill said through gritted teeth as she unlocked the driver's door. "You and your friends have a good time. I'm sure I won't be missed."

"What's your problem?" I was more than a little fed up with her snotty attitude. "Can't you at least give them a chance? You have plenty of time to stop by for a minute. It's only three o'clock, and I know for a fact that Frankie's lessons aren't over till four."

Jill whirled on me, her eyes afire. "What's my problem? What the hell's your problem? Ever since the first of the year it's been 'Lora this' and 'Lora that.'"

She turned away and threw her books into the back seat. "According to you, Lora-Fucking-Tyler hung the goddamned moon. I've been your friend since seventh grade, and all of a sudden I'm not good enough for you anymore. That's my fucking problem. Satisfied?"

Her words cut deep, but I didn't know how to handle the hurt, so I turned it into anger. "You're fucking crazy." I fired the words at her and stormed away.

"Bet your ass, I am!" Jill yelled.

Fuming, I made it to my rattletrap Datsun B-210 and yanked open the door. Ignoring the wave of heat rushing from the car, I slid into the driver's seat and slammed my books onto the floorboard. What was that all about, anyway? So what if Lora and I had become friends? I was having fun, real fun. It didn't mean Jill and I weren't friends anymore. I hadn't done anything wrong. Sure Jill and I didn't hang out together like before, but she acted like we'd been dating for six years and I'd dumped her for Lora. It was stupid, that's what it was, plain stupid.

* * *

Jackie Milano's Pizza Oven was one of those picturesque small-town establishments that thrived in Franklin. Jackie, a second-generation Italian-American with stunning dark features and a down-home drawl, had parlayed his heritage into a thriving business. After all, the mostly Irish- and English-Americans living in town didn't know squat about Italian food, so Pizza Oven didn't have to be authentic, just hot and good.

I wheeled into the space beside Lora's red Pinto, still seething over Jill's outburst in the parking lot. But when I shifted the car into park and shut off the engine, a strange calm fell over me. Sitting there looking at the Pizza Oven's rough red brick exterior and tinted arched windows, I sensed my future lay inside. Among the familiar particleboard tables and Naugahyde booths, my destiny waited like a shadowy phantom, calling me forward but refusing to reveal itself.

I burst through the swinging front door and let the aroma of garlic and mozzarella cheese soak up the remnants of my foul mood. I found my friends sitting in the booth near the jukebox, sipping Cokes and talking. Jock and Lora sat on one side of the table, his muscular arm thrown over her shoulder. As I approached, Jock's maple-syrup eyes were a little too eager as he scanned me from head to toe. If he hadn't been Lora's boyfriend, I might have been flattered by the thin smirk that crossed his lips when he gazed at my chest, but even his chiseled features and boy-next-door charm couldn't tempt me into returning his flirtatious gaze. He belonged to Lora, and his stare made my blood boil.

On the other side of the booth sat Matthew Carter. His pale blue eyes danced as he talked about the upcoming football game against our archrivals, the South High Raiders. While Jock was the undisputed, all-around prince of sports at Franklin High, on the football field Matthew was king. He had it all—athleticism, poise, and leadership skills beyond his years. Most guys would've given their right arm to be Matthew—lean, handsome, with curly dark hair and the rugged good looks of a teenage Tom Selleck. But although his looks and popularity made him every girl's dream date, and the college recruiters had been lining up at his front door for over a year, Matthew never let it go to his head. He was the same gentle, soft-spoken little boy who'd carried my books in fourth grade.

True to form, Matthew stood up as I neared the table. "Hi, Claire. I was hoping you'd make it."

Lora and Jock exchanged knowing glances. Holy crap. They were setting us up. Matthew and I had been casual friends for years, but I had no idea he might have a romantic interest in me, and I blushed in spite of myself.

I slid into the booth and Matthew settled down beside me. "So, Claire," he said. "I hear you're the new star of the basketball team."

I shrugged. "I don't know about that, but we are having a pretty good season so far."

Lora glanced toward the three sophomore boys lined up to play Pac Man, and strained to be heard over the constant *wacca wacca* reverberating over our heads. "You should go to the game tomorrow night, Matthew. She'll need a cheering section, and I have to work."

"I'll come, too," Jock said with a wily grin. "I kind of like the looks of that little redheaded water girl."

Lora gave him a playful slap with her palm and a serious punch with her eyes. "You'd better keep your eyes to yourself, hotshot."

He squeezed her shoulder. "I'm kidding, for Christ's sake. If I wanted to be with her, I would, but I'm with you, ain't I?"

"Don't let me stand in your way, stud." She tried to wriggle from his embrace, but he held tight.

Jock's teddy-bear eyes went hard. "For fuck's sake, Lora, don't get all bent out of shape. I'm only saying—"

"I know what you're saying." She stopped struggling and cut him off at the knees with one of her mother's razor stares.

He jerked his arm from around her and stood up. "See you at practice, Matthew." He shot Lora a scowl and swaggered out the door like a gunslinger at high noon.

"Geez, what's up his ass?" I asked.

Lora picked up her uniform polo shirt with the Pizza Oven logo stitched on the left breast. "No big deal. I have to set him straight about once a month. If I don't, his head gets bigger than a hot-air balloon."

"That's all it is," Matthew said. "He'll cool off in a couple of hours, and they'll be like two peas in a pod again."

"He'll be whimpering like a whipped pup by the time my shift's over." From Lora's expression, I suspected she might be getting fed up with Jock. He was basically a nice guy, but he had a bone-deep proud streak that sometimes made him a little obnoxious. He wasn't one to cut down the less attractive girls or make fun of the sissy guys; he just fancied himself a notch above the regular kids in town, and I could tell his attitude bugged Lora more than she let on.

She stood up. "I'm on in ten minutes. You guys hang around, and I'll try to sneak you out a slice."

Matthew smiled at me. "Want to have a Coke and talk awhile?" His eyes twinkled like Christmas lights. How could I refuse?

We chatted about nothing through three sodas and a stolen slice of pepperoni pizza. I liked the way Matthew looked at me, his eyes never leaving mine as I prattled on about my older brother, my parents, and my nonexistent plans for the future. He smiled at all the right times and frowned when appropriate, never interrupting my train of thought. He spoke almost reverently about his college football career. He was concerned about making the right choices. His decisions would affect his entire life.

It amazed me how he handled all that pressure and still took time to listen to me, to make me feel important. The great Matthew Carter could be a total jerk and still get any girl in school, but that wasn't his style. That's why I liked him.

We waved goodbye to Lora, and Matthew walked me to my car. In gentlemanly fashion, he took my keys, turned the lock, and opened the door for me. "Your carriage awaits, m'lady," he said, in a terrible British accent.

"Why, thank you, kind sir." I attempted a curtsy, but it was about as believable as his accent.

"Uh, Claire, I was wondering if I could ask you something?" He shuffled his feet, leaning on one foot and then the other, and thrust his hands into his pockets.

"Sure. What is it?"

"You know there's this fall dance after the game Friday night?"
I nodded.

"I was wondering, if you're not busy or anything, if you'd like to go with me." He looked like a little kid begging for a piece of candy.

"I think I can fit you into my busy schedule," I said, smiling. "But I've had sooooo many offers."

He grinned and swatted a gnat away from his face. "You've got guys all over school after you, and you don't even know it, do you?"

"Liar." I slid into the driver's seat and slipped the key into the ignition. "I'll see you tomorrow at school, okay?"

He closed the door and leaned against the frame. "Meet me in the morning by the soda machine?"

I nodded and cranked the engine. Wow! Matthew Carter had asked me out. Was this my lucky day or what?

CHAPTER 8 .

It's 11:45 by the time I break away from the office, but I'll still beat the lunch rush. As I turn into Choppy's parking lot, my palms get slippery on the steering wheel. I find a space near the door, make sure Rebecca's car is in its regular spot, and glance in the rearview mirror to check that my lipstick isn't smeared. I smooth my eyebrows with my finger and pop a wintergreen mint into my mouth—a lot of preparation for a woman who won't notice. Oh well, one never knows when a potential customer might be sitting at the next table, so maybe my primping won't be in vain.

Rebecca is at the hostess station when I walk in. My guard is down, and when she smiles, I let my gaze linger too long. Feeling hungry for her, I shift my focus to the oil print over her left shoulder. If she sees how red my face is, she might get suspicious. My feelings will be exposed, and my only relief from hell will look at me as if I've violated her.

"What are you doing up here?" I ask, trying not to grin.

She blows a lock of hair from her eyes and reaches for a menu. "Can't find good help these days." She glances behind her to the mostly-empty tables. "It's all yours. Any place special you'd like to sit?"

"Anything's fine." I follow her to a table in the back, near her office. Her hair reaches an inch below her shoulders and bounces from side to side when she walks. It takes all my composure not to walk too close—close enough to catch the scent of her shampoo or graze my shoulder against hers. God, I'm pitiful.

"Enjoy your lunch," she says, opening the menu for me.

I peek over the top of the menu to watch her walk away. I love the way her hips sway. Her walk is like the soothing flow of the ocean at low tide, and I catch myself getting lost in a fantasy of rocking to sleep in her arms. A moment later, I snap back to reality and try to concentrate on the menu as she seats four old ladies at the table next to mine.

One of the ladies turns to me. "Pardon me, but is this seat taken?" she asks, putting her hand on the chair at my right.

"No, ma'am."

She holds up a shiny metal cane. "May I borrow it to hold my walking stick?"

"Of course." I get up and help her move the extra chair to their table.

As I'm sitting back down, Rebecca sneaks up behind me and helps me with my own chair. "You're such a lady," she whispers.

I turn my head and find my lips dangerously close to her cheek. "Be kind to widows and children. I think it says that in the Bible."

Rebecca taps my shoulder lightly. "I owe you a drink."

"Why?" But she has spun around and is halfway to the front door.

She seats two businessmen at the table on the other side of me. One of them is Gerald Roth, vice-president of a large printing company headquartered in town. I met him ten years ago when I sold him a hundred-thousand-dollar filing system that cut his clerk's workload in half. This year for Christmas, Gerald sent me a Virginia ham and a fifth of single-malt scotch. The ham's still in my freezer, but the scotch has been gone for weeks.

Gerald waves. "Keeping busy, Claire?"

"Not busy enough. You?"

"Keeping the bill collector away."

"I hear you." I know he's got enough cash squirreled away to keep a family of four comfortable for life.

Rebecca glides between us. She glances first at Gerald, then at me. "Between the two of you, you know everyone in town, don't you?"

"We're working on it," Gerald says.

Rebecca returns to my table. "I owe you a drink to pay for the hose I ruined last night."

"Thank you, but..." I try to say, but she's gone again. I want to focus on the menu, but I'm too busy wondering what she'll say on the next pass. The lunch rush has followed me in, so a minute's worth of conversation could take an hour.

After seating two more parties, she comes back. "I won't take no for an answer. Besides, I want to ask you something." She spins away.

"What do you want...?"

But Rebecca doesn't hear me, and my mind starts churning. What does she want? She can't feel that bad about snagging my stockings. Could she have an ulterior motive? What if she's sensed my attraction to her and wants to confront me? That would be awful.

Don't be paranoid, I remind myself. Rebecca can't know. I've never treated her with anything but respect. Come to think of it, I've gone out of my way to be polite. I'm jumping to silly conclusions and making myself sick for nothing, and even if she has figured me out, what's the harm? It's not like I've done something wrong. If having the hots for a pretty woman were against the law, lots of people would be serving life sentences.

Despite my reassurances, my stomach is in knots, and when Sandy arrives to take my order, I can barely ask her to bring me a chef salad with ranch dressing.

I glance around to see if Rebecca is on her way back. She's standing in front of a booth filled with four good-looking men in suits. They are all staring at her, flashing their best come-on smiles. She talks to them for a minute, paying special attention to the one with the square jaw and deep brown eyes.

She's got a big grin on her face when she gets back to me. "So when are you free for a drink?"

"It's not necessary, really."

"Of course it is." She whirls away again before I can wiggle out of the invitation.

It's not that I wouldn't love to have a drink with her, but I'm not sure if I'm up to it. I know I'll end up stumbling on some comment or another and look even more foolish than I feel right now. The only reason I'm considering it is that I'm curious about what she wants to ask me. It's got to be something stupid, but I'm still intrigued.

Sandy brings my order and Rebecca seats three more couples in the smoking section before she makes her way back. "What night?" she asks.

My mouth is full of croutons, and I have dressing on my lower lip. I snatch the napkin from my lap and wipe it away. "You don't have to do that," I finally manage to say.

"Of course I do. I'm a clumsy goof." A large group of nurses meanders through the front door. "I'll be right back." She hurries to the front and finds them a table near the window.

I don't take another bite of salad for a minute. My head is confused around her as it is, making it hard to seem coherent. All I need is a mouth full of iceberg lettuce to turn my tongue into a stumbling drunkard inside my mouth.

She comes back and glances toward the door. The coast seems clear for the moment. She sits down across from me and props her elbows on the table. Her eyes glimmer. "So, what night?"

"Rebecca, it's only a pair of pantyhose. Plus, it was my fault for having my big feet in your way."

"I know it's no big deal, but I thought we might make it girls' night out. I need to get out of here for a while, and you seem like you could stand to let your hair down for once."

I finally give in to those swirling eyes. "Okay, but you don't owe me anything."

"I still might." She bites her lip. "I'm having trouble with a filing cabinet, and I thought you might be able to help—what with you designing that type of thing and all."

Now I understand. Rebecca needs a service call. If she wants service, I'll give her service. I'll work my way right up those rock-hard thighs and into her silky panties. She'll never know what hit her.

I'm not sure where that thought came from, and I mentally slap myself. She's always been nice to me. It won't hurt me to help her out.

"Have you called the manufacturer?"

"Yeah, but they're no help." She stands up as another lunch party comes through the door.

I take a huge bite of salad. Who cares if I have dressing all over my face? At least it would cover the redness creeping up my cheeks. Fair skin and a tendency to blush are not a good combination, but it's my curse.

I hope Rebecca doesn't come back before I can get the check and make for the door. Something about being so close to her and making plans to go out for a drink disturbs me. It's like I'm cheating. But I have nothing to feel guilty about. I lived up to my end of the bargain in our relationship, kept my promises. The fact that it's over is nothing I can control. It was out of my hands for months before it actually ended.

I had known it would end badly. Once the end began, I knew I'd come out of it broken and afraid. You can't spend eighteen years with a woman, watch helplessly while she leaves you, and then go on as if nothing happened. I'm like a kid lost in the supermarket, wandering up and down the aisles of my life looking for that familiar face. I search everywhere for a glimpse of someone I know, the one who loves and protects me, but she's not there. She's found another place, a place better than here.

Rebecca comes back and sits on the edge of her chair. "How about tomorrow night?"

I pick at the remnants of my salad. "Tomorrow's Friday. Don't you have a hot date or something?"

She chuckles. "I've forgotten what a hot date is."

"Tell me about it."

"So does that mean we're on?"

"Okay. We're on."

"It'll be fun." She stands up, seeming to sense my excitement is fake. As she leaves, she looks back. "Meet me here about seven. Casual."

I nod and grab my purse. After tossing a bill on the table, I head toward the door.

This could turn out to be a very bad decision.

CHAPTER 9

Autumn came late that year. The days and nights were unusually warm for early October, but the mountains around Franklin were blanketed with the vigorous colors of the season—rusty oranges, buttercup yellows, and shades of red so dark and rich you'd swear they'd come from an artist's palette. The hues danced and swirled, dappled and mottled the landscape like a patchwork quilt thrown down to protect Mother Earth from winter's icy grasp.

But winter was the last thing on my mind. It was a breezy Saturday evening, and Matthew Carter and I were on our fifth date. It was a festive hometown evening at the annual Franklin High School fall carnival.

The sophomore class had sponsored a game where the object was to toss a football through the center of a radial tire. Big mistake—Matthew cleaned them out. He won nine stuffed koala bears, three packs of baseball cards, and a black light poster of a unicorn. And at the tender age of seventeen, Matthew already knew how to work the fans. When Principal Jarvis intervened and made him quit playing, my boyfriend distributed his winnings among the crowd of wide-eyed junior high kids who'd been watching.

Later, we nearly barfed up our corn dogs and popcorn on the Tilt-A-Whirl, and Matthew spent twelve dollars playing Skee-Ball to win me a fifty-cent Kewpie doll. I told him the gift was special because he'd had to work hard for it. He seemed to like that.

I liked being with him. He wasn't like most guys. He opened the car door for me and held my chair when I sat down. He was clean-cut, handsome, and just plain nice.

We'd left the festival and were barreling down Old Simms road, a winding two-lane flanked by waist-deep ditches and a dense overgrown forest. The full moon shone through the windshield, casting a soft glow across Matthew's profile.

He glanced at me. "It's still two hours till your curfew. Want to drive down by Fuller's Dam?"

I didn't know what to say. A couple of my previous dates had suggested a cruise to the best make-out spot in Franklin, but I'd declined. Matthew was different, though. I really liked him, so I shrugged, trying to seem calm. "I don't mind."

"We won't stay long. I thought some of the gang might be hanging out."

Did he think I bought that line? No one *hung out* at Fuller's Dam. There weren't any bonfires with kids sitting around strumming guitars and singing *Michael Row Your Boat Ashore* while roasting marshmallows on pointed sticks whittled from nearby saplings. No, the teenagers who took Fuller Creek Road were like us, two kids looking for a little privacy. Make that one and a half kids—part of me wasn't sold on the idea.

We drove in silence, the chilly evening wind tousling our hair through the half-open windows and cooling the heat in my cheeks. Matthew's left hand was draped across the top of the steering wheel, his eyes fixed on the blacktop ahead.

For a moment, I almost felt normal, almost caught a glimmer of that feeling the other girls talked about in the locker room—a nervous anticipation in the pit of my stomach, a prickling excitement like ants crawling beneath my skin. But as Matthew flicked the signal light and turned left onto Fuller Creek Road, I felt a little hazy. What was I doing anyway? We'd only been out a few times. Had I gone from being a goody-goody to being a slut because the great Matthew Carter had flashed his dazzling smile and bedroom eyes?

The front tires thumped when we veered onto the gravel road, and tiny rocks pelted the undercarriage. The sound reminded me of popcorn as I watched the darkness close in around us. Nothing but trees, crowding around us till they reached out and scrubbed the fenders as we passed.

Matthew pulled the car to the side of the road into a spot worn down by hundreds of tires on hundreds of cars carrying hundreds of horny teenagers. He cut the lights, killed the engine, and turned toward me. "I hope you don't think I brought you down here to take advantage of you." His voice was gentle and timid, nothing like the roar he used to bark out play changes at the line of scrimmage.

"If that's what I thought, I wouldn't be here," I said, trying to sound coy but coming off like Rod Stewart with the croup. I coughed and tried to act sexy.

"I want to be alone with you for a change, you know?"

"Why, Mr. Carter, are you trying to woo me?"

"My intentions are honorable." He placed his hand over his chest and jutted out his chin like a bulldog.

I snickered, somewhat more at ease. "And if you happen to steal a kiss..."

"That'd be okay, too."

A wind gusted down the lane, sending multicolored leaves skittering across the windshield. Matthew's eyes went serious. He leaned close and found my lips in the near-total darkness. I leaned into him, hungry for affection, any kind of affection, but what I got was more like a bad soft porno flick, with him gouging his tongue into my mouth like a dull knife and me making indistinct wheezing noises through my nose.

Right there on Fuller Creek Road, on the very spot where half the teen pregnancies in town originated, Matthew and I were a regular comedic instruction book of what not to do with the opposite sex. Not knowing any better, I tried to enjoy the sensations and share his excitement. Besides, it was high time I explored the passions that kept other kids on pins and needles. I was tired of wondering, dissatisfied with constant self-assurances that my sex drive would eventually kick in. This was it, my moment of reckoning. I'd like it or die.

So, half an hour and a gallon of saliva later, I didn't resist when he unbuttoned my blouse. That part wasn't so bad, no worse than wearing my bathing suit at the community pool. When he clumsily reached behind my back and unhooked my bra, I didn't try to stop him. That took a little more gumption. No one but me and maybe my mother had seen my naked chest since preschool.

As he touched my breast, I closed my eyes and tried to take pleasure from it, but his hands felt like giant bear paws and were rough from years of football. Was this what all the hubbub was about, having a boy maul you, feeling his callused skin scrub against yours? Did the other girls like this?

I didn't know how much of his heavy-handed petting my untried bosom could take, and the thought of him carrying his manhandling between my legs made me shudder. No matter how determined I was to go exploring, there was no way I'd let him touch me below the waist, no way he'd thrust those huge fingers inside of me.

He didn't try to get in my pants, so I sat quietly and endured. Matthew was bound to get tired, but when he clamped his teeth on my left nipple, I let out a shriek.

"Oh God, I'm sorry," he gasped, pushing himself toward the other side of the car. "I would never hurt you, Claire, you know that." He slid back to me and took my hand. "I'm so sorry."

I gathered my open blouse, secured a middle button, and let out an embarrassed giggle. "I know you didn't mean to."

Honestly, I was somewhat glad he'd bitten me. At least it was over and we could go home.

He pulled me to him, cradling me against his chest. His heart was beating hard, and a trickle of sweat glistened on his neck. "I guess I'm not the ladies' man everyone makes me out to be."

I felt sorry for him. What kind of girlfriend was I, anyway, hoping he'd stop touching me? Matthew was a good boy; he just didn't know what he was doing. Had he been a star quarterback on the first day of Little League football try-outs? Of course not. He'd gotten good at sports the same way all the great ones did—a little talent and a lot of practice. Maybe that's all we needed, some practice. A lot of practice.

I put my hand inside his shirt, running my fingers through tufts of still-sparse hair. Reaching his left nipple, I squeezed gently. "Maybe I should show you how it feels."

"Uh, okay," he whispered, taking me much too literally. He stripped his polo shirt off over his head and guided my lips to his neck.

So much for trying to make him feel better. Now I was lost. What the heck was I supposed to do? I didn't have a clue, so I did what any high school girl would do in that situation. I sucked in a deep breath and faked it. Practice, practice, practice.

I kissed his neck for a moment and, to my surprise, found the salty-musk taste somewhat arousing. Then I moved down his chest. When I found his erect nipple between my lips, something inside me exploded. A lava-hot river of desire shot straight to my groin, and before I realized it, I clambered into his seat and was straddling him like a lap dancer.

Matthew's erection bulged through his jeans, and I pressed hard against it. My butt ground against the steering wheel, but I didn't mind. Something strange was going on inside me, and I didn't want it to stop.

We gyrated together, bucking in an odd, out-of-sync rhythm. My hair fell across his broad shoulders; his hot breath rushed across my neck. All the while, I suckled on one nipple and then the other, and ran my fingers along his chest. His hands never left my waist, but he kissed the back of my neck and nibbled my ears until he could take no more. With a gut-wrenching moan, he released himself into his brand new Levis. A bit startled by his climax, I reined in my own desire, and sat still, resting my head on his shoulder.

Matthew seemed satisfied. He held me for half an hour and then kissed me gently and slipped his class ring onto my finger. "I'd like you to wear this," he whispered.

"I'd like to wear it." I twirled the much-too-large band around my index finger. I was going steady with Matthew Carter. In twenty-four hours, I would be the envy of every girl in school.

We were quiet on the ride back to my parents' house, each deep in thought about our new maturity. I wasn't sure what we'd done, but it seemed backward somehow, like he should've been on top. Matthew seemed to like it though, and it was a new experience for me. That night, my boyfriend wasn't the only one going home with soggy underwear, but he'd reached a level of fulfillment that still eluded me, a release so exquisite that it couldn't be compared to anything I knew at the time. I would eventually understand the utter satisfaction he felt at that moment, but not for a very long while.

And it wouldn't be with Matthew Carter.

CHAPTER 10

What a way to ruin my afternoon. Why did Rebecca have to go and ask me out for a drink? Seems to me there are two things that can come of it. One, I'll end up with a worse crush than I already have on a straight woman. Or two, I won't really like her and my fantasy will be ruined. Either way, it'll suck.

I'm no good at work when I get like this, but I stay till everyone else is gone for the day, so it's dark by the time I get home. The Kingsleys' front light is on. The neighborhood watch people recommend leaving a light on when the man of the house is out, and Elizabeth takes home security very seriously.

I'm letting Jitterbug out of the guestroom when the doorbell rings. It has to be Elizabeth. She can't stand to sit in front of the TV with the kids, so she comes over whenever the good doctor is working evenings. I unlock the front door and motion her in.

My neighbor's physical beauty never escapes my notice. She's one of those tall, leggy, blue-eyed blondes who's never dieted a day in her life, and even after having two kids, still looks great in a bikini. Most of the women I know would kill to be her—or die to fuck her. But those women don't know her like I do. They don't know that beneath that pretty package is a compassionate, loving, and truly beautiful lady.

If only Elizabeth weren't straight. And married. And my dearest friend.

She enters the foyer, and I flip on the hall light as we make our way toward the den. It's the one room in the house where I feel protected. A few weeks after Lora's departure, I went on a refurbishing spree, determined to rid my home of bad memories. I bought a new matching sofa, loveseat, and chair upholstered in forest green fabric, a new wrought iron fireplace set, and the biggest freaking TV on the showroom floor at Circuit City. My spending binge kept me busy for a few days, but the high was temporary, and I decided it would be better for my bankbook not to drown my sorrows in retail hell.

"What's happening on God's little acre? Have a meeting of the silicone sisters today?" I'm referring to a weekly brunch at the country club where pseudo-genteel ladies discuss their favorite plastic surgeons with the zest of good ol' boys talking about their favorite coon dogs. In truth, very few families in Spring City are more than two generations away from sod-busting hillbillies.

"I go for the entertainment value." Elizabeth dances around Jitterbug's sniffs and slurping kisses. She settles on the loveseat and pats the dog on the head. "Old Birdie McElroy got a snoot full of sherry and dropped her pillbox hat in the lobby fountain. Took the maintenance guy twenty minutes to dig it out of the filter."

I laugh as I pull my skirt up to my waist and strip off my pantyhose. "Still going shopping with me next week?"

"Sure, if we can be back by three. The kids have some kind of practice every day next week." Elizabeth tucks a strand of her shoulder-length hair behind her ear and looks at me. Her charm seems effortless, as if she naturally has the kind of simple beauty and confident air that other busy moms have to work at.

I toss my pantyhose on the floor by the coffee table and plop down on the sofa. "We can make it a short day."

I'm glad she's decided to join me. When I'm by myself, I have too much time to think about the way my life was supposed to be at this point. Fantasies pile up until I almost believe my lover will be there when I get home. I can almost convince myself it's all been a bad dream, that it never happened, but when I slip the key into the lock and open the kitchen door, the house has that smell of emptiness, the stale aroma of lifeless air that clings to my skin until I admit the truth—Lora is gone.

Elizabeth is reading my thoughts. Her tone of voice says she's here to rescue me from myself. "Any big plans for this weekend? We're having a little get-together on Saturday night and we'd love for you to come."

I rub my temples and try to erase the images etched into my brain. "I'm going out tomorrow, but Saturday's good. Tonya's been after me to go bar whoring with her on Saturday, and I've been looking for an excuse to get out of it."

"Hold on! You're going out tomorrow night? I don't believe it." She leans toward me, her eyes expectant, ears keen.

"It's not what you think."

"Is it a woman?"

"Yes," I say in a flat voice. I have no high hopes for the evening, and I surely don't want Elizabeth to get all excited about it. If she catches a whiff of romance in the air, I'll never hear the end of it.

"So my little Claire has a date." She giggles as she leans on the arm of the loveseat. "Tell me all about it."

"There's nothing to tell. The girl that manages Choppy's asked me to look at a filing cabinet she's having trouble with. Sweetened the deal with a free drink."

Elizabeth sits back. "Let me think. Is she the one with brown hair, dimples, nice body?"

I nod.

"She's cute." Elizabeth blows a kiss in my direction. "Please kiss and tell. You don't know how I miss those raunchy girl talks we used to have. Before you came along, I had to get my jollies from those true confession rags at the grocery checkout."

I chuckle. "Don't give up on the rags. I won't be doing any kissing or telling. My racy story-telling days are over. Besides, I don't think I'm Rebecca's type."

"What's her type?"

"The one with a penis."

"You never know, Claire. Looking at a filing cabinet sounds like a pretty flimsy excuse to have cocktails."

"Shut up," I say with a groan. "She's looking to save a buck on a service call."

"But it could be something else." Elizabeth twists her gold necklace around her index finger and starts humming a sappy wedding song.

"Stop it. I don't even think she's gay."

"Oh, pooh. These days, you can't tell by looking."

"How can you tell?"

"I'm not sure, but I don't think it's by looking."

She has a point. In our younger years, my lover and I weren't an easy peg. We enjoyed being feminine even when we threw on our coveralls and put up the drywall in our first house. But when two women reach thirty-five and have lived together almost half their lives, it doesn't matter how much makeup they wear or how often they get their nails done. Chances are there's something else going on.

Some of the single ones are harder to figure, though. There are all kinds of reasons a thirty-something woman might live alone. Maybe she's divorced or separated, or maybe she just likes her independence, but I have no idea if Rebecca Greenway lives alone. I don't even know where she lives.

A thought has been bugging me for the past few hours, an undeveloped idea that seems to be coming together. Since I've been single, I've come in contact with lots of sexy straight women, charming women with beautiful faces and lovely bodies, but I've never had the kind of adolescent crush I seem to have on Rebecca. Do I suspect that she might be gay? Have I picked her up on my gaydar screen but convinced myself that she's off limits as a means of keeping my distance?

I close my eyes and snuggle down into the sofa. "I don't know how to tell about women either. I'm out of practice."

Elizabeth's voice flows over me, a soft, breathy lullaby. "It's time you got back into practice."

I open my eyes a little and see her sitting there, brows knitted together, mouth turned down at the corners. We should drop this conversation, but I go on. "I've always been with someone. I don't know anything about how to approach a woman."

"Does she know what happened?"

"No, and I'm not telling her."

"She should know, Claire, especially if she's interested in more than a filing cabinet."

"If by some crazy chance she is interested in me, I still don't want her to know." I raise my hand, telling Elizabeth to drop it.

"Why not?"

"I'm not the only person in the world who's gone through this kind of thing. It happens every day to all kinds of people. If I told her, it would make me sound like an even bigger loser than I really am."

Elizabeth looks hard at me. "Telling the truth doesn't make you a loser."

Truth? Elizabeth doesn't know the truth from axle grease. I'm the only one who knows everything, right down to the real reason I have this God-forsaken scar on the back of my hand. Or to be more precise, the real reason I have this God-forsaken scar on the back of my *fist*. But I'm not telling. If it eats a hole right though my guts, I won't tell.

Elizabeth seems to be thinking out loud. "I'm not saying there's anything wrong with being single. But there's nothing wrong with being social, either. Humans are social animals."

"I'm social," I protest. "I've got you and Tonya, and I get all the interaction at work I can handle."

"It's not the same."

"I'm not up to starting over. Anyway, who'd want an old workaholic has-been like me?"

"You act like you're a hundred years old. You had one sweet beginning, and you're plenty young enough..."

"That first sweet beginning was followed by one hell of a sour ending." I blink back tears. My sobs will come later in the evening, when only Jitterbug can hear.

"So you'll have another sweet beginning. I know how hard it must be on you to come home to this empty house every day. I miss her being here, too, but your life isn't over, Claire." Elizabeth gets up, ambles to the kitchen, and brings back a bottle of water from the refrigerator.

She sits with me on the sofa, and I shoot her a sideways look. "I've never even slept with anyone else. What if we weren't doing it right?"

"If you both liked it, you were doing it right." She unscrews the bottle cap and takes a sip of water.

"And there are so many crazy people out there. What if I end up with some psycho?"

"You've got more excuses than my kids when they get a bad grade." She's quiet for a moment. "So are you going to make a move on her tomorrow night?"

"Good God, no! I don't even know how to kiss anymore."

"Oh pooh, you never forget how to kiss." Elizabeth leans back and looks at me.

I do an exaggerated lip smack and stick my tongue out at her. "I think I have."

"Okay then. I've got an idea." She puts the cap back on the bottle and sits it on a sandstone coaster on the coffee table. "Kiss me and I'll tell you if you're okay."

I laugh out loud. "You're insane. That would be like kissing my sister."

"Come on, it's just me, for Christ's sake! And it's not like I've never kissed a girl before. In junior high, I gave my cheerleading squad kissing lessons."

I laugh even harder. "How could I measure up to a professional like you?"

Elizabeth grins and wets her lips. "When I first met Jared, he kissed like a baboon, but now he can kiss the silver off a dollar."

"I'm impressed, but I'm allergic to silver. Breaks me out something awful."

She ignores me. "Come on, I wouldn't do this for just anyone. Kiss me. I'll be honest."

"Bad idea," I say again, but she's sliding closer until our faces are nearly touching.

"Purely scientific," Elizabeth whispers, her minty breath flowing over my lips. "Get the nervousness out of your system, and you'll be ready for the real thing with the Choppy's chick tomorrow."

"I told you, I won't be kissing Rebecca." I look at Jitterbug. "What do you think about your Aunt Elizabeth? Has she gone loony or what?" Jitterbug gives me a quizzical look and licks her chops.

"See? Even Jitterbug agrees." She slides closer. "Pucker up before I have to use force."

"What's Jared going to say about this?"

"He won't care. It'll probably turn him on."

I want to ask what happens if it turns me on, but think better of it. I don't kid myself. Even before my relationship fell apart, I'd entertained a couple of whimsical daydreams about kissing Elizabeth. She's an enchanting woman inside and out, and I could easily be swept away by her sapphire eyes and honest charm, but I always think of something disgusting like maggots before I let my fantasy get too far. I can't have her as a lover, and there's nothing like sexual tension to ruin a friendship, and where would I be without Elizabeth?

I look at her again. "I can't believe you're serious."

"As a heart attack." She motions for me to move closer as a smile skips at the corners of her mouth. "Come here and kiss me, you sexy thing."

"Oh, good Lord!" I slide toward her and plant a smacky dry kiss half on her lips and half on her cheek, the same kind of kiss I lay on her children every time I get close enough. The kids used to love it, but now it embarrasses them beyond belief. I do it a lot.

"That was pitiful." Elizabeth takes my shoulders and turns me to face her. "Close your eyes and pretend I'm some hot babe."

"You are a hot babe." I frown and close my eyes. "This is stupid."

"Think of it as a warm-up exercise. Now give me all you've got."

She leans toward me. Her breath hits my cheek. The powdery scent of her perfume drifts into me. When her lips touch mine, every cell within me swirls and swishes in a clumsy tango of mixed emotions. Out of sheer instinct, I open my mouth and meet her tongue, soft and warm. Her lips are full and wet, sliding across mine with a relaxed caress. I kiss her from inside myself, a place deep but alive, and I'm lost, drifting through a desire I thought was gone long ago.

I move my hand to the back of her neck, running my fingers into her hair, and pull her to me, gliding my tongue into her mouth. She welcomes me with a light sigh and entices me to stay, tickling my lips with hers.

I know I'm kissing one woman, but I feel as if there are three. I feel my lover, the one I'll never know again. I feel Elizabeth, the need I've held chaste and secret. I feel Rebecca, the passion I want to know but never will. Then a seed of common sense takes over, and I slide my hand away from Elizabeth's neck, stroking her cheek as I pry my lips from hers.

I'm hot and embarrassed, but try to sound cool. "How was that?"

"God almighty." She sounds breathless. "You need to give Jared lessons."

"I thought he could kiss the silver off a dollar."

"He kisses like a baboon." Elizabeth scoots back to the end of the sofa and grins as she fans her face with her hand. "Damn, girl. You turned me on."

"You're just being nice." I settle into the corner of the sofa and cross my legs. No sense letting my groin get any big ideas; that kiss was a once in a lifetime thing.

She catches my eyes as she reaches for her water bottle. "I'm not being nice, and don't try to tell me that didn't turn you on a little."

I stifle a giggle. "I'm not comatose, you know."

"Well, I know one doctor who's going to get lucky tonight." Elizabeth fans her face again before taking a long swallow of water. "And if you've got one lick of sense, I know one restaurant manager who'll get lucky tomorrow night."

"Don't tell Jared about this, okay? We're silly for even doing it."

"I'm not going to lie to my husband. Besides, we're not talking about wife swapping here. It was just one little friendly kiss to work up your courage. He'll understand."

"But he'll look at me funny." I cover my face with both hands.

"He won't look at you funny."

I drop my hands and stare at her. "How do you know? Men can get defensive about things like this. I don't want him to think I'm trying to move in on his wife."

"Honey, men don't get defensive about girl-on-girl action. They get excited. Truth be told, he'll probably be mad that he wasn't here to see it."

It hits me harder now. I just kissed Elizabeth. I slap my hand to my forehead. "Oh, my God."

She doesn't seem worried about what her husband will think, and it strikes me as a little odd. But there are all kinds of relationships in this world. Maybe Jared won't mind.

Elizabeth sits up and dead-eyes me. "If I'd thought it would create a problem, I wouldn't have suggested it. And it was my idea, not yours. Besides, think about it. If you can kiss me, you can surely lay a big wet one on Rebecca."

"My neighbor's going to think I'm a pervert."

"He's thought that since you moved in." Elizabeth grabs my elbow. "Don't worry. I promise, it's okay."

I look at Jitterbug, who is busy licking her privates. "Jit, don't ever poop in Dr. Kingsley's yard again. I've left enough mess in his territory for the both of us."

Elizabeth laughs as she stands up. "I'd better go make sure the kids aren't burning the house down." Before she opens the front door, she looks back at me. "Bring a date Saturday night. Larry Maxwell is coming, and I don't want you to suffer through his boring stories at dinner."

I wave her away and watch the door close. The house is quiet except for the sound of Jitterbug's incessant licking. The silence pushes against my eardrums and makes my head throb. I reach for the TV remote, turn the set on, and flip through the channels. The choppy news dialogue and intermittent commercial music warms the chill inside me. Finally, I get up, pick up my discarded pantyhose, and wander toward our bedroom. Jitterbug knows the drill and leads me down the hall.

"Jitterbug," I call from behind her. "What do you think of me? The first person I kiss is Elizabeth. How does that make sense?"

Jitterbug stops and glances at me before entering the bedroom. For some reason, she'll wander all over the house in pitch dark, but she won't go into our bedroom till I turn on the light. On some level, I think she knows something isn't right. After all this time, her instinct still tells her someone is missing.

I toss my pantyhose into the hamper, take off my work clothes, and put them back on their hangers. A quick snap of my bra hook, and I crawl under the sheets naked.

I still have the urge to reach for her, to feel her hand slip into mine as I drop away into darkness. Some nights I swear she's beside me, whispering nonsense in her sleep, snuggling against my back when she hears distant thunder. I rub my hand across the sheets, but she's not there. I am alone.

I shudder and reach for the sleeping pills on the nightstand. No way am I going to fall asleep without help tonight.

CHAPTER 11

It's scary how your life can change so quickly. In one instant, you can turn into a whole other person, someone you'd never have recognized in the mirror. The day my life changed didn't start out so different from any other Sunday. I'd gone to early church services with Mom and Dad, had our usual Sunday fried chicken lunch at home, and headed to Lora's house to catch *Terror Theater* on channel six.

The afternoon lingered on like the dreary black-and-white movies flickering on the ten-inch portable TV sitting on Lora's dresser. Jock and Matthew were out of the picture on Sundays. Vincent Price and Boris Karloff were our boyfriends of the moment as we gobbled up handfuls of popcorn and Oreo cookies and tried to scare each other to death.

It wasn't hard to be frightened in the Tyler house. Between Mrs. Tyler, the prison matron, and Grandpa Kane sitting like a huge, bleary-eyed yard gnome on the front porch, I walked on eggshells. But Lora's bedroom was less intimidating. Although the room was kept immaculate as a result of her mother's orders, Lora had managed to put a bit of herself into her private space. She had draped a red scarf over the lamp on her bedside table, making the room glow like the fortuneteller's tent at the carnival. A brass-framed picture of Jock sat on the dresser by the television, and a half-dozen snapshots from her younger days were taped neatly to the full-length mirror on the back of the door. But Lora's bed was as hard as her mother's disposition, and I could never get comfortable on it.

The second film in a mummy trilogy was well into its first hour when Lora looked at me and out of nowhere asked, "Claire, are you a virgin?" She never took her eyes off my face as I squirmed for an answer.

I figured with Jock as her boyfriend, she was pretty experienced, and I wasn't about to confess my naiveté. Looking like a prude to Lora would embarrass me to no end.

"Are you?" was my best reply.

"Yeah." She shifted her gaze back to the toilet-paper-covered actor chasing a buxom brunette down a darkened country path.

"Me, too," I murmured.

It would've suited me fine if she'd dropped the subject, but she added, "Jock wants to do it, but I'm not sure."

"If you don't want to do it, don't." I looked at her but couldn't get a read on how she felt. She seemed confused and frustrated.

"I want to—kind of." She puffed out a grunt and leaned back against the headboard. "I don't know. It's like one day I'm ready and the next day I'm not."

"Think it would hurt?" I asked.

"They say it does the first time." Lora seemed twisted up in her clothes. She wiggled onto her side, then rolled onto her back. She stared at the ceiling, her unblinking eyes focusing on a thought I couldn't read but somehow understood.

I popped a caramel in my mouth and sucked on it. "Well, it's a big step. You should be sure before you do anything. You can't take it back, you know."

She looked at me from the corner of her eye. "I don't think I want Jock to be my first."

I was stunned. "Who, then?"

She shot me one of her devilish grins. "What's the most you've ever done with a boy?"

My thoughts turned to the night with Matthew as we flapped against our clothes, covered with sweaty need. Neither of us understood exactly what we were striving for, only that we had to have it. The incident was three weeks old and hadn't recurred, but it had left a mark on me, and my heart skipped.

"Come on," Lora said. "Tell me."

"It's too embarrassing." I hid my face with my hands.

Lora sat up and leaned toward me. "I'll tell, if you will."

Normally I would've held out, but I felt a unique fascination with the idea of hearing about Lora and Jock. My stomach tightened at the thought of him kissing her, roving her body with his lips and hands. A spark flickered through me when I imagined her pressing against him, caught up in the heat of forbidden passion.

"Okay." I was warm with anticipation.

"I've let him take off my bra a bunch of times. About two months ago, I started letting him touch me down there." She pointed toward the zipper of her Calvin Klein jeans.

The vision of his hand between her legs, her hips gyrating with his touch, had a strange, erotic effect on me. My palms got damp, my face flushed, and a hot, trembling sensation settled into my groin. Almost like the feeling I'd had with Matthew that Saturday night at Fuller's Dam, but much more intense, almost unbearable. Was this normal? Was this how other girls felt when they talked about their boyfriends?

I had trouble looking at Lora and focused on the television as I asked, "On top of your clothes or under?"

"On top for now."

"Are you going to let him go under?"

"Sometime, I guess." She looked hard at me and settled back into the feather throw pillows resting against the headboard. "I know that's not going very far when three girls in school are already pregnant, but I don't want to rush it, you know?"

"Me either. Who wants to drag a kid to the prom?" A distinct tremor rattled my voice.

Lora giggled and caught my eye, her own voice low and throaty. "Okay, your turn."

I tried to tell her, but words wouldn't come. "I... I can't. I'm sorry."

"I told you, so you have to at least give me a hint. I won't tell."

When I looked into Lora's eyes, an unusual burst of recklessness rose within me. "It was with Matthew a couple of weeks ago. I guess..." But my courage retreated, and I turned away.

"It's okay, you can tell me. We're best friends, right? I swear, I won't tell a soul." Lora touched my arm, sending an odd vibration through my skin.

Reaching down into the pit of my quivering stomach, I looked back at her. "I think I got to second base."

Her eyebrows knitted together. She frowned, then smiled. "You mean *he* got to second base."

"Kind of. But I think I did, too."

"What did you do, get *him* out of *his* bra?" She chuckled.

"Well..." I couldn't go on. What I'd done with Matthew was the most natural I'd ever felt with a boy, but now it seemed freakish.

"Come on, tell me." Lora's expression got serious. She bit her lip as she searched my eyes.

It all seemed stupid. I wanted to hide under the covers, but the bedspread was tucked neatly and I had nowhere to run. Feeling exposed and perverted, I started to get up, but Lora tightened her grip on my arm. In her eyes, I saw something I'd never seen there before, almost like the hungry look Matthew sometimes gave me before we kissed.

"Show me," she whispered.

Lora's words hung in my ears, and her expression unnerved me. For the first time in my life, the idea of touching a girl crossed my mind, and for an instant, I saw myself kissing Lora. I had to be misreading her, had to be misinterpreting the visions in my mind's eye. She couldn't be suggesting that I show her what we'd done. She didn't really want me to put my hands on her. Surely I couldn't be considering it.

"What did you say?" I muttered.

"Show me." Her eyes were level, but her voice wavered.

I was mesmerized by her stare. "Are you serious? You want me to demonstrate?"

She slid an inch closer. I smelled sex on her breath, felt it radiating from her eyes. Something very strange was going on, and I found myself caught up in it, wanting to take it a step farther.

"I don't know how." I wasn't sure she heard me, wasn't sure if I'd said the words out loud or only thought them.

"Did you touch his chest?" she whispered, inching still closer.

"Yes." I couldn't move, didn't want to.

"Then show me."

Never taking my eyes off hers, I placed my hand across my own chest as if about to pledge allegiance to the flag. My heart thrashed so hard I thought it would break through my ribs.

"Show me like this." Lora took my hand and placed my damp palm flat on her chest, just above her bra. Her skin seemed to burn through her blouse, searing my fingers.

I was on the verge of hyperventilating. Did she want me to do this? Was she going to follow through, or was she toying with me? Would she stop at the last second and say it was a joke?

"Over or under his shirt?" she asked between shallow breaths. Her voice trembled. If she was acting, she deserved an Academy Award.

"Under." I let her control me, unwilling to instigate the wild and erotic acts racing through my head, for fear of retribution. If Lora wanted me to touch her, she'd have to make it so clear a blind man could see.

Holding my hand against her, she reached for the top button of her cotton blouse. "Do you want to show me what you did with Matthew?"

Yes! Holy shit, yes! My mind and body screamed, but I couldn't speak. She'd already loosened her last button and was slipping her blouse off her shoulders. When the fabric fell from beneath my hand and I touched her naked skin, I almost stopped breathing. She was so soft, so small, yet her sheer intensity overpowered me.

"Don't suppose Matthew had a bra on, did he?" she asked.

I shook my head.

Holding my hand against her, blouse dangling by one sleeve from her elbow, she reached behind her back and unhooked her bra. It fell away, showing me all of her. My head started to hurt. I took a slow breath and let my gaze linger on her shoulders and eventually come to rest on her full breasts. She sat before me, bare and venerable, exposed but not ashamed. I was in awe of her.

For the first time in my life, I felt a connection with someone, a bond stronger than my raging hormones, deeper than our friendship. Lora *trusted* me—with her reputation, her body, but most of all, with a part of her more meaningful than either. She knew I wouldn't hurt her. Somehow she understood that I didn't want to take anything from her, that I only wanted to please her.

A craving rose in the pit of my stomach, a physical and emotional longing so intense it brought tears to my eyes. When I saw these feelings mirrored in her lovely face, my breathing went shallow and I thought I would faint.

It seemed natural when she released her grip on my hand and allowed my fingers to trace down the curve of her cleavage. It was like reaching toward heaven and experiencing the pure and simple beauty of a perfect white cloud. I touched her the way I wanted to be touched, with respect and appreciation for what she was giving me, a gift that, until that moment, I didn't know I needed.

Lora slid closer. Her blouse slipped away as she wrapped her arm around me. I leaned in and kissed her shoulder. She smelled of baby powder and honey, and I lingered in the curve of her neck, sliding my lips against her skin.

She moaned and pulled me closer, killing me with pleasure. I kissed her skin again, this time along her chest. She ran her fingers through my hair and grazed her nails along my shoulders. My lips found the place over her heart. It pounded even harder than mine. Guided by instinct, I traced my lips along her breast and, without hesitation, drew her erect flesh into my mouth. Sweet and ripe as a summer strawberry, her taste set me free. I reveled in her—the silky feel of her skin against mine, the rhythm of her breath, the subtle moans escaping her as my lips and hands touched her.

When she shuddered and stroked my cheek, I was overwhelmed by the need to kiss her lips. I had to give her part of me, accept her as she'd accepted me, but as I rose to find her mouth, an ice-cold pain pounded me between the eyes.

"Lora!" Her mother's voice sliced down the hallway. "Chop, chop, young lady. You're going to be late for choir practice."

Lora jumped up, and I slid off the bed and tossed her the discarded blouse. When the door flew open, I was sitting on the floor, staring at a dog food commercial while Lora fastened the last of her buttons.

Lora turned her back to her mother and tucked in her shirt. "Geez, Mom, I'm changing clothes. We'll leave in a minute."

Her mother glared at me, then at Lora. "I would think you two could find something better to do with your Sunday afternoons than watch trash on television." She turned to leave, then paused in the doorway. "And for God's sake, Lora, take that scarf off the lamp. It looks like a whorehouse in here."

Mrs. Tyler knew what we'd been doing, I was sure of it. She'd shape-shifted into a fly or a gnat and flown through the keyhole, or turned herself into a fog and crept under the door. She'd watched us and was now plotting a slow and agonizing death for the girl who'd done unspeakable things to her daughter.

"Come on." Lora's tone was edged with frustration. "I have to go."

The moment was over, but I was swimming in passion—and drowning in fear. We'd made a terrible mistake, a horrible, wonderful blunder. What would the kids at school say? Oh God, what would my parents think? It wasn't right. It wasn't normal. Lora and I would be cursed for life if anyone found out. Worse than that, we'd go straight to hell. Everyone knew that's what the Bible said. Touch a girl, go to hell. That's what it said, right?

But why did it feel so good? Her arms had felt so small around me. Her skin had been so soft, not like a boy's. Not at all like a boy. Guys were big and rough, usually taking what they could get. Lora hadn't taken anything. She'd given me something—a part of herself.

I struggled to my feet and followed Lora from the room, my eyes lingering on the seat of her jeans as she walked me to my car. I tried to stop looking at her but couldn't. I tried to stop imagining how she'd look naked, but my mind's eye worked of its own accord, stripping off her clothes and returning my lips to her breasts. Oh, God, I had to be insane.

It was October 24.

My new birthday.

CHAPTER 12

It's six o'clock on Friday night, and I'm meeting Rebecca in an hour.

I step out of the shower and towel-dry my hair. Jitterbug tries to lick the water droplets from my calves, but I'm too fast for her. I learned a long time ago to dry my legs first, or I'll get a doggie tongue-bath, and Jitterbug will get an upset stomach from drinking hot water. Tonight of all nights, I don't want to spend my time cleaning up after a sick dog.

I dry my hair and put on my makeup. Dressed only in my underwear, I go to the walk-in closet and stare at the rows of blouses, slacks, and pullovers. Rebecca said casual, so a pair of jeans, tan v-neck sweater, and Birkenstock mules should do.

I pull on my leather jacket, put Jitterbug in the guestroom, and check the time. 6:50. I'll be about five minutes late. Perfect—don't want to seem too anxious.

When I get to Choppy's, the lot is packed and I have to park at the dry cleaners across the street. Rebecca's car is not in the usual spot, and for a second, I consider turning around and going back home to Jitterbug and a TV dinner. Think of the embarrassment if she's forgotten our plans. I'll feel dumber than dumb if I wander in and wait for her for half an hour only to find out she's ditched me for some hunk driving a Jag.

But if I turn back now, I'll never know for sure, so I grit my teeth and prepare for the worst.

Inside, I find the restaurant as full as the parking lot. Not accustomed to being in Choppy's on Friday night, I take a long look around. The crowd, ranging from business people in suits and dresses to university students in jeans and sneakers, is crammed around tables, hovering around the bar, and leaning against the exposed-brick walls. I scan the faces but don't see Rebecca. I saunter to the hostess stand and ask the college-age girl in a low-cut black dress if Rebecca is in. The girl gives me a huge grin and points to the bar. "She's the worst bartender I've ever seen."

"Thanks." I slip by and head for the bar.

Sure enough, Rebecca is there, juggling highball glasses and customers. The woman talking to her through a tequila sunrise is the regular bartender. As she watches, Rebecca measures the liquor and mixer like she's in a chemistry lab.

I slip sideways between a rough-looking biker in a black leather jacket and a geek in aviator frame glasses. My smile feels huge, but when Rebecca looks at me, it grows.

"Hey," she says. "I'll be right there."

"No rush."

She looks muddled and tired, but she's grinning when she steps toward me and slaps a cocktail napkin on the bar. "Might be a few minutes. How about a drink on the house?"

"What's your specialty?"

Rebecca leans in close to my ear and cups her hand beside her mouth. "I suck at this. To be safe, you'd better have a beer or a glass of wine."

I like the way her sweet perfume mixes with the alcohol on her hands, so I fake indecision, savoring the closeness. "Make it a Bud," I finally say, wishing to inhale her again.

When Rebecca turns away and bends over the cooler for my drink, I stare too long. I'm still thinking how good she looks in khaki pants when she puts the frosty mug on my cocktail napkin and pours the beer.

She glances toward a man with a droopy mustache and an empty glass. "One of my regular bartenders called in sick. His backup is on the way, but it might be thirty minutes or so. Is that okay?"

"I'll take a free beer any time I can," I reply, hoping I don't sound like an alcoholic.

She laughs and turns her attention to the biker beside me. "Ready for another?"

"Ready for you, darlin'," he says. "Why don't you come out from behind there and let me take you for a ride?"

Rebecca grabs a clean highball glass from the drainer and fills it with whiskey. "Now, George, you know I can't go for rides with customers."

George turns his bloodshot eyes to me. "How about you, darlin'? Wouldn't you like to feel the wind on your face and my hog between your legs?"

I recoil. Men like him always throw me off. "No thanks. I'm waiting for someone."

"Hell, darlin', a looker like you shouldn't wait on a man. I'm here for you now." A wave of his booze breath washes into my face.

Rebecca puts her hand on his arm. "The lady said she's waiting on someone. Let's keep it clean, okay?"

"I ain't going to start no trouble." George looks at Rebecca, then at me. "But if you change your mind, you know where I am."

"I'll remember that." I pick up my beer and head for another open spot at the bar, finding a safe-looking space between a middle-aged woman with no makeup and a skinny kid with a crew cut. I slide up on the stool and check my watch. It's 7:15.

I watch Rebecca take orders and pour drinks. Her hair is in her eyes and the front of her blue button-down shirt is soaked with God knows what, but I can't take my eyes off her. She's working the crowd like a good politician, and every time one of those gleaming smiles falls my way, blood rushes to my head—and elsewhere.

Every minute or two, she looks at the employee entrance and then at the clock on the neon Miller Lite sign. Time keeps ticking away, but there's no evidence of the back-up bartender.

At 7:40, she brings me a clean mug. "Sorry this is taking so long. He should be here any minute. How about another beer?"

"We can make it some other time. Besides, you look exhausted."

Rebecca blows a strand of hair from her eyes. "I've been here since six this morning, and it's been this busy since lunch. There's an insurance convention at the civic center." She leans close and whispers, "These people are more interested in getting drunk than going to an insurance seminar."

"Do you blame them?" I breathe her in again before slipping off the stool and pushing the empty mug toward her. "You've had a bad day. I should go on home."

Rebecca puts her hand on mine. "Please don't go yet."

Something in her eyes says there's more to this evening than I thought, and as she lets go of my hand, I feel a spark skip between us. Could be my imagination, but I slip back up on the stool and tap the empty mug. "One more, but promise me if you're too tired, we'll call it off and shoot for another time."

"Promise." She crosses her heart before turning away.

By eight, the bar is packed, and there's still no sign of the bartender. The geek in the aviator glasses is trying to pick up the middle-aged woman. He starts by asking her if she'd like another drink. She says she just got one, but she'll take another round when she finishes. He asks her if she comes here much, and she replies once or twice a month. The geek says he's glad he stopped in. Says it's his lucky day to meet a woman as pretty as her. She giggles and thanks him.

If this guy can relate to a woman, surely I can, but the geek has one thing on me—he's not afraid to try. She could have shot him down, made him feel like a loser for even trying, but he didn't let that stop him. He marched right up to her and struck up a conversation.

Wonder if I should tell Rebecca I'm interested in going out with her, as a date instead of as pals? I imagine her throwing her arms around me and saying that's what she's been hoping for. She kisses me and leads me to her bedroom, a romantic candlelit chamber with a canopy bed and a chilled bottle of champagne. She teases my lips with plump red strawberries while erotic strains of soft jazz drift over our naked bodies.

Then I imagine her getting a disgusted look on her face and calling me a deviant who needs to be locked up. She slaps me and says she'll rent billboard space and plaster my name all over town as a lesbian masher.

I shiver and take a long gulp of beer. I don't expect either scenario would be exactly accurate, but the visions keep my brain seesawing till I feel sick.

It's 8:20 and Rebecca brings me another drink. "Sorry about this."

Between the beer and my indecent daydream, I'm starting to sweat. I try to smile, but my lips stick to my teeth. "I'm fine."

She looks downhearted. "Maybe we should make it another time. I hate to keep you waiting like this."

"Sure, but I think I'll hang out for a while anyway. Entertaining crowd tonight." Taking a sip of beer, I glance around as if amused by the drunken insurance agents and college kids, but her grin seems to say she's knows why I'm staying.

"Good. Maybe Rich will show up before you leave." She turns away and takes a drink order from a balding man in a blue sport coat.

By 8:55 I'm feeling a little light-headed and decide to pack it in. Looks like the elusive Rich won't show, and I'll be driving home early. Another night shot to hell.

However, at nine, as I push my mug away, a boy in baggy chinos and a Choppy's logo sweatshirt rushes in, ducks behind the bar, and taps Rebecca's shoulder.

Rebecca hands him a towel before catching my eye.

Maybe I'll stick around a little longer.

CHAPTER 13

Like an infant forced from the security of her mother's womb, I was blinded and confused by my birth. Everything was different. People I'd known all my life looked different, like zombies unaware of the pleasures I'd experienced. The air smelled fresher. Even food didn't taste the same.

But the things around me hadn't changed. I had, and something in my chest longed for the familiar safety of the place where I'd been for so long. Yet another, stronger part yearned to breathe free and bask in the new sensations flooding my senses.

I was obsessed with Lora. Every time I looked at her, I wanted to take her in my arms. The inexplicable need to touch her haunted my thoughts, robbing me of sleep and the desire to eat. The emptiness in my stomach wouldn't be satiated with mere food.

I needed Lora.

We hadn't even kissed that day in her bedroom, and that bothered me. Would she have kissed me if her mother hadn't barged in, or was kissing too personal? Was it something she saved for Jock and wouldn't share with me?

I considered the possibilities, bouncing them around over and over in my head. Maybe Lora had had a wet dream the night before, and I'd happened to be around to ease the frustration. She could've been testing me, trying to find out if I had a kinky bone in my demure body. Maybe Jock wasn't giving her what she needed, and she'd wanted to feel someone else's touch without technically cheating on him with another boy. All these notions played against the one thing I wished for—that Lora wanted me.

But Lora seemed to have selective amnesia. Four days after our clumsy attempt at lovemaking, she still hadn't mentioned the incident. It was like it had never happened. She treated me just as she had before that afternoon in her bedroom—like a best friend—and it was killing me.

I sat in the back row of comp class and watched the door, starving for a look at her. She breezed in, her trendy plaid skirt whipping about her knees and penny loafers slapping the tile floor. She dropped her books on the desk beside me.

"Hey, Claire, there's going to be an excellent party at Rachel's house Saturday night. Think you and Matthew would like to go?"

"Yeah." I feigned exuberance. "I'll tell him not to make plans."

"Great. We can all go together." She glanced toward me, catching my eye for an instant. Her expression almost sparkled as it had when she had laid my hand on her chest a few days before. Almost. "I was thinking maybe you could sleep over at my house Saturday night. My parents are going to visit my brother at college for the weekend, so we'll have the place to ourselves."

Something like a huge wad of cotton lodged in my throat, and I nodded. I struggled for something to say, but Mr. Burns had followed Lora in, and he brought the class to order. As our teacher analyzed *The Scarlet Letter*, I watched Lora from the corner of my eye. She was drawing cartoon mice in the margin of her book.

Thinking about spending the night with Lora made my scalp crawl. The feelings that had passed between us were so intense, so real. She must have felt it, too. But what if I had read her wrong? What if the need in her eyes was a figment of my imagination and Lora had only wanted a one-time experiment to explore a dormant and now-dead side of her sexuality?

From the desk in front of me, Gina's booming voice shook me out of my trance. "That preacher was a spineless coward. He knocked that girl up and then let her take all the heat."

Toward the front of the room, Joey Kennedy piped up. "Hester knew what she was doing. If you can't take the heat..."

"But it takes two to tango," someone voiced another cliché from the window aisle.

"His sin was secret, and that's worse," I said, more to myself than to the class.

"What's that, Miss Blevins?" Mr. Burns peered at me over his black-rimmed bifocals and laid his worn copy of the book aside.

"Sin is worse when you can't tell anyone about it." I fiddled with the cap of my ballpoint pen.

"Elaborate, please," Mr. Burns said, that intimidating stare of his plastered on me.

I drew a deep breath. "If you did something and couldn't tell anyone about it, wouldn't it drive you crazy, even if what you did wasn't a sin?"

"You don't believe they sinned?" Mr. Burns asked.

I felt that Lora wasn't looking at me but went on despite her indifference. "They thought it was a sin because that's what they'd been taught, not because it was true. All they did was love each other, but everyone else thought it was a sin so they kept it a secret. But Hester got pregnant and everyone found out. That's when everything started going wrong."

Mr. Burns pressed his lips together and drummed his fingers on his desk. "Go on."

"What if no one had ever known about it?" I was trying to make a point, but my thoughts kept derailing and jamming up. The problem with making a point is that you have to *have* a point, and I was just a kid with a head full of confusion.

"Sin and secrecy," Mr. Burns said. "These are our quandaries. Is forbidden love a sin only if it is discovered? Is sin based on societal perceptions? What is real sin? In the case of Hester and Dimmesdale, I would presume that in a Puritan society, they would see their actions as less than virtuous, even if their affair had remained hidden." He waggled his hand. "But then the contrast would be lost. It would be a very different story if Hester's actions hadn't been revealed by her pregnancy."

"He's still a creep," Gina muttered.

Mr. Burns lifted a cautioning finger. "Ah, perhaps, but we have much to read, much to discover. Reverend Dimmesdale might surprise you before we get to the final page."

I nodded, but wasn't sure why. I didn't want to talk about it anymore. When I looked toward Lora, she was doodling Jock's name on her notebook.

* * *

After class, Lora and I walked together down the hall.

"You're awfully quiet lately," Lora said, waving at another student as we passed.

I shrugged, shifting my load of books from my right arm to my left. "Just a little worried about this assignment, I guess."

"Don't lie to me, Claire. You've got that Hawthorne and morality crap down cold."

I shook my head. I wanted to tell her we should talk, needed to tell her how that afternoon in her room had affected me, had to tell her it was making me crazy. But the words wouldn't come, and I just looked away.

Lora stopped and I did, too. We blocked the hallway, but she ignored the swarm of kids pressing around us. "Claire, look at me," she said quietly.

I faced her. Tears puddled in my eyes. I tried to fight them, but I was frustrated beyond belief and more than a little fed up with her nonchalance. "What?" I mouthed the word, unable to speak around the lump in my throat.

Lora's expression changed. A mix of revelation and confusion flooded her eyes. At last, she was getting the picture. I wasn't just her study buddy or even her best friend. But I wasn't a potential boyfriend or prom date, either. I was something different altogether, a thing neither of us knew how to deal with.

She swallowed hard. "Come on, we'll stop at the soda machine." She bumped me with her shoulder to urge me forward, then walked on ahead.

I was past the point of containing my anguish. I went in the opposite direction and ducked into the girls' restroom. Unable to hold it in any longer, I found a vacant stall, sat down, and cried. All my questions and fears tumbled around one another and beat against my insides like fists. They gnawed on my brain, driving me crazy. What sin had I committed to deserve this? What deed was so horrible that I'd be forced to endure this pain? I was seventeen, for Pete's sake, how bad could I have been?

I couldn't take it anymore. I wanted it over and began to pray. I begged God to end my torture, promising Him anything, vowing to never do anything wrong again if He'd commute my sentence and give me peace.

But now my feelings weren't just between God and me. Lora had read my mind in the hallway. She'd seen past my façade and looked into the real me, a person I hardly knew myself. Just like in *The Scarlet Letter*, my sin had been revealed and I felt a blazing mark upon my breast.

When the restroom's door opened and flooded the room with echoing voices from the hall, I shifted gears in my prayer. Please don't let it be Lora. She couldn't see me like this, delirious and snot-nosed—I'd die.

A gentle rap came on the stall door. "Claire? It's me. Open up."

I wiped my eyes. Feeling like a freak, dreading the look on Lora's face, I lifted the latch and opened the door. Instead of standing aside so I could come out, Lora pressed into the stall with me, wrapped her arms around my shoulders, and closed the door with her foot. "Please don't be upset," she said softly into my ear.

I settled into her arms and grabbed fistfuls of the back of her sweater. "I don't know what's wrong with me. Everything's so confusing."

She squeezed me tight for a second and touched her lips to my ear before stepping back. She looked down into my eyes, sighed, and glanced away. "I guess we need to talk. And we will, I promise. But we can't do it here, and not over the phone either. For now, just blow your nose and go on to class. Act like you've got a cold or something." She wiped a tear from my cheek before stepping out of the stall.

I watched her leave, more confused than before. Her words had sounded as though she wanted to forget the incident in her bedroom. But she'd held me so tight, touched me with such compassion. She was pulling me to her with one hand and pushing me away with the other. All I knew for sure was that we'd better have our little talk before I went berserk.

Good luck with that, though. I had a basketball game coming up on Thursday night, Lora had the football game on Friday night, and she had to work on Saturday before the big party at Rachel's house. If she didn't want to discuss our tryst over the phone, it would be days before we could have a private conversation, and by then, I might be in a straightjacket.

So I did all I could do, blew my nose, sucked in a deep breath, and prepared for three days in hell. But if Lora was going to say what I thought she was going to say, my hell days would look like a trip to the beach compared to the lifetime of torment that was sure to follow.

CHAPTER 14

Rebecca gives Rich, the tardy bartender, a few quick instructions and tosses him a towel. She takes a deep breath and shoots a last look around as she brushes her hair from her eyes and comes around to my side of the bar. She walks up behind me and puts one arm around my shoulder and the other around the geek in the aviator glasses who is still moving on the woman beside me.

Rebecca looks at him. "Hey, Frank. Ready for the weekend?"

"Sure am," he replies, pushing up his glasses.

Rebecca squeezes my shoulder. "How about you, still feel like hanging out for a while?"

"Sure," I say, smiling. She's different tonight, more relaxed and open. And I like the feeling of her hand on my shoulder. It's just a friendly gesture, but it still feels good.

As I slide off the bar stool, that nagging sting of guilt hits me between my eyes. For all my conscious efforts to keep it at bay, it hits me every time I think about another woman. I promised to be faithful, and no matter how hard my head tries to be reasonable, my heart throws silly emotions into the mix.

Rebecca squeezes my shoulder again. "Are you okay?"

"Yeah, but I think I'm physically attached to this stool. My legs are asleep."

She gives me a scan, and when she seems satisfied that I'm capable of walking, leads me through the crowd, stopping a couple of times to speak to the regulars. She uses the same tone with them she usually uses with me, friendly but professional.

When we reach her office, she flips on the fluorescent light and drops into her high-backed leather chair. So far, I've only known Rebecca as an uncompromising restaurant manager or the sultry star of a few erotic dreams. In her office, I have my first opportunity to find out a little more about her.

I catch a snapshot in a metal frame on her desk. It's of Rebecca in younger years, maybe around sixteen, standing in front of a Christmas tree with an older woman. They're both wearing red winter dresses and brandishing holiday smiles. Judging by the older woman's eyes and the dimple in her right cheek, I assume she's Rebecca's mother.

Next, I notice her college diploma hanging on the wall over her desk. It's in a fine oak frame and has a gold honor student seal in the lower left corner. Her middle name is Lynn, the same as mine. By the graduation date, I figure she's about thirty-four, older than I thought.

Rebecca lets out a sigh and looks down at the front of her soaked shirt. "Lord, I look like a drowned rat."

"You look fine." I fold my hands in front of me and shift my weight to my left foot. It's my natural business-meeting stance. I've been doing it so long, I don't know how to stand any other way.

Rebecca glances through a stack of papers on her desk before putting them aside and standing up. "Mind if I go upstairs to change?"

"Upstairs?"

"My apartment. When I came back to town to take over the business, I renovated the upstairs. It's small but it's free, and I can always get to work on time."

We leave the office, and she leads me through the kitchen, which is still bustling to prepare late orders. The dark-haired dishwasher stares at me through a steamy fog rising from the sink and watches me all the way to the back door. I shiver in the kitchen's muggy heat and pull my jacket closed.

Rebecca takes a quick glance down the stainless prep aisle. Seemingly satisfied with the kitchen's condition, she shoves the heavy back door open. In the frigid night air, the smoky aroma of grilling meat mixes with the acidic odor of rotten tomatoes from the dumpster a few yards away. The smell is at once appealing and revolting.

I hold my breath and follow Rebecca along the back of the building to a long flight of stairs. She warns me to watch my step as we climb the rickety metal staircase to a square landing in front of a wooden door.

She slides a key into the lock, opens the door, and motions me in. "It's not much from the outside, but it's kind of homey inside." She follows me in and flips on the overhead light. "Sorry for the mess," she says, but the apartment looks well kept.

I'm taken with the studio-style flat. The small kitchen area is decorated with yellow sunflowers of all descriptions: a tiny plaque, a square clock, and a metal napkin holder at the center of the two-chair table. In the middle of the great room is a green leather sofa fronted by an oak coffee table. A big screen TV is angled in the corner between the kitchen and the living area. On the far side of the room, a king-sized bed with a patchwork comforter and a dozen throw pillows sits under three arched windows. All around the apartment, the exposed brick walls are dappled with framed photographs and what appear to be original watercolors. Near the bed are a computer desk and filing cabinet.

My eyes zoom in on the filing cabinet. One of its drawers is half-open, with green and red folders spewing out, and I remember why I'm here. This isn't a date, it's a service call.

Rebecca crosses the room and drops her purse on the bed. "I've got to get out of these clothes. Make yourself at home. I'll be right back." She disappears behind a door to the left.

I stand around for a minute with my hands in my jacket pockets, unsure what to do. Telling myself to relax, I slip off my jacket, fold it across a kitchen chair, and wander into the living area.

"Is this the filing cabinet you wanted me to look at?" I ask.

"What filing cabinet?"

"The one with the stuck drawer."

"Oh, man. I forgot." She rushes back into the room, wearing a green satin bathrobe. "Think you can do anything with it?"

"I don't know. It's about a hundred years old, and I'm not too familiar with the workings. Maybe if we can get the drawer open, we can see what's going on in there."

Rebecca is still securing her bathrobe's sash when she joins me at the cabinet. She stands close behind me and watches as I try to reach into the drawer with my right hand. I smell the alcohol from the bar on her skin. Its strong, sweet aroma settles over me and makes my brain go numb.

"Maybe we need to take the files out. I don't think your hand will fit." She moves even closer, touching my back with her body and resting her chin on my shoulder. The motion is not sexual, but it's intimate and not the move of a straight woman—not a touch I expected from Rebecca.

Startled by the contact, I jerk my hand from the drawer, spin around, and almost trip. I try to clear my throat but it's too dry. I manage a cough.

Rebecca's eyes are wide, her cheeks flushed. She seems about to say something when she looks down at my hand. "You're bleeding." She turns and goes toward the kitchen, motioning for me to follow.

Sure enough, there's a small, shallow cut along the heel of my hand. I cup my left hand under it to catch a drop of blood as I step to the sink.

Rebecca takes my hand and inspects the jagged red wound. "Sorry if I frightened you. I'm tired and I wasn't thinking. I didn't mean to... Please don't be offended."

"Why would I be offended?"

She takes a kitchen towel from the counter and dabs the blood. "I don't usually do things like that."

"Like what?"

She catches my eyes again, those swirls of green looking into me, through me. "Get too close."

I've seen that look before and know what it means. But I'm no fool. When it comes to women, it's best to assume nothing. The old lips-say-no-but-eyes-say-yes crap doesn't carry any clout with me; never has. I have to hear it, and more than once, before I'll consider acting on it.

"You weren't too close."

"You're sure?"

"I just didn't expect it."

Her eyes brighten for a second, then narrow with skepticism. "Are you—?" She bites off her words.

What a comical picture we must be—two grown women standing in a kitchen not big enough to cuss a cat in, playing verbal peek-a-boo to keep from insulting one another.

She stares at the gold refrigerator for a second, then draws a deep breath. "Can we keep this just between us?"

I nod.

"The truth is, I've been getting these vibes from you for a while."

"What kind of vibes?"

"Like maybe you'd be interested in getting to know each other better, like maybe you... But I might be reading you wrong, and if I am, I'm very sorry for putting you on the spot like this."

Outside, a car's alarm beeps twice and the sound of rambunctious laughter drifts into the loft. Pretending to be distracted by the noise, I steal an instant to collect my thoughts before saying, "Is your gaydar going off?"

"A little."

"It should be."

She sighs as though a weight has been lifted off her chest. "Oh, thank God. All I need is to ruin the restaurant by talking out of turn to a customer." She grins and leads me to the sofa. "Sit down. I've got some Band-Aids in the bathroom. We'll get you fixed up."

When she disappears behind the door again, I'm glad to have a minute to regroup. My head feels like it's full of glue. All the thoughts inside are sticking together and oozing through the cracks in my skull.

She returns with a box of bandages and an alcohol pad, sits down beside me, and takes my hand. "I'm sorry for acting so ditzy tonight. I just hate the thought of doing something wrong."

"I understand. I'm a little ditzy myself."

The very air between us seems different than before, clearer, free from the conjecture and speculation that clouded our previous conversations. We're being honest, and it feels good for a change.

Rebecca tears open the alcohol pad and dabs it along the cut. "I haven't been back in town very long, and I work all the time, so I didn't know anyone to ask about you."

I wince at the alcohol's sting, but don't pull away.

She fixes a sterile strip across the cut and gives me a warm glance. "I think you'll live."

She traces her fingers along my palm. "You can tell a lot about a person from their hands. That's the first thing I notice about a woman."

I don't think she can see anything other than the obvious, but I want her to keep touching me. "What can you tell?"

"You take good care of your skin. That's obvious." Her eyes narrow as she takes my left hand and rubs her thumb across my palm. "You play some kind of sport, something with a racket. Tennis?"

"Racquetball. How did you know?"

"You've got a tiny callus below the ring finger on your right hand, but you don't have one on your left. You keep your nails short, but manicured. That tells me you're particular about your appearance, but you don't mind getting your hands dirty." She turns my hand over and tracks the jagged scar running from between my knuckles to above my thumb. "What happened here?"

"I broke a mirror." My reply is oversimplified, but the details would make me look like a maniac.

"Seven years bad luck. How old is the scar?"

"About three years."

Rebecca sits back for a second, then reaches toward me and touches a spot between my breasts. "You've got blood on your sweater."

I look down and see about six red specks on my chest. "Ah, crap! I just had this darn thing cleaned."

She lingers on the blood spot for a moment, then leans back. "You seem nervous. Are you sure everything's all right?"

"Yeah, I'm fine, just a little out of practice with this sort of thing."

"What sort of thing?" She tries to look me in the eye, but I won't let her.

I shrug and pick at a string on my jeans.

She giggles and brushes her hair back. "Guess I'm not helping anything by being so evasive. It's just that you never know if you might be hitting on the wrong woman."

"Are you hitting on me?"

"Maybe. I mean if it's okay with you, I'd like to get to know you better."

"I think I can live with that." I try not to let my grin touch both my ears.

"So you're not married, or involved, or whatever?"

"Not for a while." That twinge of guilt tickles my throat.

My head is starting to hurt. I don't want to get into this right now. Besides, it's a complicated subject. It gets even more complex as the months pass and I seem to forget little things about Lora. Sometimes I'm desperate to recall the way she brushed her hair or that throaty laugh that erupted from her when I tickled her feet.

Rebecca looks at me with a strange sadness, as if she can see my emotions going from white to black, from red to blue. Worse, she seems to understand.

"Bad breakup?"

"You could say that."

"Was there someone else?"

I look at the ceiling. I can't stand for her to read me like a dime-store romance novel where she'll scan a few pages and put me back on the shelf.

"Sorry, I don't mean to pry." She glances toward the television, then back to me. "I've had a couple of nasty breakups myself. We don't have to talk about it if you don't want to."

"Thanks, I'd rather not." I'm trying to find my earlier grin but it won't come back. I shake my head and look away. "This is too bizarre."

Rebecca crosses her legs and slides closer to me. "At first, I couldn't tell about you because you're so distant sometimes. And after a while, I got the feeling you might be interested, but I never dreamed you'd be single." She holds up her hand as if swearing to tell the truth. "And I don't play in anyone else's yard, if you know what I mean."

"I appreciate that."

Rebecca looks down at her robe, then to my bandaged hand. "This isn't exactly what I had in mind for the evening. I guess we've gotten off to a rocky start."

"Does that mean I'll see you again?"

"I hope so." She looks at her hands before peeking up at me. "I'd like to be a little more presentable next time."

I feel an urge in the pit of my stomach, but it's not the kind of craving most women would have in this situation. Panic is pounding through me, insisting I excuse myself and head for the door before I get into something I can't get out of.

I know the intricate waltz of relationships is not meant only for those who possess a natural ability for the dance, or for those more deserving than me. It is for us all, but a trace of doubt lingers, a tiny seed of self-loathing that says I don't deserve a second chance.

I focus on the good that might come of this situation. I picture her in my arms, imagine kissing those perfect lips, and think how soft her hands were when she touched me. The thoughts curl around one another, squish together, and flow through my body. Spurred on by them, I tell her about the Kingsley's dinner party and ask her if she'd like to join me. She accepts eagerly. Outside, a car horn blows and boisterous voices drift up from the parking lot, but her attention is focused on me and she doesn't seem to hear them.

I give in to my desire to run before those eyes make me say things I'll regret. "It's been a long day. I'd better go and let you get some rest. We'll try this again tomorrow, okay?"

We stand up, and she takes my arm as we walk toward the door. "I'm glad you came over. Sorry it's been such a disaster."

"I wouldn't call it a disaster."

"I'll see you tomorrow." She leans in and gives me a lingering kiss on the cheek.

Nice move. Letting me know she's interested without going too far. But part of me wishes she would, and I let myself imagine her leading me toward her comfortable bed, where we'd explore each other for hours. I hate to admit it, but if she asked, I'd consider staying. I'd run away like the coward I am, but I *would* consider it.

She doesn't extend the invitation, so I say goodnight and slip out into the freezing night air. As I head toward the parking lot, I feel like I'm walking on water. Hope I don't sink.

* * *

By the time I get home, it's eleven, and as I pull into the driveway, I see Jared in his bathrobe sitting on my front steps, smoking a cigar. I'm not looking forward to this. Even if Elizabeth didn't tell him about our little experiment, I still know what happened. The memory of her gentle lips and the way she tilted her head has haunted me all day and made the confusion worse. Even if it wasn't the real thing for her, it was for me, and I hate the way it made me feel. How do I look a man in the eye after I've kissed his wife?

I leave the garage door open and go up the front walk. Each uneasy step brings me closer to his even gaze, his strong jaw and thick chest. Stricken by the urge to fall at his feet and beg forgiveness, my knees wobble and my hands start to shake. My senses sharpen. I can hear the evening dew crackle as it freezes on the grass. The tulips beside the steps are still frozen under the ground, but I smell their earthy sweetness tonight as easily as I will come spring.

"Elizabeth run you out again?" I ask.

He looks at his cigar's glowing tip and puffs out a heavy blue cloud of fumes. "She understands my need for a good smoke."

"She's afraid the kids will, too." I sit on the step beside him and hunker down against the wind. Even through my jeans, the bricks are cold.

"Thanks for letting me sneak over for a puff." A dime-sized circle of ash drops from the stogie, and he kicks it off the walkway with the side of his sneaker.

"Hey, smoke here all you want. I know how Elizabeth feels about tobacco in the house."

"Funny how many doctors smoke. You'd think we'd know better." He folds his arms across his knees, keeping the cigar away from me. "Nice night, huh?"

"Yeah. Smells like snow."

"It won't, never does." He takes a long pull and peeks at me from the corner of his eye. "It was nice last night, too, wasn't it?"

"I suppose."

He leans back and looks at me. "I don't know what's gotten into Beth. She attacked me last night, after breakfast this morning, and twice before the kids got home from school. Sure am glad I had the day off."

I'm sweating. It was a bad idea to kiss Elizabeth. I knew it and did it anyway. "What?"

He grins. "Whatever got her so torn up, I hope it happens again."

"Excuse me?"

Jared takes another puff and blows a smoke ring over our heads. "Beth is a complex woman. Sometimes it takes something unusual to get her going."

I remember the kiss in vivid detail and the way it made me feel, all squishy and hot from the inside out. How could I have done it, let myself get so torn up over my friend, my married friend?

He waves his cigar in front of him. "A good smoke is my thing. It relaxes me, makes me nicer to her and the kids after a hard day, so she doesn't give me much flak about it. If she needs a little something of her own to make her feel good, who am I to tell her not to do it?"

We're not talking about a shopping trip here. We're talking about the good doctor's wife fooling around with her next door neighbor—her female neighbor. And from where I sit, it looks like a porno movie with lusty nymphs wearing fishnet stockings and stiletto heels making out on the kitchen counter.

I shudder and try to read Jared's expression, but his thoughts are hidden behind the cool detachment of a man who's seen too much suffering, someone who's pronounced dozens of teenagers dead while their anxious parents pace the emergency waiting room at Mercy Hospital.

He stands up and tamps out his cigar on the bottom of his running shoe. "Coming to dinner tomorrow night?"

"Okay if I bring a date?"

"Only if she's pretty." He touches my cheek before sauntering down the walk and across the yard.

I wonder if Elizabeth is waiting.

CHAPTER 15

The Saturday-night party at Rachel's was a total disaster. The small house was packed with drunken, horny kids guzzling beer and dancing to music so loud I was sure the sheriff could hear it at the police station three miles away. Those with enough alcohol in their systems and a willing partner stumbled to the upper floor bedrooms for a quick romp while they could still function without throwing up.

I was miserable. Matthew and I lingered around the fringes of the madness, nursing one beer for hours. I held his hand while we tried to talk but I couldn't take my eyes off Lora and Jock. They were on the downstairs sofa, surrounded by a mob of Jock's admirers as he related one tale after another about how the Yankees' scouts were looking at him but he'd rather play for Pittsburgh. Every minute or two, he'd pull Lora to him and grope her ass with one hand as he smothered her with his lips. She'd giggle and squirm away, playfully chastising him for being so aggressive. Every few minutes, Lora looked at me with a disgusted expression.

If she were mine, I wouldn't treat her that way. I'd respect her, I thought over and over.

But she wasn't mine. She belonged to the golden boy, the one who had it all figured out, a nice life plan. He'd play in the minors for a year or two, sign a fat contract, and hurl fastballs at Yankee Stadium in no time. Jock could give her everything—money, cars, a fancy home.

What could I offer? I didn't have a dime, drove a junker, and had no idea what I wanted to do with my life. Then there was that other little problem—I wore a B-cup instead of an athletic cup. Hell, if I were Lora, I'd pick him, too.

After a hundred years in the party's madness, Matthew managed to pull Jock from his pedestal and load him into the back seat. On the drive to Lora's house, the sounds from behind me told an age-old tale.

"C'mon," Jock slurred over and over.

Lora didn't speak loud enough for me to make out the words, but she didn't seem receptive. I wanted to leap over the seat and save her, but all I could do was stare out the window into the cloudless sky. There must've been a gazillion stars out that night, but their radiance was masked by a torment that was driving me over the edge.

When we made it to the Tyler's front porch, Matthew gave me a warm goodnight kiss while Jock begged Lora to let him stay the night. After a few minutes, she planted both hands on his chest and shoved him away. "Not this time, hotshot. Go home and sober up."

He grumbled something about being the only guy in school not getting any, but staggered off, leaning on Matthew as they went toward the car. Jock proceeded to stumble into the yard and throw up. Matthew dragged him to the Thunderbird and dumped him into the passenger seat. He closed the door and turned to us. "Don't worry. I'll take care of him."

I was glad to be away from the party, but when we locked the front door behind us, I realized that Lora and I were alone for the first time since our afternoon encounter of almost a week ago. I'd yearned to talk with her about it, explain how it made me feel, tell her how I felt about her. But now that the confrontation loomed before me, I wasn't so sure it was a good idea.

I shuffled to the bathroom, splashed my face with cool water, and glared at my reflection in the mirror. What was I, a masochist, or something? Why didn't I slit my throat and get it over with?

I dried my face and brushed my teeth, taking comfort in the fact that it would be over soon. I'd go straight to bed, be comatose for a few hours, get up early, and run home. I set my jaw and made my way toward Lora's room. Each step got heavier than the one before as I imagined Lora, my best friend and the source of my worst pain, curled up in bed thinking of Jock.

When I stepped into the room, Lora was sitting on her bed facing the wall, the veiled lamplight casting a crimson glow on her profile. She looked fragile and in need of comfort, but I knew better than to give in to the urge to go to her, wrap her in my arms, and love her.

My frustration was beginning to get ugly, growing stronger and more vile as I realized I'd never get what I wanted. "Have fun tonight?" I asked, bitterness edging my question.

"No," she said and glanced away.

"Looked like you were. I thought you were going to choke Jock with your tongue."

Lora spun around, eyes narrow and teeth clenched. "Is that what you think? You think I like having him paw at me like that in front of people?"

She'd never raised her voice to me, and the sheer pitch of it was unnerving. Flabbergasted, I searched her face and saw the same kind of confusion that clouded my own thoughts. "But you seemed so..."

"So *what*, Claire, so happy to be on the arm of the best athlete in school? So tickled to be his trophy?" She drew her knees to her chin, hugging her thighs against her chest.

I sat down on the other side of the bed. "I thought you were having fun."

She avoided my stare, tracing her finger along the hem of her black pants. "All he wants is a girl on his arm, a girl that's not too easy but might give in and fuck him. I thought I loved him, but I don't."

With an exaggerated chuckle, I said, "Why not? Everyone loves good old Jock. Everyone knows how perfect he is."

"People don't know shit about Jock. Have they ever been left standing outside the stadium in the pouring rain while he ducked out for a beer with the boys? Have they ever had him cuss them out and make them feel like a piece of shit for not giving him a blow job?" She shot me a quick look, her eyes blazing with hurt. "Everyone thinks we're such a perfect couple, but we're not. Not by a long shot."

"I'm sorry." I leaned closer. I wanted to touch her, but didn't dare. I looked around the room, and when my eyes caught Jock's picture turned facedown on the dresser, I lost my breath.

Lora looked at me, a timid determination etched into her face. She slid across the bed and threw her arms around my waist. "I just get so fucking confused sometimes." As she rested her forehead on my shoulder, a tear dropped onto my hand.

I wanted to say something, do something, but couldn't. We just sat there for the longest time, rocking like frightened children. It was like a dream, sitting there with my arms around her, her legs touching mine, our faces so close I could feel the heat of her skin against my cheek. Was it heaven or hell? It felt like a little of both.

Lora raised her head, misty eyes half-hidden by a wild shock of dark hair. "You wouldn't treat me the way Jock does, would you?"

"Never." I studied her eyes, memorizing the line of her lips and the curve of her chin. I had never wanted anyone the way I wanted Lora Tyler, not even close.

She looked up at me and stroked my cheek with her slender fingers. That's when everything in my head went straight to hell—all my restraint, and more important, all my fear. If I never did anything else, I would kiss her. I put my hand on the back of her neck and brought her lips to mine. She closed her eyes and slipped her tongue into my mouth, exploring me—timid at first, then growing confident and assertive. As I nibbled and sucked at her lips, I focused on everything about her, on the sweet aroma of beer lingering on her breath, the warm smoothness of her tongue, the growing eagerness of her touch.

Lora moved her mouth to my ear. "This is wrong," she whispered, and flicked my earlobe with her tongue.

"I don't care."

She sat back and, holding me spellbound with her stare, freed the top button of my blouse. Still watching my eyes, she undid another button, then another until my blouse was open. She sat motionless, and seemed to be studying my reaction. "Do you want me to stop?"

I slid my shirt off my shoulders and took her hand. Just like she'd done with me the week before, I placed her palm over my heart. Lora skimmed her fingers up my chest, across my shoulders, and up to my cheek. She lowered her hands, slid her fingertips along the lace cup of my bra, and unhooked the front fastener. She sat there, staring at me, drinking in my naked skin as if she'd found an oasis in the desert of her existence. By that time, the ache in my untried flesh was almost unbearable.

"You're so beautiful," she whispered, tracing her slender fingers up my arm and toward my breast. My cheeks flushed and my body trembled.

Lora tugged her sweater off over her head, slipped off her bra, and pulled me to her. When her breasts touched mine, a primal instinct took over. I couldn't seem to get close enough to her. Of their own will, my arms squeezed her tighter till my lungs could barely draw breath. I found her lips again and kissed her with more certainty.

"Can we take off the rest of our clothes?" Lora whispered roughly.

"Are you sure?"

"I'm sure—I think." She smiled and brushed my hair from my eyes.

As I took off Matthew's class ring and put it on the bedside table, I wondered if I'd ever be able to face my boyfriend again. At that point, I didn't care.

Lora flipped off the bedside lamp, and we giggled as we slipped under the blankets. In the less intimidating semi-darkness, I felt freer to tug at her zipper and peel her slacks over her hips, and she became much more aggressive, nearly ripping my remaining garments at the seams until we were both nude and lying a foot apart.

We lay still for a moment, summoning the courage to do things we'd never done, to discover each other—and ourselves. Lora slid closer and pressed her body against me. It was wonderful, her skin sliding against mine, the triangle of coarse hair between her legs tickling my thigh as we rolled together from one side of the bed to the other.

I studied her, touched her face, her hair, her chest. My body trembled when she rolled on top of me and kissed my neck, inching her way down to my breasts and back again. But when she guided my hand down her flat stomach toward her most private self, I hesitated.

"I want it to be you," she said.

"You're sure?"

She removed her hand from mine, pulled me to her, and kissed me with the passion of a thousand boys. She did want it to be me—I knew it. I traced my fingers between her breasts, down her stomach, and into the edge of her pubic hair. I stayed there for a minute, tangling my fingers in the wiry curls, wallowing in the fulfillment of my secret desires. She wrapped her arms around my shoulders and kissed me deeply.

"Together," she whispered and slid her hand between my thighs.

I gasped as I found her wet warmth and she found mine. Overwhelmed, we stopped kissing, stopped moving, almost stopped breathing. By the green glow of her clock-radio light, we stared into one another's eyes, lost in the unbreakable connection that would be with us forever.

"Oh, God," I whispered.

She smiled. "I love you for this," she said as we began to move in a slow and steady rhythm.

I didn't speak. It would be corny to tell her I loved her more than life, that I could have died at that moment and been happy. Maybe someday I wouldn't be afraid of being trite, but for the moment, I wanted to be better than me—to be perfect for her.

We stayed locked together well past dawn until, exhausted, we drifted to sleep. Neither of us found our orgasm that night, but we didn't need to. Lora and I had touched as lovers, forging a bond stronger than any physical release.

The sex would come.

CHAPTER 16

The phone rings. It's 3:15 a.m., so it has to be Tonya.

"Didn't I say to call on Saturday morning?" I growl as I pick up the phone.

"It's after midnight, isn't it?"

I roll over and accidentally kick Jitterbug. She hits the floor with a thud and whimpers before jumping back on the bed and curling up around my feet again. Cockers aren't known for their brilliance, but then neither am I. I should've let the answering machine pick up and let Tonya stew till a more reasonable hour.

The cell phone static whistles into my ear. I consider hanging up and blaming it on the phone company, but she'll call right back and keep calling till I answer, so I try to stay awake.

"Where are you?" I ask.

"On my way home. I stopped by Sister Moon's for a drink."

"Sounds like you've had more than one. Should you be driving?"

"I'm okay. Besides, I'm going slow so what's-her-name can follow me."

"Who?"

"Girl I picked up at the bar." She pauses and clears her throat. "You should see her, Claire, legs all the way up to her neck."

"Anyone I know?" I yawn and pry my eyes open.

"She's in town for the insurance convention."

"Oh, my God! You don't even know her name, do you?"

"Give me some credit, please." She pauses and I begin to think she's hung up, but she adds, "Starts with an A. Don't tell me... it's Andrea... no, Amber... that's not right either. Give me a minute, I'll get it."

I'm starting to fume. It's one thing for Tonya to be so rude as to wake me in the middle of the night, but calling to fill me in about picking up some leggy chick? That pisses me off.

"What time do you want me to pick you up tomorrow?" she asks.

"Oh, shit, I forgot. I can't make it."

"You're not backing out on me again!" The echo over the line punctuates her disappointment and makes me feel like a pig for canceling.

"I'm going to the Kingsleys."

"Goddamn it. I should've known you wouldn't go."

"Fly, I've got a..." The word *date* won't come out.

"You've got what, a bug up your ass? Fine by me. Sit in that fucking house till you rot, for all I care."

"Call me tomorrow." I hang up without saying goodbye. There's no reasoning with her when she's got a gut full of hooch and a pair of long legs waiting. I'll explain after the booze has worn off and the scent of sex has been washed away.

Jitterbug crawls up and slurps my face. I push her to arm's length and scratch the back of her neck. "Jit, one of these days, I'm going to slap the piss out of her."

* * *

It's only 6:30, but I'm already dressed for dinner and pacing the living room. I scuff across the carpet, trace my finger along the sofa table as I pass, and stop at the bar before spinning on my heels to reverse the trek. When I ramble to the foyer and touch the front door knob, I've built up enough static electricity to shock the bejesus out of myself. I swear under my breath and start to pace again.

Jitterbug's whimpering is driving me crazy. She hates being cooped up in the guestroom, but her raving greetings can be over the top for new visitors. She will have to meet Rebecca later—maybe.

I play in my mind what I'm going to say when Rebecca gets here, but everything sounds wrong. She's bound to look nice—she always does—but would it sound cheesy to tell her? Would it come out as awkward as it feels and hit her like a wad of sticky bubble gum, or would she be impressed by a sincere compliment?

What does she expect from me? Women want different things when it comes to being with other women. Some want to be gentlemanly and hold the door for you, while others would be insulted if you didn't hold the door for them. Still others would be mortified if any woman dared to assume what they considered a masculine position. I'm uncomfortable playing roles, so I decide to be myself. Screw her if she doesn't like it. Only problem is, I'm not sure how to *be* myself.

Knowing my luck, I'll get a phone call from Tonya as soon as Rebecca arrives. Tonya hasn't called yet, and when I tried to get her earlier, she didn't answer. She has a nasty way of interrupting at the worst times. When I'm in the tub, say, or when it's three in the morning, or when Jitterbug needs a walk. Plus, she's apt to put the moves on any woman in sight, and it'd be like her to show up on the front step and seduce Rebecca before she can ring the bell.

I shudder, envisioning Tonya all made-up and sexy in spiked heels and a little black dress wheeling into the drive behind Rebecca. With lust on her breath, she growls a lascivious remark into Rebecca's ear and lures her away from my timid grasp.

When the doorbell rings, I snap back to reality and count to ten before strolling into the foyer. It's hard to stay cool around Rebecca, and I wonder if she'll sense my unrest. As my fingers touch the knob, panic races through me. What if this is a mistake?

With a gulping breath and another count to ten, I grip the knob and open the door. One glimpse of her eyes is all it takes to sweep the fears into the back of my mind and focus my attention on the beautiful woman about to enter my home.

Rebecca returns my smile, her hair shimmering with streaks of gold in the dim light. "Hi there. Am I on time?"

"Perfect." I step aside and motion her in. As she walks past, I catch a whiff of her perfume and let my eyes linger on the curve of her hip.

Sometimes I wish I had a little of Tonya in me, an ounce of her confidence or a dab of her unrestrained nerve. I'd make a move on Rebecca right now. I'd pull her close and kiss her with three years' worth of pent up passion, and who'd blame me if I did? She's stunning in her skin-tight blue dress, sheer stockings, and three-inch heels.

But I'm a cowering lamb instead of a mighty lioness, so I adjust the collar of my black satin blouse and hope my buttons are straight. "I'm not looking forward to this. Elizabeth and Jared will be watching us all evening."

"They're cool with us being together, right? I don't want to slip up and say something wrong." Rebecca shifts her weight from one foot to the other and looks around.

"They're okay. We just can't make out on the dining room table or anything like that."

"I'll try to control myself." She nudges me playfully as we go out the door.

Down the walk, across the Kingsleys' driveway, and up the front steps is only a twenty-yard stroll, but it seems to take forever. The night breeze is stiff and cuts through my blouse, and I lean close to Rebecca, savoring the relative warmth of her body.

Elizabeth greets us at the front door and gives Rebecca a polite scan. "It's about time you two showed up. Can I get you a cocktail?" She takes Rebecca's arm and leads her toward the kitchen, leaving me to tag along behind. "Rebecca, I'm so glad you could join us this evening. Claire's one of our dearest friends, and we hate to see her alone so much."

I squeeze in between them. "You're not helping me look good, here, Elizabeth. You make it sound like I'm a hermit or something."

"Oh, hush," Rebecca says. "I have a feeling Elizabeth and I have a lot to talk about."

Elizabeth gives me a sly grin and a peck on the cheek and pulls Rebecca away, letting me know I shouldn't follow. "Rebecca and I will get your drinks. We can compare notes."

This is backward—I've kissed my neighbor, but not my date. I hope they don't compare too many notes, but I leave them to their talk and meander toward the great room where boisterous laughter erupts and dies. Jared must be comparing golf scores with Larry Maxwell again.

They are. Larry nods as Jared demonstrates his chip shot. Four other men encircle Jared, feigning interest in a story they must have heard twenty times. They also nod, stirring their drinks with monogrammed swizzle sticks and making their ice cubes clink.

The Kingsley home is a lot like its owners, elegant and tasteful. The great room boasts a floor-to-ceiling stone fireplace, which flickers constantly during the long winter months. Along the right wall, a cluster of comfortable furniture upholstered in sky-blue leather creates an intimate conversation area, and tucked in the far corner sits a beautiful but well-used baby grand piano.

The other guests linger in two groups, one huddled around the piano and the other around the sofa. It's the standard Kingsley dinner party crowd, mostly married couples. Some are doctors, others are lawyers, still others are business folk like me. Some are older, some are middle-aged, but none are under thirty. This group doesn't have time for those they consider children.

My host stops in mid-swing and glances at me. "Back me up on this, Claire. Remember when I chipped in on the seventh green at the Pines?"

Jared and I have played golf exactly twice, but he always pulls me into his stories with that seventh-green shot. I smile at him. "One of the best shots I've ever seen."

Jean Newberry, a rail of a woman with graying hair and gold eyes calls to me from the sofa. "Why, if it isn't Claire Blevins! Haven't seen you in a coon's age." She pats the cushion beside her, beckoning me to join her.

I bite back the temptation to ask how old a coon is and sit down. "Jean, you do have a way with those old sayings, don't you?"

"I may be married to a fancy-pants CEO, but I remember where I come from. My dear grandmother, Lord rest her soul, had more old sayings than a dog's got fleas."

"And that's another one, I'll bet."

Jean tells me about her son making partner at Bentley, Newberry, and Davis as Jared continues with his golf story. There are at least four other conversations going on at the same time, but I catch only snippets of each. "Pitched it up easy... buying a new house on Park Street... rolled about six yards... getting a divorce... saw it on the news..."

I watch the doorway with a mix of anticipation and dread. If we're lucky, Elizabeth won't make a big deal of introducing my date, but I'm not counting on it. The news of Claire Blevins having a female companion is front-page material, and she won't bury it among the stories of golf scores and sons doing well. When Rebecca appears, all eyes will be on her, and then on me. They will be gracious, but they'll splinter into groups of two or three, all whispers and innuendo.

I catch my breath as Elizabeth leads Rebecca into the room. They're both smiling.

Elizabeth stops at the doorway and makes a production of clearing her throat. When she's satisfied that she has everyone's attention, she says, "This is Rebecca Greenway, Claire's friend." She punches the word *friend* for effect and glances in my direction.

Utter silence. You could cut it with a knife, but it only lasts a second, because before I can get to my feet, Rebecca is working the room. She looks at each face, saying, "I believe I know almost everyone here," and extends her hand to Larry Maxwell. "Hi, Larry. Are the bears still giving you fits?"

"For the moment, but the bull market will be back any day." Larry leans in and kisses her cheek. His broad shoulders block my view of Rebecca, but I hear him say, "Surprised to see you here. I didn't know you and Claire were friends." Thank heaven he didn't emphasize *friends* the way Elizabeth did.

I rise and move toward Rebecca, but another guest, Greta Jennings, a short woman with huge breasts and tiny hips, beats me to her.

Rebecca turns to Greta. "Hey, there. That e-mail help you any?"

Greta wraps her arm around Rebecca's waist and gives her a quick hug. "I and the Historical Society thank you. You saved me months of digging through the newspaper's archives." Greta turns to me. "She's a real lifesaver."

Elizabeth gives me a full-body bump from behind and hands me a scotch on the rocks. She murmurs, "Looks like you've got a crowd pleaser there."

After a long pull on my drink, I turn to Elizabeth. "Thanks for making a scene."

"My pleasure." She twirls into the crowd and disappears.

I balance on my left foot, then my right, as Rebecca chats with the other guests. I've known these people for years, and they didn't even notice when I came in, but they're swarming around her like bees on a clover patch. Go figure.

When the excitement abates, Rebecca takes my hand. "How am I doing?" she whispers.

A broad smile finds my lips. She's doing great.

CHAPTER 17

"Claire, wake up!"

Lora's voice rattled me. I pried my eyes open, confused by my surroundings and by the events of the night before. Was it a dream? My eyes focused, and I saw Lora struggling to get her panties on and grabbing for a nightshirt. It was true. Holy crap! I'd had sex—and with Lora Tyler, of all people.

"Hurry! My parents are home. Get dressed." She hopped on one foot, still tugging at her underwear, and peeked out the window. "Oh, God, I'm in deep shit. I wasn't supposed to have anyone over."

I rolled out of bed, spurred on by the image of Mrs. Tyler literally catching us with our pants down, and acid rose in my throat. If I didn't make tracks in about seven seconds, my illicit lover and I would be dead where we stood.

I scrambled around the floor looking for my clothes. "What time is it?"

"After 12:00. I can't believe we slept this late." She kept her voice low as she tossed me a long tee shirt and a pair of her panties. "Here, take these. I'll find yours later."

I wrestled the shirt over my head and yanked the underwear on. "Christ, why didn't you tell me I wasn't supposed to be here? We could've set an alarm or something."

"I wasn't exactly thinking clearly last night." Lora shot me a dry look as she tugged the blankets back onto the bed.

"What's that supposed to mean?" I scurried to the other side of the bed and found my khaki pants beside the nightstand.

"It doesn't mean anything. Just get dressed and get the hell out of here." She threw my penny loafers at me. "Go out the front door. They're coming in the back, so maybe they didn't see your car."

I jerked my pants over my hips and gathered my shoes in both arms. "Lora, we need to—"

"Not now! If we get caught, I'm grounded for life."

I stood there for a second, not knowing whether to laugh or cry. It wasn't supposed to be like this. We'd done something wonderful, something we shouldn't rush away from. We should've been in bed holding one another, talking and kissing like lovers, not running around like a couple of cornered mice.

As I turned away, Lora grabbed my arm. "I'll call you later, I promise."

"Okay." I slipped into the hallway and tiptoed toward the front door as fast as I could. For an instant, I thought I'd left my keys on her nightstand, but heaved a sigh of relief when I found them in the side pocket of my purse. I looked out the door to be sure the coast was clear before making a mad dash toward my car. I scampered across the lawn, dodging Jock's vomit from the night before, and skidded up to the car. I tumbled into the driver's seat, eased the door closed, and started the motor.

In another moment, I was on my way home, but home didn't seem like the same place it used to be. I imagined the familiar beige walls of my room, the outdated tawny carpeting and curtains, the yellowed 4-H ribbons taped to my vanity mirror; but those things held no comfort. That room had been mine all my life, but now it felt like a distant and lonely place, a place where I couldn't be me anymore.

But I *wasn't* me anymore. A cheerleader with a great big grin and bruised up shoulders had changed me. She'd found a part of me that no boy could ever begin to understand, a thing so baffling it made my head hurt every time I thought about it. But when I didn't think about it, when I simply accepted it without logic or rationalization, it made perfect sense. I wasn't alone. Whether she wanted to or not, Lora Tyler now shared my soul.

I groaned when I pulled into my parents' driveway. Mom and Dad were already home from church. Great. Mom would be in the kitchen whipping up our usual Sunday dinner of fried chicken and mashed potatoes. She'd get in too big a hurry and wind up with a mood on by the time the food hit the table. Dad, on the other hand, would be laid back in his La-Z-Boy snoring like an asthmatic grizzly.

I breezed in the back door, hoping to slip by unnoticed, but when I saw Mom and Dad standing in the living room, still in their church clothes, I choked. I'd have to face them. They'd know what I'd done. They'd see it on my face as surely as I still felt it in my groin.

"Good morning, party girl. Did you have a good time last night?" Mom asked. She was busy picking a piece of lint out of Dad's hair and didn't look at me. Small favors.

"It was okay," I said, never breaking stride.

Dad brushed Mom away from his head. He loosened his blue-striped tie and undid his collar. "We're going out to lunch with the Osbornes. Why don't you put on a dress and go with us?"

"Nah. I haven't had a shower. I stink. Besides, I've got studying to do." I tried to slip on by, but Mom's bull crap detector must have gone off the second I opened my mouth.

"Oh, come on. Your old folks aren't that bad to hang around with, are they?" Mom practically sang the words as she fell in step behind me. "We're going to Dutch Boy. You used to love Dutch Boy."

"It's okay, but I've got to finish my comp paper," I replied, quickening my pace. I heard Dad ramble to the kitchen, his wingtips clunking on the tile, but Mom was on my heels, her steps nearly silent on the worn carpeting.

"Robert called last night," she said.

"Really?"

"He wanted to talk to you." Mom could be quick as a cheetah when she wanted to, and she made it to the doorway before I could escape. She leaned against the frame and watched me kick off my shoes. Her gray dress matched the color of our eyes and revealed a modest amount of pale skin above her breasts.

"Why did he want to talk to me?" I asked, avoiding her knowing gaze.

"He said he'd been thinking about you. He sounded worried."

"Worried? Why?" A knot twisted up inside my stomach as I tossed my shoes in the closet.

Mom sat on the edge of my bed, tucked her skirt beneath her, and crossed her ankles. "Is something bothering you, Claire? You haven't been yourself lately."

I'd tried so hard not to be obvious, but no one knows you like your mother. She's the one who could identify your sick crying from your temper tantrum crying, who woke up in the middle of the night out of pure instinct when you had a fever, and who could tell you'd flunked an algebra quiz by the way you walked. I must've been nuts to think that I could have gone through a life alteration without Mom noticing.

"Nothing's bothering me." I started to unbutton my pants, but realized I was wearing Lora's panties. I stopped and left the chinos hanging on my hips.

"Honey, you've got your whole life to worry. Don't waste your youth on it." Mom paused and pretended to adjust her belt, a nervous habit she'd tried to break for years. "If you need to talk to me, you can, Claire. I won't be a hysterical mother."

Okay, Mom. I had sex with my best friend last night. I think I'm a queer. How's that grab you? A swell of nausea rose in my stomach.

I turned and forced a smile, wishing away the hurt I would eventually cause her. "I'm fine, Mom, really. I guess I'm a little scared about going to college next year. You know, stuff like that."

She smiled back, but the worry in her eyes deepened. I tried to put myself in her place as she sat on her child's bed, not sure what was wrong, not sure how to help. She must have been terrified.

Mom looked out the window. "If it's a boy... if you're in some kind of trouble, any kind of trouble..."

I wished it were that simple. If I'd gone out and gotten myself knocked up, at least she'd have some idea how to deal with it. They'd be upset and disappointed. They'd shake their heads and wonder where they went wrong. They'd be ashamed by what the neighbors would think, but we'd sit down and discuss my options. The real problem was unknown territory, something so unthinkable that my parents would have no idea where to start.

I forced another smile. "Honest. I'm okay."

She looked at me, and I saw myself in her. As I'd matured, I'd developed more of Dad's features—round cheeks and long, dark lashes—but I was still the spittin' image of Maureen Blevins, like Babbling Betty at the Woolworth's lunch counter had said more than ten years before. I ached with emptiness. I would never make her proud like Robert had, never give her the things a daughter should, but she still smiled. "Sure you don't want to go to lunch?"

I nodded, unable to speak. The monstrosity of the family would remain hidden for at least another day.

She got up and left, and the phone rang. I jumped on my bed and picked up the receiver. "Hello?"

"Can you meet me in ten minutes?" Lora's voice lifted my spirits and dampened them at the same time.

"Where?"

"By the tennis courts."

"Give me fifteen. My parents are going to lunch, and they haven't left yet."

"Fifteen, okay."

She didn't say goodbye.

CHAPTER 18

The brittle night air is good for my head. It blows away the echoes of idle dinner conversation and allows me to compose myself for a moment alone with Rebecca. We stroll silently along the sidewalk and up the front steps.

"Feel like a nightcap?" I slip my key into the lock.

"Sure, but just one. I've got an early day tomorrow." She follows me to the den and drops her purse beside the sofa.

"Make yourself at home." I go to the kitchen and pull a bottle of chilled Chardonnay from the refrigerator and two glasses from the cabinet.

When I return with the wine, she's sitting square in the middle of the couch. Shucks. I have no choice but to sit close to her—very close.

"You have a nice home," she says as I give her the drink.

"Thank you." I'd like to say something else, something witty and charming, but the line between my brain and my voice has disconnected.

She goes on. "I had a nice time at dinner. Jared and Elizabeth are good people."

"I don't know where I'd be now if it weren't for them. Probably on the street selling pencils."

"I'm glad you're here instead." She sips her drink. "I hope you don't think I'm being too forward, but I couldn't take my eyes off you tonight."

"Did I have spinach in my teeth?" I take a long swallow, but this sissy wine couldn't tranquilize a sloth. Should've poured myself a nice tall scotch or shaken up a vodka martini.

"No, silly. You didn't have spinach in your teeth. I like looking at you, that's all." Rebecca giggles and tentatively slides her hand onto my thigh. When I don't protest, she relaxes, leaving her hand near my knee.

"*You* like looking at *me*?" I ask.

"Does that bother you?"

"It's ironic, that's all. Do you know how many times I'd eaten at Choppy's before three months ago?"

She shakes her head, looking puzzled.

"About four. Now, how many times have I been in this winter? Every single day."

"You come in to see me?"

"I'm not a stalker or anything like that. It's just that... well, this sounds pitiful, but you were always so nice, and I kind of started looking forward to seeing you. I swear it was completely innocent. I had no idea we'd end up going out."

"Why?"

I shrug and hit the wine again. "I don't know. Guess I thought you were straight."

"Is that a compliment or a jab?"

"Neither, just a comment."

She leans closer, eyes dreamy, lips pouting. "This is the south, darlin'. It doesn't pay to be too obvious around here."

"Exactly." I tap my glass against hers. "I'm not about to put a lambda tattoo on my forehead."

"Me neither." After an awkward silence, she takes another glance around the room. "How long have you lived here?"

"Five years, give or take a few months. That's when I first met Elizabeth. She contacted me about speaking at a Junior League luncheon, and we hit it off right from the start. When she told me about the neighborhood she'd just moved into, she made it sound so nice that I drove through one day on my way home from work. This house was for sale, and I fell in love with it. I didn't realize at the time that Elizabeth and Jared lived right next door."

"So you bought this house by yourself?" She casts the question casually, but I know what she's fishing for.

I get up and head toward the kitchen, answering her question over my shoulder as I leave. "No. I had a partner."

As I refill my glass, I can almost hear Rebecca's mind processing the data. *Let's see, she moved here five years ago, must have been a serious relationship for them to buy a house. What happened? Did she tell me how long they were together? She's been single for how long?*

I step around the corner, obviously interrupting her thoughts. "More wine?"

"No, thanks."

What to do, what to say? I put the wine bottle back on the counter and join her on the sofa. With the most honest expression I can muster, I say, "Look, Rebecca, let me clear up a couple of things for you. Yes, I was in a very serious relationship for a very long time, but it's done, and yes, you're the first woman I've been out with since it's been over."

Rebecca's eyes widen. She takes a sip of wine and composes herself. "Thank you for telling me."

"I thought you should know why I'm so clumsy around you. Like I said, I was in a relationship for a long time and haven't dated since, so this is pretty new to me."

She won't look at me now. Her gaze darts toward the fireplace. "Is that what you want from me, a relationship?"

"I like you, but I don't know what I want right now."

"Fair enough." She puts her glass on the coffee table, turns to me, and clears her throat. "Since we're being so honest, I'll tell you a little about me. There have been a lot of women in my life—well, not that many—but the point is, I've never found one who fit just right. Maybe I never will."

"Maybe you expect too much."

"Could be, but I don't think a sense of decency is too much to ask for." She looks disgusted, but then a glimmer of hope twinkles in her eyes. "It's like I keep dating the same person over and over again. After three dates, they're in love. After three months, they're history. Guess I want to break my cycle, you know?"

I trace an X across my heart. "I promise not to fall in love with you after three dates."

Rebecca gives my thigh a playful smack. "That's very kind of you. I've been chasing the wrong type all my life. It's nice to know you're not like them."

Boy, is she in for a surprise. I've been trying to put my best foot forward, but in fact I'm burned out, used up, and ill-tempered. On the wrong-type scale of one to ten, I'm a seventy-two, and if I had one sliver of the decency she seeks, I'd thank her for a lovely evening and send her packing before one of us gets hurt.

But I don't want her to go, not yet. Searching her eyes, I say, "I'm carrying around all kinds of baggage, stuff you might not want to deal with. We've had some fun tonight, and I'd like to see you again, but consider yourself warned. I'm a basket case."

"Claire, we've all got baggage. It's what makes us who we are." She pauses. "So what do you think? Can two disillusioned old broads like us let our hair down and see what happens—no promises, no regrets?"

"Maybe."

"So I'll see you again?"

"I'd like that."

Rebecca laughs and squeezes the ticklish spot above my knee. "We're being way too serious."

She's right. My neck muscles are on the verge of cramping. I take a slow breath and roll my shoulders. "It's my fault. I'll try to lighten up."

Rebecca peeks at her watch and pats my leg. "It's late. I should go. Big day tomorrow."

Fighting the urge to ask her to stay and talk a while longer, I stand up and walk her to the door. As we reach the foyer, Rebecca turns and takes a coy step in my direction. She takes another, more determined step, her eyes fixed on me.

A second later, as if driven by an uncontrollable force, her body is pressed against me, her lips on mine. Her hands are on my face, easing toward the back of my neck. I accept her kiss, and a shiver pours down my back. The shiver transforms into heart-pounding heat, and I grab her waist and pull her closer. I slide my thigh between her legs and feel the gentle pivot of her hips.

As quickly as she lunged at me, she pulls away. We stare at one another, unblinking, eye to eye. I've got to get this on level ground, but I'm not going to do that with Rebecca straddling my thigh and breathing down my neck.

She leans in and touches her lips to my ear. "I don't usually attack someone on the first date." She relaxes and rests her forehead on my shoulder. "But you don't know how long I've wanted kiss you."

"I think I have an idea." I stroke her back with both hands. Her body is lean but soft, a wonderful mixture of athleticism and feminine contours.

I kiss her lips again, this time softer, sweeter. Rebecca traces her fingertips along my cheek, lingering a moment on my neck before continuing down my chest toward the top button of my blouse. I'm on fire, almost wishing she'd open the button.

She kisses my throat and whispers, "You make it hard for me to be a good girl."

"I don't *want* to be good. But I *need* to be good for a little while." I'm forcing my hands to stay on her arms.

She moves her lips back toward mine. "If you do everything the way you kiss..."

"You're crazy." I rub my cheek against hers, wallowing in her gentleness and wishing she were someone else.

Rebecca brushes her hands down my arms and steps back, avoiding my eyes. "I'm sorry."

"Don't be."

She looks up, a weak smile tickling her lips. "You must think I'm a real slut."

I wrap my arms around her shoulders and hug her tight as our bodies sway to the music in my head. "Just surprised. Pleasantly surprised."

My antiperspirant gave out the second she touched me, and my stomach is fluttering around somewhere between my knees and my ankles. But I'm not complaining. I'm just not accustomed to such gleeful confusion swishing through me, making clear thoughts as elusive as desert rain.

Rebecca touches my cheek again before she leaves.

I like that.

CHAPTER 19

Fifteen minutes. I had fifteen minutes to meet Lora at the tennis courts, and my parents were lingering in the kitchen like they had nowhere to go. As seconds ticked away, another of my already frayed nerves unraveled a little more and sent my senses into overdrive. Every noise was unbearably loud. The sound of Mom's shoes clopping on the linoleum reverberated down the hall and into my head like a gong. Dad opened the refrigerator door, then closed it, sending another thunderous boom into my ears.

I wanted to shout down the hall, "Bet the Osbornes are getting hungry!" But I bit my tongue. I jumped up and paced across the room. I'd been pacing a lot over the past week, so much that I noticed a slight rut in the carpet along the foot of my bed. Finally the back door closed, the Impala's engine sputtered, and the sound of crunching gravel gave way to silence.

I paused in front of the dresser, just to give Mom and Dad a good head start. Glancing in the mirror, I groaned. Gross. I was red-eyed, pale, and wrinkled. What a mess. Lora couldn't see me like this. I stripped off my clothes and tossed everything but the borrowed panties into the laundry hamper. I folded Lora's underwear and tucked it in the back corner of my sock drawer, then dashed toward the bathroom. I grabbed a washcloth from under the sink, sponged off as best I could, and rolled fresh deodorant under my arms. My greasy hair was hopeless, and I brushed it out with a sigh. It would have to do. After throwing on a pair of sneakers, jeans from the clean laundry bin, and a Lady Warriors T-shirt, I bounded out the back door.

Within five minutes, I had steered into the parking lot behind the high school. It was a secluded place, surrounded on two sides by the school and on the third by the football field house. Only the narrow road leading to the parking lot was open. A knee-high pile of brown leaves had blown against the field house wall. An intermittent breeze swept the ground, making the pile swell, collapse, and swell again like the frazzled breathing of a sleeping monster.

When I saw Lora's Pinto parked in front of the field house, my mouth got dry and my hands got wet. I swallowed hard and rubbed my palms across my jeans.

Her windows were rolled down, and Blondie's *The Tide is High* blared on the car radio. She didn't look at me as I parked. I dried my hands again, braced myself for the worst, and got out. Despite the cool wind tousling my hair, a fine sweat broke out on my forehead. I threw open the Pinto's passenger door and toppled into the seat.

Still not looking at me, Lora turned down the radio and dropped a wrinkled brown paper bag into my lap. I unrolled the top and peered in—my lost panties, folded into a perfect white square and Matthew's class ring perched on top like a blue and gold cherry on a virgin ice cream sundae.

"Shit," I muttered.

"I don't think Mom knew you were there. If she did, she didn't say anything." Lora glared at the brick wall in front of the parking space.

"Lora, I think—" I started to talk, not sure where I was going.

She cut me off. "I'm not a queer." She turned and looked at me with desperate eyes. "Are you okay?"

"Fine." I snuffled back the fullness swelling behind my eyes.

"Are you sure? I mean... I don't know what I mean." When she shook her head, all sad and confused, Lora Tyler had never been more beautiful.

We were silent for a moment, but a question gurgled in my throat. I tried swallowing it, but it wouldn't stay down. I considered a dozen ways to ask, but couldn't find one that sounded right. "Do you wish... are you sorry about what we..." The words got lost somewhere in my chest, and I dropped my head. I blinked hard and waited for her to strike my deathblow, but she didn't speak right away. She brushed her hand through her hair, sucked in a deep breath, and held it.

When you're waiting to be disemboweled, a few seconds can feel like forever. I fully expected Lora to turn blue and pass out before she breathed again, but she exhaled slowly and propped her elbows on the steering wheel. She buried her face in her hands. "Why won't it go away?"

She looked so scared, so vulnerable that I wanted to reach for her, comfort her, and say something understanding, but all I did was grunt, "Huh?"

Head still bowed, she looked at me. Her eyes glistened. "This has bothered me for so long, since grade school. Hell, since forever. I've begged God to make it stop, prayed till my knees are blue, but He isn't listening. It goes against everything I've ever been taught, everything I believe in, but I just can't get it out of my mind. I can't stop thinking about you. I can't stop thinking that I might really be... Jesus, I can't even say it out loud."

Lora's pained expression cut deep. I dropped my head again and gazed at the floorboard. "I'm sorry."

"Don't be sorry. It's my fault. I started it, and now I have to finish it. I'm just sorry I dragged you into it."

I looked away and stared at the pile of leaves. The monster was still breathing. In and out. In and out.

Lora sat up and wiped her eyes. "Have you ever... been with a girl before?"

"No."

"But you've thought about it?"

"Not really. Not before now." I faced her. "Have you done it before?"

"No. Never."

"Why me?"

"I don't know." She paused. "I feel like I can be myself with you. That Sunday in my bedroom, anyone else would've told the whole school, but I knew you wouldn't. I knew you'd keep my secret." She stopped, and her voice went hard. "Claire, no one can ever know what we did."

"I won't tell. Besides, if I rat on you, I rat on myself." My shoulders slumped as my last shred of hope began to fade away. Lora's desires were in a fight with her principles, and it looked like the principles would win out. I just had a ringside seat—my urges didn't count. I dried my hands on my jeans again.

Lora propped her hand on the gearshift and squeezed the worn knob till her knuckles turned white. "I have to go. I'm meeting Jock before work."

"Lora, wait... I... I don't know what to say." *Bullshit!* But she didn't want to hear what I had to say. My confession would turn her against me, and I wouldn't even have her as a friend. But could I be just a friend to Lora Tyler? Could I see her and not want her? Would I ever forget our night together? Could I bear watching her stroll down the halls of Franklin High, hand-in-hand with Jock Richardson? I didn't think so.

A vision of Lora with Jock formed in my head. When she'd first told me about her sexual escapades with her boyfriend, it had turned me on. Now the thought of him kissing her made me sick. I gulped down the acid rising in my throat and blinked hard. Who was I trying to kid? Jock was her boyfriend and I was nothing. He would be the one holding her hand during lunch break. He would dance with her at the prom and stand with her before the minister. It wouldn't be me. It couldn't be me.

But I was young and brash. And worst of all, I was in love. Something rose inside my chest. My hands began to tremble, and the skin on my arms broke out in gooseflesh. Then it hit me. I had to go for it. What did I have to lose? Like a tsunami crashing over me, the realization sent my thoughts tumbling and thrashing till they smacked together and melded into a single question. Why *not* me?

A geyser-like pressure forced my words out. "Break up with Jock. Be with me." Stunned by my own statement, I stared at Lora.

Her eyes went wild, her face suddenly pale. "What?"

My heart was on cruise control, ignoring my brain's protests to exercise caution. I sped on. "He's full of shit, you said so yourself. I won't treat you like he does. I'll treat you like a queen. I'll give you anything you want, anything. Lora, I've never felt the way I feel with you. I don't want to forget this ever happened."

The muscle in her jaw twitched. "You're serious, aren't you?"

"I am."

She looked away. She looked at me. She looked away. "I want to be normal. I don't want to be a freak, to have everyone pointing at me and laughing behind my back."

"They'll never know."

"People will find out."

"No. I promise, it'll be our secret."

One corner of her mouth turned up. "Our secret?"

"Besides, wouldn't you rather be a freak and be happy than be normal and unhappy?"

Lora sat quiet for a moment. A rumble from the nearby highway drifted over us, and the Pinto trembled. She timidly reached for my hand. She didn't have to say another word. Lora wanted me. We could deny it, ignore it, try to forget it, or even fight it, but it wasn't going away. It couldn't. We were bound together by a rudimentary need that seventeen years of programming couldn't erase. It was at the core of our being, and without it, we couldn't live. But with it, what did our future hold?

Lora's hand was damp and clammy, but her touch sent a surge of blood to my groin. My heart beat faster. My head swam. "What now?"

"I don't know." She looked toward the empty street, then leaned across the console and kissed me.

I met her lips and tasted her sweet breath. I was starving for more, but we were in the open and exposed. We pulled apart as quickly as we'd joined.

Lora's face was flushed with the same excitement that raged through me. "This is crazy. We're asking for a world of trouble, Claire. If anyone even suspects what's going on, we're toast."

"I've never felt right with anyone but you, not even with Matthew. I don't care what people say, this is what I want."

She brushed my cheek with delicate fingertips. "If you can handle it, then so can I."

With that, Lora and I started our journey. For the first time in his life, Jock Richardson had been benched, but I was a rookie and didn't understand the game. Only time would tell if I had what it took to keep Lora Tyler on my team.

CHAPTER 20

I can't sleep. I've been bouncing around the bed for hours and regularly kicking Jitterbug. The dog is used to it; she just grunts, rolls over, and goes back to sleep. I wish it were that easy for me, but my brain seems to have a short circuit. Every time I drift off, some spark of thought flares up and I'm wide awake again.

If it weren't so late, I'd pop a pill, but I don't want to spend all day in a stupor, so I prop my pillow against the headboard and flip on the bedside lamp. When my eyes adjust, I grab this week's copy of *Time*. Without looking at the cover, I flip through a few pages and stop on a full-page cosmetics ad. Before me, in all their undernourished glory, two models stand side by side. One has an exotic Oriental look, olive skin, satin black hair, and almond-shaped eyes. The other is pure California surfer dudette, bobbed blonde hair, bronze skin, and blue eyes that would make Paul Newman look twice. The caption reads, "Because no two of us are exactly alike." There's a truth that hits home.

Tonya has told me a thousand times that all women are physically unique, but my lack of experience with anyone but my lover has made me skeptical. Now, after kissing Rebecca only once, I see that Tonya is right. Rebecca's body feels small, more compact than the one who shared my bed for so long. Her lips are full, her hands dainty compared to my former lover's. But there's something else about Rebecca, something I can't define, that makes her different. Maybe it's her smell—like apricot brandy—or maybe it's the way she tilts her head a bit to the left when she smiles.

I push those thoughts aside and turn a few more pages, stopping on an article about genetic engineering. The tag line reads, "Is sexual reproduction becoming old-fashioned?"

Sex. All I have to do is see the word, and it makes me nuts. How could something so simple drive me so insane? Now that I don't have a ready supply, I'm as frustrated as a one-armed juggler. One hand will do the job, but how exciting is that? What I need is a partner with energy to spare and skin like velvet. I need hot breath on the back of my neck, a body responding to my touch, and the final bliss of oblivion that for the past three years I've achieved vicariously through sleeping pills and vodka.

But as my imagination creates a passionate love scene, replacing the blank visage of a stranger with Rebecca's face, I see that reality wouldn't live up to my hopes. I will never completely release myself with someone I don't love. Tonya would say that my attachment of love to sex is a childish fantasy, and maybe she's right. If real people had to be in love to have sex, no one would be getting any, so if I expect physical relief, I'll have to put those silly ideas out of my head. I'll never love again, but by God, I'll have sex and will find some middle ground where at least my physical needs can be fulfilled.

When the doorbell rouses me from sleep, I'm disoriented. I don't remember nodding off, yet it's nearly 8:00 a.m. I stumble toward the front door while I wrap my long cotton bathrobe around me and scratch places I wouldn't go near in polite company. Jitterbug skitters along in front of me like a car driving on ice. Her rear fishtails and looks like it might reach the door first.

Without looking through the peephole, I swing the door open and see Tonya standing on the step holding a red and white striped bag from Thompson's Bakery. She looks fresh from the shower, her blonde hair half-dry, its perfectly cropped ends clinging to the sides of her neck and falling around her forehead. With no makeup, her eyes seem innocent instead of seductive. It's a good look, but try convincing Tonya of that. Who wants a kitten when they can have a tigress, she'd argue.

"Put on the coffee, girl. I've got fresh bagels and those apple muffins you like so much." I catch a sniff of vanilla body spray as she charges by and tosses her leather jacket on the sofa.

"Nice outfit," I say, eyeing her gray sweatpants and orange University of Tennessee sweatshirt. "Did the jacket come with it or did you put it together all by yourself?"

"Bite me." She swings too fast around the bar into the kitchen, and her sneakers send a harsh squeak through the house. She grabs a paper towel from the cabinet over the stove and drops the bakery bag on the table. She then stops dead and stares at me. "Are you going to make coffee or what?"

Still in a sleepy daze, I force one foot in front of the other and ramble to the counter to put on the pot. I yawn and toss Jitterbug a treat from the pantry. "What's got you up at this hour?"

Tonya falls into a kitchen chair and stretches her arms above her head. "Up from what? Haven't been to bed yet. Not to sleep, anyway."

"Slut."

"Prude."

If I didn't know her so well, I might not take her carousing so casually, but considering the atrocities she's suffered, she's bound to be somewhat eccentric. As a matter of fact, she's remarkably well adjusted.

I don't know why Tonya confided in me when she did. We hadn't been friends that long, and she'd never spoken of her past. But one night, as we struggled over a sketch, she began to speak of her drug-addicted mother and alcoholic father—tales so wicked I couldn't sleep well for weeks. But Tonya spoke as if the memories belonged to someone else, recounting the events like a TV commentator, detached and dry-eyed, stating the facts and ignoring the suffering behind them.

Her words gave me some insight into the infamous Fly By Knight, told me at least part of why she behaved the way she did. Now, as I consider my own sexuality and how I feel so isolated from the rest of the world, I understand her even better. Not to say my experience is anything like hers, though. I've been shot in the heart. She was emotionally slaughtered, maimed before she even had a chance.

I sneak two cups of coffee from the half-full carafe and join Tonya at the table. Taking a bite of apple muffin, I savor the cinnamon and brown sugar, letting it roll around my mouth before washing it down with a hot gulp of black coffee. "So who was it this time?"

"She was in town for the insurance convention. I think she said she was from Atlanta."

"Hitting on out-of-towners, huh? Think that's a sign you've done everyone in town?"

"Hey, I saved her. You should've seen the woman who was hitting on her when I got there. I swear to God, she looked just like Bob Dylan, scruffy beard and all."

I laugh, spewing crumbs onto the table. "I know who you're talking about. Her name's Priscilla. I met her through Joanna and Karin about a hundred years ago."

"Anyway, after a few drinks, she tells me her husband doesn't understand her needs as a woman."

"Why does she have a husband if he doesn't do it for her?"

"Didn't ask." Tonya intentionally drops a piece of bagel on the floor, and Jitterbug snatches it up before I can protest. "Her name is Alison, by the way—with an A—and we had a very nice time together." She leans forward and grins. "But I'd much rather hear about your evening."

Elizabeth Kingsley is a dead woman. I bet she was on the phone to Tonya the minute Rebecca and I left the party. What a juicy talk they must have had, guessing how long my date would stay, how far we'd go. I can just hear them going on and on about how wonderful it was that poor little Claire had finally taken her first step toward healing. Holy Mother, they were probably on the phone for a solid hour.

"Hope you've got free weekend minutes," I say. "Bet your cell phone was smoking by the time you two got through."

She exposes her ear. "It wasn't exactly smoking, but it did get a little warm. See? My ear's still red."

"So what was my neighbor's take on the evening?" I pull another muffin from the bag.

"Said she seems nice and that she's pretty." She swallows a bite of bagel. "Got any cream cheese?"

I nod toward the refrigerator. Jitterbug collapses by my chair and lays her head on my foot. "Yes, Rebecca is both nice and pretty."

"Fuck her?"

"Fly, for God's sake!"

"Didn't think so." She ambles to the refrigerator, snatches a container from the shelf, and sits back down. "Going to fuck her?"

I try to answer, but no words will come. If I can't tell Tonya how I'm feeling, I can't tell anyone. It was Tonya who spent a month living out of an overnight bag, shuttling between her own house and my newly empty one, her arms that rocked me to sleep after a hundred crying fits. She's the one who told me it was okay to feel bad for a while.

I scan her face and wonder how she stays so young. She looks only a day older than when we met, smooth skin unmarred by laugh lines or crow's feet. Her eyes still dance to the rhythm of her different drummer; her heart still longs for something she can't name.

I swallow my last bite of muffin. "I don't know if Rebecca wants sex from me."

Tonya's glance lingers on me for a second before her attention returns to the cream cheese and bagel. "Here's a good rule of thumb: if she doesn't try to fuck you by the second date, she's not interested."

"Where'd you get that rule?"

"Made it up."

"Well, it's stupid."

"You got a better one?"

"No."

"Then believe it." Tonya takes a small bite and swallows quickly. "When are you and this Rebecca person going out again?"

"We didn't talk about it. Thought I might call her later." I stuff the rest of the muffins back into the bakery bag and dust the crumbs into my palm.

"You should. Maybe she'll be free this evening, and you'll be a new woman by this time tomorrow."

"Rushing things a bit, aren't we?"

"Rushing? How can it be rushing? Maybe if you were a nun or something, but by my standards, you should've bagged her last night."

"By your standards, I'd have been screwing every woman in town the day after—" I chop off the words, letting them linger in my brain. The day after. The worst day of my life. How can the feeling still be so vivid, hurled from nowhere like an ice pick stabbing me between the eyes? I reach for the counter to steady myself. It won't come back to haunt me, not today. I'll never go through that again, even if I really do have to become a nun, or duct-tape my knees together for the rest of my life.

Tonya yawns. "I'm tuckered. Mind if I crash for a while?"

She leads me down the hall, and we crawl into bed together. My best friend wraps her slender arms around me and kisses my forehead. "Sleep now," she whispers, as she has a hundred times before. "You'll feel better when you wake up."

I snuggle into her breast and thank God she's here.

Tonya will always be here. I'll make sure of that.

CHAPTER 21

During our first few months together, Lora and I were careful to hide our relationship. We always maintained an appropriate distance, never touched in public, and never let anyone know how much time we spent together.

It was unbelievably frustrating. I wanted to hold her hand. I needed to kiss her. As often as possible, we'd meet after work. Lora would steal a couple of leftover slices of pizza, we'd stop by Pic Kwik for a fountain soda, and off we'd go, roaming back roads and logging trails, looking for a secluded place to share an intimate moment. But we weren't the only ones in search of privacy, and most of the places we found saw a fair amount of traffic from straight kids. So, even alone on a country road, we had to be careful. Climbing into the back seat for a quickie was out of the question. It was one thing for two girls to get caught at a make-out spot but quite another for them to get caught in the back seat with their clothes off and the windshield fogged up.

So my lover and I held hands and talked, which was probably a good thing. Instead of building our relationship on sex, we built it on bonds forged during those long talks. We talked about everything—school, religion, how narrow-minded our parents were, and we even had a lengthy discussion once about which was better, sanitary napkins or tampons. How many boys could you talk about that with? It was marvelous. I had a confidante, a best friend, and a sweetheart all rolled up in one neat little package.

On a sunny April afternoon, I sat in Pizza Oven's parking lot tapping my foot in rhythm to the Devo music crackling through the dashboard speaker. Lora's shift would be over soon, and we'd take off and leave the real world behind. I cranked down my window, laid my head back, and closed my eyes. The county road crews had mown the median along US 19, and the cool, clean aroma of cut grass filled the car.

Springtime had always been good for my spirit. It awakened my love of the outdoors and sparked a renewed sense of purpose. But that year, the red and purple April tulips seemed more fragrant, the forsythia a brighter shade of yellow, and the sun a bit warmer on my face. I felt alive, more than I ever had before.

I opened my eyes and saw Lora sauntering toward me. Her hair was pulled back in a floppy ponytail that looked as though it might break loose in the slightest breeze. She'd changed into Levis and a pink button-down shirt and carried the usual duffel bag under her arm, no doubt stuffed with her dirty work garb. She shielded her eyes with her hand and smiled. I leaned over to unlock the passenger door, but she shook her head.

"I want to drive today," she said and dug her keys out of her purse.

"Aren't you tired?"

"No. Come on."

I locked up the Datsun and joined Lora in her Pinto. She tossed her duffel bag into the back seat and jabbed the key in the ignition. She turned the key, the engine came to life, and we were off. As soon as we cleared the parking lot, I reached across the console and took her hand. She held my hand tightly but didn't speak as she steered onto Bluff Head Road and headed out of town.

Something in her demeanor seemed a little off. She only nodded or shook her head when I tried to make conversation. By the time we left the main road and pulled onto a rutted tractor path, I was exhausted from trying to get her to talk.

Lora navigated the path cautiously, avoiding deep ruts and fallen branches. The sun was beginning to dip into the western sky, and as we worked our way into the forest, shade fell around the car, hiding us, protecting us.

We sat in silence, and for at least thirty minutes, Lora wouldn't look at me. She just held my hand and picked occasionally at a loose stitch on the steering wheel.

"I can't do this anymore, Claire," she finally said. A faint shaft of evening light danced through the surrounding trees and cast swaying shadows across her face. She squeezed my hand but kept staring straight ahead. "I can't stand what we've been doing."

Can't stand it? I lived for these moments. My heart stopped for a second, and my hands went cold.

I struggled to talk and finally managed to whisper, "Has Jock started calling you again?"

"He hasn't called in weeks."

That was good. The one thing Jock Richardson had taken more seriously than sports was trying to get Lora to come back to him. He'd sent dozens of roses, called ever day, and even tried to get me to talk her into reconsidering. I had promised to talk to her, and I had. What poor Jock didn't know was that my talking to Lora had nothing to do with her going back to him and everything to do with keeping her for myself. Now I feared I would soon share his fate.

Lora turned to face me. "I've been thinking that since we're both going to State in the fall, maybe we should find an apartment close to campus. It wouldn't have to be anything big, but at least we could be alone. Think about it. We could make love in a bed instead of sneaking around all the time."

"Oh, God." I gasped as air found my lungs again. "I thought you were breaking up with me."

"I'll never do that." She put her other hand on my knee. Something rose in her eyes, a look I'd never seen on her or anyone else. "I love you, Claire."

She'd spoken the words before, but never with the purity I saw in her face, the devotion I heard in her voice. Tears welled in my eyes.

She went on. "I don't want to spend another night wishing you were beside me. I don't want us to act like a couple of kids anymore. It's time we grew up."

"You really want us to live together?"

She nodded. "I think you want it, too. I see it in your eyes every time I have to go home. I hear it every time you say goodnight over the phone."

"But State is only thirty minutes away. My parents expect me to commute for the first year. They say it's a good time to learn to be independent but still have them to fall back on."

"What do you want?"

The thought of living with Lora quickened my pulse. We'd been dodging boys and prying eyes for six months—not a perfect way to start a relationship. Since our first night together, we'd managed to make love a few times, but each occasion left us more frustrated. We always ended up focusing on not getting caught instead of each other. What a luxury it would be to have our own space where we could be ourselves instead of what everyone thought we should be. At that point, I was ready to sell my soul for one night alone with her, and I became light-headed at the prospect of spending every night together.

"I want to live with you, honey, but can we do it? Apartments in Spring City are expensive. I've only been working at the pharmacy since Christmas, and I don't have much saved up."

"That's what I've been working on." Lora pulled a folded piece of notebook paper from her purse, opened it, and handed it to me. On one side, she'd listed expenses along with an estimate of their monthly costs. On the other was a list of apartment complexes.

She pointed to the list. "These apartments are all close to campus, some even within walking distance, and they're cheap."

I recognized two or three of the complexes. They weren't exactly in fancy neighborhoods. "We'll have to find new jobs."

"It's a college town. I found all kinds of places that will let students schedule work around classes." She grabbed a folded newspaper from under her seat. On the help-wanted section of the *Spring City Tribune,* she'd circled a dozen ads with red ink.

I stared at her. "You've done your homework. Think we could do it?"

"I know we can. I've been saving all my tips since November. We can use them for deposits on the electricity, phone, and whatever else we need." She glanced in the rearview mirror before leaning her head on my shoulder. "I want to be with you, Claire. I'm tired of having to look around every time I want to touch you, and I'm sick to death of trying to love you in a car."

"Me, too."

The dusty gravel road was empty. Only the budding maples and possibly a low-flying robin could see us. I lifted her chin and pressed my lips to hers. Her kisses always set me free. Sometimes she was soft and gentle, tasting me, caressing me, but other times she was hungry, pulling me into her, setting me on fire with her hot breath and roaming hands. Either way, I was exactly where I wanted to be and would do anything to stay there.

A cardinal lit on the limb of a nearby spruce and sang, *pretty, pretty, pretty*. It sat there watching us, red and black nestled in a sea of green. It flew away and dropped a splat of poop on the windshield.

I pointed at the mess. "Hope that's not an omen."

"I hope it is. Shit can fly at us, but it can't hit us."

"You sure are optimistic."

Lora gave me that pouting lip routine she always used to get her way. "Tell me, baby. Are we going to try it?" She didn't have to ask—she knew she had me.

It wouldn't be easy to convince my parents. They'd argue I couldn't afford it, I needed to save my money, I wouldn't be able to work full time and keep my grades up. They could've been right on all counts, but they couldn't understand my motivation.

"Let's do it," I said.

Her pout turned into a huge grin, and she glanced in the rearview before lunging over the console toward me. She squeezed me so tight I almost couldn't breathe. "Baby, I love you."

Seeing Lora so thrilled was the best thing I'd ever known. I'd do whatever it took to keep her that way, even if it meant working eight days a week and eating soup from a can for the rest of my life. I'd give her an apartment. One day, I vowed to myself, I'd give her the best mansion money could buy.

CHAPTER 22

The phone rings. For a minute I don't know where I am or what day it is. Jitterbug sniffs my face. Okay, I'm at home. I glance at the clock—10:30. Oh yeah, now I remember. It's Sunday. Tonya brought muffins from Thompson's.

I roll over and punch my friend. "Get that, will you?"

She picks up the phone and answers in a groggy voice. "Hello. No, this is Tonya. Sure, she's right here, hang on." She hands me the phone.

I press the receiver to my ear. "Hello?"

"Claire, this is Rebecca. Is this a bad time?"

Wonderful! The first time she calls, I'm in bed with another woman. "Uh... no, it's fine," I stammer. "My best friend, Tonya, and I fell asleep watching a movie."

"I see." She pauses and clears her throat, sounding a bit confused. "I wanted to thank you for last night. I had a great time."

I wipe the sleep from my eyes and look at Tonya, who's giving me a thumbs up. "Me, too. I hope Elizabeth wasn't too pushy. She's decided you and I need to move in together."

"One of these days I'm going to have a long talk with Elizabeth." Rebecca giggles and lets a couple of seconds tick away. "I would like to see you again."

"Maybe we can get together sometime this week." I glance at Tonya, who's now sticking her tongue out at me.

"I'd love to, but my evening manager had a baby last night, so I'll have to cover for a few days. Maybe by Friday, though."

"We can work something out."

"Will you come by for lunch tomorrow?"

"Wouldn't miss it."

I hang up and drop the phone on the bed. My stomach is in knots. On one hand, I want to see Rebecca again. Her smile makes me feel good; her kiss makes me feel better. But on the other hand, I don't want to get carried away. All these conflicting ideas are teetering back and forth, making me more anxious than ever. This whole charade may be more trouble than it's worth.

Tonya rolls toward me and sniggers. "My little Claire is growing up."

"I think your little Claire is going insane." I run my hand through my hair. It feels greasy.

"What do you mean?" She props herself on one elbow and gives me a rare serious look.

"I don't know, I'm just so moody these days. Sometimes I feel great about things, you know, almost like my old self, but sometimes I'm on the verge of suicide."

Tonya purses her lips. "No middle ground?"

"A little."

"How long do your mood swings last?"

I sit up and stare at my friend. Tonya seems concerned, and that bothers me. Fly By Knight doesn't give a horse's patoot about much of anything that doesn't wear fishnet stockings, and if she smells trouble, I might need professional help.

"Hello, in there. Anybody home?" she says, tapping my forehead.

"Oh, the mood swings, right? They might last a day or two, but I can be happy as a clam and just start crying."

"Probably a good sign." Tonya falls back on the bed and closes her eyes. Jitterbug hops across me and sniffs her sweatshirt.

"A good thing?"

"Think about it. As angry and depressed as you've been, at least you have some up time now. Maybe the depression is easing up. You know, working its way out of your system." She smiles. "I have to admit, you've seemed a little less intense for the past couple of weeks. I think you're getting better."

"Is that your professional opinion, Dr. Knight?" I slap her stomach, and she acts like I've knocked the breath out of her. She rolls onto her side into a fetal position and jabs at my ribs.

I curl up, trying to make a smaller target. "Hey, cut it out!"

Tonya grabs my wrists and wrestles me onto my back. "Don't even try to fight me. I can still take you down." In one deft move, she's straddling my hips and smiling.

"Get off me, you beast!"

"You can't fight destiny, my dear," she croons, doing a horrible Cary Grant impression.

A silent alarm goes off in my head. We can't do this, and there are a thousand good reasons why. I've always told myself that my main reason for not pursuing a physical relationship with Tonya is because it might ruin our friendship, but there's another reason, a more basic excuse which I've kept to myself. On the outside Tonya is all woman—curves and long legs, lipstick and perfume, high heels and little black dresses. But on the inside she's stone butch—one of the most extreme cases I've ever seen. No one will ever touch Tonya Knight again, not even me. I respect it, but I don't think I could stand it.

I struggle against her grip and she releases me.

"Damn, I'm tired." She rolls away, saving us from the conversation that usually follows one of these moments. She pulls the blanket over her shoulders, and I tuck it under her chin.

I brush her hair from her cheek. "Sleep as long as you want. I'll be here when you wake up."

"I know." Tonya closes her eyes and snuggles up to my chest.

Staring at the ceiling, I wonder what will become of me. I'm too old for all this indecision and emotional mayhem. My life wasn't supposed to be this way. Lora should be here, like we planned. Why won't she just come home?

CHAPTER 23

I never convinced my parents it was better to have an apartment off campus than stay at home or live in the dorm. The debate turned into a contest of wills. Both Mom and Dad had fiery stubborn streaks, but they hadn't counted on me being as ornery as a borrowed mule. We argued for three days.

Dad insisted that it was too dangerous for two girls barely out of high school to live alone. "Lord only knows what goes on in those shabby apartment complexes. There's probably more drugs in just one of them than in all of Franklin."

"Don't kid yourself, Dad," was my snotty reply.

Mom said, "If you live here and commute, I guess we'll have to buy you a new car. That old Datsun won't last much longer, and I know you've had your eye on that blue Mustang down at Keener's."

But her serene expression didn't faze me, and I smarted off again. "Bribery will get you nowhere." Boy, was I ever a nasty little twerp then.

After the initial battle, we all retreated into silence. Then it was just a matter of who sent up the white flag first. So when Mom came creeping into my room one afternoon, I smelled victory.

She leaned back against the wall, arms crossed, looking defeated. "I don't know why this is so important to you, but I guess we have to let you go."

The truce was simple. My parents would pay for my tuition and books as long as I kept a 3.5 grade point average. As for rent, utilities, and food, I was on my own. I was determined to grow up, and they were determined to give me a good dose of it.

Three months later, on a scorching July afternoon, I stood in the middle of a tiny living room, surveying what would be our home for the next four years. Home—the word sent a tingle though me. Lora and I were beginning the long journey of carving our niche, a space unbound by bricks and mortar, which we would share through good and bad.

It didn't matter that the tiny kitchen had barely enough room for a small table, or that the gold refrigerator and stove looked like they'd come over on the Mayflower. We didn't care that the shower hadn't had a good scrubbing since before we were born, or that the bedroom carpet was so full of cigarette burns it looked like an old slab of wormy chestnut. We were intoxicated by new freedom and by each other. Nothing could bring us down.

I'd wangled a job working four nights a week in the archive room at Mercy Hospital. It paid just a dime over minimum wage, but I'd settled on a business major, so it seemed a good place to start.

Lora, with her great big grin and unusual good looks, had found a waitress job at Spangler's Steak House. At the time, it was the only place in Spring City where you could get liquor by the drink and a good meal in the same building, so it stayed busy with doctors, lawyers, professionals of all kinds—the types who ordered big and tipped bigger.

I stumbled around a few unopened boxes and wondered how in the world we'd ever get the place cleaned up. The sun was already casting long shadows through our lone living room window and forming a rectangle of amber light against the paneling. We'd stirred up a good bit of dust moving in, and the lingering particles swam through the beam of light like snow in one of those Christmas globes my Aunt Trudy collected. The air smelled like mothballs and turpentine.

Lora had gone to K-Mart for cleaning supplies and was taking her time getting back, so I was alone, sticky hot, and irritated. Already things weren't going as planned. For months, I'd been dreaming of our first night alone, imagining soft music and candlelight, but it looked like I was going to spend more time with Mr. Clean than with my lover.

For the moment, two empty pillowcases served as curtains. I pulled one away from the window and peeked out. A dozen cars dotted the yellow-lined parking spaces. Most of them looked like my poor old Datsun—beat up and in need of a paint job. Across the way, in the window of the first floor apartment closest to the Dumpster, an obese cat sat licking its front paw. I slid up the window and flicked an ant off the sill into the yard below.

As I watched the black speck tumble to the ground, Lora's Pinto lumbered into the parking space in front of our apartment. She scrambled out of the car and hoisted three brown bags from the back seat. On her way up the sidewalk, she stopped and put down the bags. She stepped into a deep patch of clover and plucked something from the grass. Then she retrieved the bags and bounded up the steps.

I opened the door for her. "What took you so long?"

She set the bags down and held up a four-leaf clover. "Look what I found out front. It's a sign, a good-luck charm."

"We need all the luck we can get," I said, picking up one of the bags and heading toward the kitchen.

She brought the other two, and we put the bags on the floor. Lora pressed the clover into a textbook on the counter and turned to face me. "Looks like we've got our work cut out for us, honey."

I opened a roll of paper towels and set them on the table beside a bottle of Windex. "Where do we start?"

"I say we christen the place first." She gave me that little devilish grin and pulled a bottle of champagne from one of the bags.

"How'd you get that?" I took the bottle and inspected the label as if I knew something about sparkling wine. Truth was, I'd only tasted it once, at my cousin Reba's wedding when I was in the ninth grade.

"That's what took so long. I bugged a guy at the liquor store till he went in for me." She put the champagne aside. "We can clean later. Now we celebrate."

She wrapped her arms around my shoulders and kissed me long and sweet, like in the movies. We'd been playing hide-and-seek for so long, I didn't quite know how to hold her without glancing over my shoulder first.

"Does this mean I might get lucky?" I asked.

She gave me a playful look and smacked my backside. "Honey, you're going to get luckier than a whore on a submarine."

We laughed for a minute, but we'd been making corny jokes for months. Now it was time to get serious.

"Can we do that thing?" I asked, breathless and embarrassed.

Lora took my hand and led me through the living room mess, dodging cardboard boxes and suitcases. Once we were in the bedroom, she kissed me again.

The bed was nothing more than a mattress and box springs sitting on the floor with a borrowed comforter and K-Mart sheets that might have carried a guarantee to exfoliate your skin from head to toe while you slept. But we had a bottle of unopened cheap champagne getting warm in the kitchen and love getting hot in the bedroom. As far as we were concerned, we were in the honeymoon suite at the Ritz.

We tugged at our clothes, needing to know each other in a way we had yet to experience. A stitch in my tee shirt snapped as Lora stripped it off over my head, and her bra whirred as it flew across the room. After we tore the rest of our clothes off and fell onto the bed, I pulled away from my lover and looked at her. We'd done a lot of things over the past months, but I'd never seen her completely nude, only caught glimpses here and there by the dashboard lights. I knew she had long, shapely legs, but I'd never seen how they flowed into her hips, how her hips rounded and dipped into her waist, how her waist blossomed into her breasts. The whole of Lora really was greater than the sum of her parts. She was perfect in my eyes, made by God and impossible to duplicate. I was so young, so goofy in love.

She reached out and her fingers touched my face, tracing my lips. "I love you."

I pulled her close, bathed her in fluttering kisses, and rolled on top of her. Looking down into her eyes, I said, "Can I?"

Lora brushed my hair from my face. "Of course."

I buried my face in the slope of her neck, drew her into my mouth, and tasted her salty sweet skin. She wrapped herself around me and pressed her hips against mine. I eased down her body, kissing her chest, her breasts, her stomach until I found my cheek brushing against the patch of twisty fuzz between her legs. I'd wanted to kiss her there, the place where life begins and reason ends, but Ford Pintos were never known for their luxurious seats. We wanted to do it right, so we'd decided to wait. The wait was over.

I was timid at first, fearful of doing something wrong. I kissed her with easy strokes, finding places I never knew existed, but I soon became caught up in her motion, her breathing, her hands running through my hair, pulling me in. Then I devoured her, consumed with an awkward hunger, and in a few minutes of blinding sex, six months and eighteen years of pent-up desire climaxed in Lora's body. She thrust herself to me, lost her breath, then pulled away as she passed the point of being touched.

She lay very still for a full minute. Then, damp and exhausted, she shivered and pulled me to her, wrapping her arms around me as her tears spilled on my shoulder. Outside the window, a dog howled, low and mournful, compounding the mix of ecstasy and sadness in her eyes.

With trembling fingers, I combed her hair from her face. "What's wrong, honey? Did I do it wrong?"

She shook her head and didn't speak for a second, but when she did, all she said was, "I'll show you."

She then kissed my lips and gently escorted me to the place she'd discovered, the one unearthly plane where we could hide and never be found. Then I understood. What we'd done felt so pure and beautiful that it ran the gamut of emotion, starting at bliss but stopping at a strange feeling of loss. It almost hurt to be so close, to let even Lora take me that far.

We lay together for hours, enveloped in the rough sheets and rocking to the steady beat of our hearts. The intimacy overwhelmed our young minds and bodies, and the journey back to reality was slow. But voices, slamming doors, and heavy footsteps reverberated deep into the night, reminding us we weren't alone. We were out in the world, on our own. Together.

I'd finally given Lora all I physically could. It would never feel quite the same again, but it would be good for a long time.

CHAPTER 24

I hate it when the boss calls sales meetings in my office, especially on Monday morning. For the past two hours, Reggie and our lead sales rep, Bob Carlisle, have discussed the Wayland County Court proposal in agonizing detail.

Before Bob came along five years ago, I'd been the lead sales rep, spending four nights a week away from home, beating the bushes from daylight to dark in search of anyone who might need a filing system. I built our little empire from nothing and wasn't about to hand it over to just anyone, but Bob proved efficient and loyal. Turning the territory over to him was a relief, but the damage had already been done. By the time I started staying home every night, Lora had spent too much time alone.

I stare at the framed photograph on my desk. After all this time, her Mona Lisa smile still renders me defenseless, and several times a week, that stupid picture ends up in the bottom drawer. But in less than five minutes, it finds its way back to the spot between my CRT and the stapler. The space seems bare without it. Besides, the cherry frame matches my desk.

Bob shakes me from my trance when he lets out an exasperated groan and loosens his silk tie. He looks the part of a super sales rep—tall and lean, with a grin that turns most women to mush and most men into his best buddies. Yet he's a coward when it comes to putting his foot down with a customer.

"You've been around long enough to know this counteroffer is just a negotiation tactic," Reggie says. He tosses his legal pad on my desk and glances toward me. He wants me to take the ball and baby-talk Bob through this, but I sit quietly.

Bob's not convinced. "This is a big deal, Reg. All we have to do is shave the profit margin a few percent." He wants this sale, but he'd be smart to listen. Reggie knows his stuff. More than once he talked me out of cutting a price just to make the sale. "It's like poker. When the other guy bluffs, you can't flinch," he'd say.

Reggie looks at me. When he frowns, his eyebrows rush together like two lovesick caterpillars. "We're not going to budge on this quote."

Bob shakes his head. "Give me five percent."

Reggie waves his hand in my direction. "Claire, tell him. Never be afraid to walk away from a deal. When you give up your walk-away power, you've lost. You'll get screwed every time."

I lean back in my chair and watch a black spider try to build a web across the fluorescent light fixture. "Reggie's right. If I'd had the nerve to walk away from the Lexicon deal ten years ago, we'd still have made the sale, and we would've made about twice the profit."

Maintaining your willingness to let go of something is good advice for sales, but even better for life in general. When you're ready to do whatever it takes to achieve a goal, you'll end up losing something else. It's a pity I learned that lesson too late, but it's ingrained now, and I plan to walk away from anything or anyone who might end up costing me more than they're worth.

"Come on, guys." Bob's eyes are pleading. "It's just five percent."

I look at Reggie and know he won't go for it. "Offer him one percent." I watch my boss's reaction. When he doesn't protest, I continue. "If he doesn't take it, pack up your briefcase and thank him for his time."

Bob squirms but closes his portfolio and says he'll meet with Jennings next week.

Reggie looks at his wristwatch. "Time for lunch. Where would you two like to go?"

"I've got plans," I say. This time, Rebecca really is waiting, and the darn photo on my desk knows it. "You guys go on and do your male bonding. I'll catch you back here later."

After leaving the office and wheeling into Choppy's parking lot, I stop and take a deep breath. I've been looking forward to seeing Rebecca more than I care to admit. Although the memory of her lips on mine is almost two days old, it sends a hot streak down my spine. But it's best not to overanalyze the situation. My brain keeps telling my squeamish stomach that it's nothing serious. I can walk away at any time.

It's a little after noon and the place is crowded. Rebecca spots me and works her way toward the hostess station.

"Hey, girl," she shouts over the crowd's noise. She looks me over, eyes lingering on mine. "You look great."

But she's the one who looks good enough to eat in her red dress with the scoop neck. It takes a lot of willpower not to gaze at her breasts as she walks beside me toward a table near her office. The ice is getting thin, but I'm skating like a fool.

"Like hot stuff?" she asks as I sit down.

I give her a sly grin. "Depends. What have you got in mind?" When I try to flirt, everything sounds slutty. That damn picture on my desk must be laughing out loud.

Rebecca smacks my shoulder. "Hot wings, you nut. I found a great recipe and put them on the special menu today. I'm thinking about adding them as an appetizer permanently. They're a little messy, but they're really good. Want to try some?"

I unfold the napkin and drape it across my lap. "I'm going to trust you on this, but if I breathe fire all afternoon, I'm holding you personally responsible."

"Fair enough." She disappears into the kitchen.

When she returns, she's carrying a glass of Sprite and a plate piled high with wings. She knows what I want to drink without asking. A bad sign or a good one? It could be a restaurant pro knowing her customer's preferences, but it could also mean she's been paying more attention to me than I realized. Have I been so blind that I couldn't tell an attractive woman was trying to get close to me? Maybe I should hit Tonya up for some tips on picking up women.

Rebecca goes back to the kitchen and returns with two bread plates. She sits down across from me. "Thought I'd join you for lunch, if you don't mind."

"I guess it'll be okay." I stab a wing with my fork and drop it on my plate. Good thing I've got antacids in my purse. The sauce is thin and spicy-red, and I inhale its fiery aroma. "So what's in this secret sauce?"

"I'd tell you, but then I'd have to kill you."

We make small talk for a few minutes, discussing the weather and speculating on when spring will arrive. Her eyes dance as she tells me about the new menu she's working on and the new vendor she's hired to provide higher-quality steaks. She seems to turn nervous when she mentions that her father is coming back into town next week, and that she doesn't know how he'll react to the changes.

"Dad's always kept the building updated, but he's not big on changing the menu," she says as she puts a bone on her plate, "but how am I supposed to improve the bottom line if I don't shake things up?" She sucks a drop of red juice from her index finger.

It's really getting hot in here. I gulp down some Sprite. "Your ideas sound great. Any business has to change with the times or it'll go under."

"Enough shop talk." Rebecca pushes her plate aside and dabs the corners of her lips with the napkin. "Still up for getting together later in the week?"

"I'd like that." I can't feel my tongue, but it's in there, stuttering like a broken lawnmower.

"I've rearranged the manager schedule, and I think I can get Friday night off. If you're free, maybe I could come over and cook dinner for you."

When I think of Rebecca in our kitchen, using our stove, setting our table, a sudden pang of guilt spears me. I had this woman in our house, for God's sake. I kissed her in our foyer. What's worse is I want to do it again. In my mind, I'm taking her to our bed, having sex with her in *our* bed. How can I be doing this?

She sobers at my expression. "Friday's no good?"

A redheaded busboy dashes by. The green and black dragon tattooed on his forearm writhes and seems to spit orange flames as he clears the table beside us. He tosses dishes and silverware into the plastic bin as if they were made of lead and creates an annoying racket of clanks and jingles. His obvious indifference disappears when he notices his boss sitting across from me. He slows down and places the glasses into the bin instead of dropping them.

"Uh, no, Friday's fine. Say about seven?" I dig through my wallet and toss a twenty on the table, but Rebecca hands it back to me.

"Lab rats eat free," she says with a grin, but her brow is still wrinkled.

Rat. That's what I am, a big fat rat. I thank her and drop the bill back into my purse. Citing an important meeting, I dash for the door and tell her I'll talk with her later.

Outside, the sun blinds me, but the cold air smacks my cheeks, as though rebuking me for my weakness. A lone raven flies overhead, and its sharp caw rings in my ears. Nevermore. How appropriate. I haven't thought of Edgar Alan Poe's classic poem in years, but its truth hits home like an axe splitting my ribcage.

The breeze sends a cluster of dainty clouds skittering across the sun. My mood is much like the surrounding landscape, first draped in shadows, then in light, then in darkness again. At times I think it's better to dwell in constant gloom than to endure the maddening extremes of sun and shade. Am I prepared to be a creature of the night, like a vampire in a horror movie who exists only in darkness and lurks on the fringes of humanity? Can I give up on the promise of a new day? And how do I know about this new woman in my life? Is Rebecca Greenway my new dawn, or the final nail in my coffin?

I'm so befuddled that by the time I get into the car and start the engine, I'm crying like an idiot. In the parking space beside me, a woman gets out of a green Subaru and gives me a worried glance. I must be a sight, a grown woman sitting in a Lexus sobbing and blowing her nose into a leftover Burger King napkin.

When I regain some control, I call Reggie and tell him I'm taking the rest of the day off. I'm in no shape to discuss profit margins or proposals. The only thing I'm good for now is going home and wallowing in self-hatred till bedtime.

CHAPTER 25

Time moves slowly when you're young, but when you're functionally destitute and in search of a dream, you feel like you're crawling through the Sahara in search of water. Every inch seems like a mile, every parched breath feels like your last, but you keep moving. The goal is out there somewhere.

For two years, Lora and I scraped by. We ate condensed soup and store brand macaroni and cheese, clipped coupons, worked extra hours, and carpooled. We changed our own oil and set the apartment thermostat at sixty in winter and eighty-five in summer. Our idea of a big night out was to grab a Big Mac and go for a walk in the park, but it was worth it. Lora kept me focused. Without her, I would have folded the first month and moved back in with my parents.

In that time, we'd grown. We'd done everything we could imagine in the bedroom, learning what we liked and what we didn't. We'd discovered different ways to bring each other to shattering orgasms and found out how to put the exhausted pieces back together. But we'd experienced more than sex. Lora and I had nursed each other through colds and bouts of the flu. We'd spent hours studying, forcing trivial facts into each other's heads, and lazed away Sunday afternoons in bed watching low-budget horror movies, content to share a few quiet moments. Being together was our life. Apart, we were lost.

I'd learned little things that made me love her more. She always rolled the toilet paper under. She loved puppies and kittens and would drag a stray all over the neighborhood to find it a home before taking it to the animal shelter. To her, pizza was nature's perfect food, and after an especially good meal, she could break wind with the gusto of a drunken sailor. But her most amazing quality was her capacity for love.

If she'd stayed home with her parents, Lora would've had nice clothes, cable TV, a VCR, and a new car. It broke my heart to see her do without those things just to be with me.

Some nights I'd wake up and watch her sleep. She mostly slept on her back, one arm across her stomach, the other curled around her head.

I often wondered what she was dreaming when her eyelids fluttered and her breathing went shallow. Did she see a better life, one that wasn't so hard, one where she didn't have to break her back for pennies just to be with me? I swore to myself that I'd make that life a reality.

But our best intentions often cause us the most trouble, and in my case, my obsession with giving Lora a better lifestyle became my biggest regret. Over time, I had become determined to make money. If we just had a little more cash, things would be so much easier. Little did I understand that once you become obsessed with money, enough is never enough.

My undoing started on a Monday night. Eight hours into my last shift of the week, I was feeling the strain. My neck ached, and I'd been though a bottle of eyedrops just to keep blinking.

I'd started twelve-hour shifts six weeks before so Lora could take a lower-paying job at an adult group home. She'd decided to continue her education and get a Ph.D. in psychology, and the experience at the home was invaluable. Longer hours were my way of supporting her, but my body wasn't adjusting well to the change.

Monday nights in the archive room were the worst. I'd already worked thirty-six hours since Friday and been in class all morning. To beat it all, seven of my main storage units had stuck drawers, and I had to zap them with WD-40 every time I tried to cram another lab report into the folders.

I yanked at the top drawer of the filing cabinet near the counter. It didn't budge, which added to my frustration. I spent several minutes of pulling, tugging, and cursing before the drawer skidded out with an ear-piercing screech.

There's got to be a better way, I thought, as I peered at the workings. Another half-inch here, better balance there, and it would all be so much easier. Plus, if the thingamabob that connected the whatchamacallit to the doohickey was a little wider, the whole thing would slide like grease on a doorknob.

Not certain what I hoped to accomplish, I found an old measuring tape in the desk drawer and jotted down the cabinet's dimensions. I then attempted to sketch a design that would solve the sticking problem. At the time, building a better mousetrap—or filing cabinet in my case—didn't seem like a fork in my career road, only a way to make my shifts more manageable. However, my artistic skills left much to be desired, and the design ended up looking like the guts of a wrecked Chevy. I dropped it on the counter.

I glanced at the rows of filing cabinets behind me. They didn't look much better than my pitiful sketch, like big green dominoes that might tumble down at the slightest provocation.

I took a long breath and sat down at the desk to sort birth certificates. The archive room was always quiet, and the ticking of the old Seth Thomas clock was lulling me to sleep. I put my head on the desk and closed my eyes.

When the door flew open, I jumped and pretended to be busy, but the girl who came in and dropped an armload of manila folders on the counter didn't seem to notice I'd been napping.

"So you're the night girl. I've heard about you," she said.

I stood up and went toward her, observing this stranger. She was pretty, with her hair cut short around her ears and in the back but longer on top. The sandy mop softened her face and brought out her high cheekbones.

"What have you heard?" I asked with a yawn.

"I hear you've got this place in tip-top shape for a change." She leaned over and propped her elbows on the counter that separated us. Something in her gaze told me I should be wary. We'd never met, but she was reading me like a roadmap.

"If alphabetical order is tip-top shape, then it's far from it." I gathered the folders and placed them on the corner of the desk.

She tapped a finger on the drawing I'd attempted of the filing cabinet. "What's this?"

"I'm trying to figure out how to make these filing cabinets open easier, but I can't draw worth a crap."

She picked up a pen. "Maybe I can help. What is it you want to change?"

"The drawers roll fine when they're empty, but the folders weigh them down, especially when they get crammed full like this one." I pointed to the bottom of the open drawer. "This latch catches on the roller. If you moved it over just a little and extended this bar about a quarter of an inch, it could handle the weight, no matter how much we squeeze in there."

"I see what you're saying. I can do that." As she started to sketch, the phone rang and I picked it up

"Archive room."

"Hey, how's your night going?" Lora's voice was distant and faint.

"Same. How about you?" I replied, still watching the girl at the counter. She looked at the picture, then at the drawer, and kept drawing.

"Doreen shit her bed again. Took me an hour to clean up the mess, and she's still crying about it."

It was beyond me why Lora would rather be up to her elbows in excrement than earning good tips at the restaurant, but she loved her new job. Every night she came home with a story about how she'd worked with a resident, helping her learn to pick up after herself or hugging her after someone had made a rude comment.

I glanced back at the stranger, who was inspecting her work. "I'd better go, honey. Someone's here."

"Okay," Lora said. "I love you."

"Me, too."

When I hung up the phone, I saw the girl watching me, her elbows once more propped on the counter. "Heard that new song by Madonna?" she asked. The finished sketch lay before her.

"All fluff. In two years, no one will even remember her."

I picked up the picture and was amazed at its quality. In three minutes, she'd created a perfect rendition of what I'd wrestled with for a half hour. "This is just what I had in mind. How'd you do it?"

"Got a knack for drawing, that's all." The girl stood silent for a long moment. She looked at the clock on the wall, glanced at the growing pile of paperwork to be filed, and tugged at the gold earring in her left lobe.

"So where are you from?" she asked.

"Franklin."

"Hmm. I think I've been there once."

She'd never seen me, but in two minutes, she'd scanned me head to toe and seemed to know everything about me.

"Anything I can help you with?" I sorted through the birth certificates that I'd already alphabetized.

"You can go to dinner with me."

I stepped back. "Why would you want me to do that?"

"I like to eat with pretty women."

Good Lord, this girl is crazy, I thought. Spring City wasn't the kind of place to hit on any woman you met; it could be dangerous.

When I didn't answer, she stuck out her hand. "Sorry, I forgot to introduce myself. I usually work the mailroom, so most everyone knows me. Name's Tonya. But you can call me Fly By."

"What kind of name is that?" I shook her hand, but let go when she rubbed her thumb along mine.

"I'll explain over dinner." Her confidence bordered on obnoxious, but something in her eyes caught me off guard.

"Sorry, hotshot. Not interested." With a cocky tilt of my head, I spun around and returned to the desk, hoping she'd be on her way, but she just stood there looking at me, staring at me. She didn't say anything, but her thoughts were obvious. This pretty, brash girl was mentally undressing me right there in the paper morgue, and I got the impression she would've done the same in the real morgue with sheet-covered stiffs lying all around.

"Anything else?" I asked.

One corner of her mouth turned up, and she winked. "Not right now, but let me know when you need some more artwork. I'll be happy to help." She turned and opened the door, then stopped. "See you later, Claire."

The door slammed behind her, and I let out an exasperated breath. What the hell did she expect? Did she think I'd fall at her feet, grateful for the opportunity to go out with her? What nerve! What utter disregard for propriety.

What legs. What a smile.

A hot flush colored my cheeks. How could I stand there, weak-kneed and heart fluttering over some bimbo with the tact of a charging rhino, while my kind and compassionate Lora was across town, working her butt off with disabled adults? All those eyedrops and WD-40 fumes must've gone to my head. That's what I told myself, anyway.

For the next four hours, I filed medical transcripts and felt guilty. Lora had always been wonderful to me, treating me with the utmost respect and love. That's what life was all about, not a quick fling with a hot babe.

When my shift was over, I went home and found Lora sitting up in bed reading her abnormal psychology textbook. Only the well-worn sheet covered her body, the skin I knew so well, the flesh I adored.

She looked up and smiled. "Hey, honey. How was work?"

"Usual." I stripped off my clothes and crawled into bed.

She put her book aside and draped the red scarf across the bedside lamp. "I've missed you," she whispered as she snuggled up and kissed me.

If I'd ever had the slightest doubt about my feelings for Lora, it disappeared at soon as she touched me. And even though we both had early classes, we made love all night.

CHAPTER 26

After changing clothes, I grab a bag of popcorn from the pantry, a Sprite from the refrigerator, and fall onto the den sofa. Jitterbug follows, all sniffs and slurps. I punch the remote and flip a few channels before half-watching a cable movie about a crazy investment banker who gets his jollies by disemboweling buxom blondes.

"Don't go in the basement, you idiot," I say.

But I can't stop her. The bimbo with the big teeth and bigger boobs goes right on down the dusty steps to meet her untimely end. The expendable cast member squeals, a light bulb breaks, and by the time the scene is over, she's on her way to Denver inside a Samsonite suitcase.

I toss a piece of popcorn to Jitterbug and ask her why I keep watching these stupid horror flicks. She shoots me a weepy gaze and gobbles up the kernel.

It used to work like a charm. Anytime I'd had a bad day or was feeling depressed, I'd throw on a pair of ratty pajamas and settle on the sofa with Lora for a thriller. After a couple of hours with Vincent Price, the slump would be over. Not anymore, though. It hasn't worked in three years, and the reason is plain. Vincent wasn't the medicine—she was. The cure has become the affliction.

Rebecca called an hour ago. She'd checked the office, and panicked when Mary told her I'd gone home sick. "It's not from the wings, is it?" she asked.

I blamed a migraine and assured her it would be over in a few hours. She made me promise to call if I needed anything. The poor girl has no idea how deep my needs are, but then, neither do I.

When the doorbell rings, I put my popcorn bag out of the dog's reach and shuffle to answer it. It's Elizabeth. She's smiling when I let her in, but after looking at me, she frowns. "What's up with you? You look like hell warmed over."

"Bad day."

We go back to the living room, where all the blinds are closed and the lights are off. The only illumination is coming from the flickering

TV screen. Another blonde is about to get whacked. I hit the mute button on the remote and sit back down on the sofa.

"No wonder you feel bad. It's dark as a dungeon in here." Elizabeth opens the blinds.

"Cut it out, will you?" I squint in the brightness and order Jitterbug off the sofa. I sit up and peek out the window. The backyard is brown and lifeless this time of year, and I wonder if the bulbs and seedpods will ever rouse and fight their way through the frigid sod.

Elizabeth plops down on the love seat. My eyes are starting to adjust to the light, and I see her glare at me. "I've about had it with you, Claire. I thought you were getting your shit together, but you're as bad now as you've ever been." Fire flashes behind my friend's eyes. Time for another sermon. "I thought if you went out with Rebecca, you might feel better."

"She's making it worse." I hadn't thought of it before, but it might be true. As long as there's no one in my life, I'm not giving up.

Elizabeth grunts and rolls her eyes. "Rebecca seems great. You should give it a chance. You don't have to fall in love, and it won't hurt you to have some fun."

I see the compassion on Elizabeth's face. For an instant, I want to kiss her again, to feel her near me, but I force the desire away. I can't have her. She has a husband and a family I adore. I cinch my pajama top to my chest. "The women I want, I can't have. The women I can have, I don't want."

She laughs out loud. "Ain't that the truth? Fly By is so in love with you she can't see straight. All you'd have to do is give her a sign, and she'd be right here, but you won't do it. Last week, you wanted Rebecca. But now that you might have a chance with her, you're chickening out."

"I am not." I look away, knowing she's right. "And as for Fly By, we both know why that would never work out."

"Listen, I don't care if you date Rebecca, or Fly, or anyone else. Don't date anyone if you don't want to, but whatever you do, get yourself out of this funk. It's been going on way too long." Elizabeth runs her hand through her hair, and it falls back into place perfectly. "Throw on some clothes and come over. I'm making pork chops for dinner."

"Thanks, but I'm not up for it right now." I stretch out full-length on the sofa and fold my arms across my chest.

"Well, get up for it. You look like a corpse lying there like that." She gets up from the love seat, grabs my arm, and drags me down the hall to the bedroom. She opens the closet door and prods my ribs till I go in. "Find something comfortable. The kids might want to take you on in a wrestling match."

Knowing I don't have a choice, I drag my hand along the hangers and snag a flannel shirt and a pair of jeans that have seen better days.

"If you're not there in ten minutes, I'm coming back." Elizabeth scowls at me as she leaves. A few seconds later, I hear the front door open, then close behind her.

When the doorbell rings, I hop down the hall, tugging on a pair of rag socks as I go. "You said ten minutes," I yell. I open the door, and Rebecca is standing there, holding a Styrofoam cup.

"Chicken soup. Good for what ails you."

She's still wearing that red dress from lunch, and I can't help looking her up and down, catching a glimpse of her thigh when a gust of wind flips at her skirt. Nice view.

"An angel of mercy." I motion her in, and she hands me the cup.

Rebecca lingers in the hall, teasing Jitterbug with baby talk. "Hello there. Aren't you a pretty girl?" Jitterbug does a quick drop and roll and exposes her pink belly. I quickly set the cup of soup in the kitchen and return, while Rebecca kneels and scratches the dog's stomach, sending Jitterbug into a doggie trance.

"That's Jitterbug, resident pest."

"She's adorable."

From this angle, I get a nice glimpse of Rebecca's cleavage. A brief smile crosses my lips.

I'm not sure what to do, but I give in to the lingering ache in my chest and step toward her. "Can I have a hug?"

Rebecca stands up and steps out of her heels, and we're face-to-face. There's a hint of worry in her eyes. "Come here, you. I could use a hug myself." She opens her arms, and we wrap around each other.

I snuggle into her shoulder. "You've had a bad day, too?"

"The worst. I've got to get some reliable help. I can't keep working like this."

I don't want to let go, but I pull back and lead her to the couch. "Come in. Sit for a minute."

"I don't have time. I have to go home and change clothes before the dinner crowd hits. Looks like I'll either be bartending or cooking tonight." She follows anyway and collapses beside me on the sofa. I cradle her in the crook of my arm. It feels pretty good to be on this side of the hug for a change.

Rebecca drapes her arm across my waist. "Maybe we could stop time and sit here like this for a day or two."

"Suits me." I squeeze her shoulder and touch my lips to her forehead. Her skin seems damp and feverish. "Do you feel okay?" I press the back of my hand against her cheek. It's a little too warm.

"I'm fine, just a little case of the sniffles. Nothing contagious."

I pull back and take a good look at her. Her skin is pale, her eyes hollow. "The restaurant can do without you for a while. Why don't you lie down for a few minutes?"

"Don't be silly, I'm not sick." She dismisses my concern with a casual wave and glances toward the TV. "What are you watching?"

I'm not convinced but decide to drop it. "Some made-for-TV horror movie. I'm kind of a thriller buff."

"A buff, huh? What's your all-time favorite?"

"*Night of the Living Dead.* Best horror movie ever made. Bet I've seen it at least fifteen times."

"I've heard of it." Rebecca picks a stray piece of lint off my flannel shirt and balls it up between her fingers. "Maybe we can watch it together sometime."

"Tell you what. You need to rest on Friday, so don't worry about cooking. We'll order a pizza and watch the movie. I've got it on video."

"That sounds like a perfect evening after the week I'm having." She snuggles closer and rests her head on my shoulder.

I sniff a hint of aloe in her hair and basil on her dress, and I'm overwhelmed by the urge to kiss her. As if on cue, she raises her head and touches her lips to mine. She's so gentle. I wish she didn't have to go back to work. Maybe we really could stop time and stay like this forever.

Forever? Stop it, you idiot! There's no such thing. But I keep kissing her. We won't have forever, but we've got this minute and I'm not going to let it slip by.

After a moment, she pulls away and glances at her gold wristwatch. "I hate to rush off, but duty calls."

I touch her chin and make her look at me. "Take it from someone who knows, your first duty is to yourself and the people you care about. All the money in the world won't keep you warm at night."

"Maybe not, but I've never slept in a cardboard box. I don't think I'd like it." She stands and pulls me up with her. "Call me later?"

"Count on it."

We hold hands as I walk her to the door, and she kisses my cheek before she leaves.

My heart is in chaos, full of passion, remorse, and lust, all topped off by loneliness. It's an emotional abstract of divergent shades, culminating in absolute blackness at my core. Am I strong enough to strip away the dark, separate the light, and allow beauty into my soul again?

I wonder.

CHAPTER 27

I was sitting in an amazingly uncomfortable straight-backed chair with no armrests, looking across a veneered desk at an old man who bore a remarkable resemblance to Uncle Joe on *Petticoat Junction*—bald and puffy cheeked with a cheesy smile. He wore an open-collared plaid shirt and clip-on suspenders, but I was in no shape to be handing out fashion tips. I had on a cheap navy blue suit and an imitation silk blouse, and I carried a fake leather briefcase. What a sight the two of us must have been, acting like we were doing real business.

Mr. Johnson reared back and tapped his stubby fingers on the desk. "Drawings are good. Do them yourself?"

"No, sir. A friend helps me with the artwork, but the designs are all mine." I tried to maintain eye contact, but his gaze darted to the coffee-pot in the corner, to me, to the copier by the door, and back to me. The stuffed moose head on the wall seemed more interested in my ideas.

He picked up the first sketch and peeked at the initials at the bottom of the drawing. "F.B.K?"

"Yes, sir. It's a nickname. Her real name is Tonya Knight."

"She's talented."

"Yes, sir, she is."

It must have been ninety degrees in his office. I mopped sweat from the back of my neck, leaned toward the desk, and pointed to the third drawing. "If you look here, Mr. Johnson, you'll see how this—"

"Yes, yes, I noticed that." He brushed my hand aside and stared at the coffeepot again.

"So you agree that my ideas are good?"

Mr. Johnson's stare didn't shift as he rubbed his chin with the back of his hand. "Sure you don't want a cup of coffee?"

"Yes, sir. I'm sure."

"Tea?"

"No, sir, nothing, thank you." I leaned forward again and caught a whiff of bourbon and almond-scented pipe smoke from his side of the desk. "Getting back to this particular unit, I believe that by extending the roller I can—"

"Tonya Knight, huh?"

"Yes, sir, that's her name."

"Talented girl." He stacked the drawings on the desk. "Where're the prototypes?"

I took the drawings and cleared my throat. Here came the killer. I'd said the words eighteen times over the past month, and eighteen times they'd gotten me kicked out of someone's office. However, most had been nice offices with Rembrandt reproductions and double-loop carpeting. Old Nate here had a 1981 calendar with a picture of a red convertible Corvette on the wall and a multicolored Dollar Store throw rug on the floor.

I tugged at the high collar of my blouse. "I don't have any prototypes at this time."

He hawked out a smoker's cough without covering his mouth. "Well, little lady, you don't know for sure if these units even work, now do you?"

Disgusting old geezer had me on the defensive, and that "little lady" remark had raised my blood pressure, but I was desperate. Johnson's name was the next to last on my list.

I forced myself to envision the nice little house I was going to buy Lora when I got this thing going. One story. Flat yard. Black shutters. That's right, see it? But it won't happen if I don't make some sacrifices along the way.

I leaned closer to Mr. Johnson. "I don't have a prototype at this time, but with the right backing—"

"Backing? You want me to put cash into something that might not even work? What're you selling here, kid, fairy dust? You got to have some kind of prototype." He looked at me with a mocking glare.

"It will work, sir. I know it."

He clenched a Sherlock Holmes pipe in his teeth and spoke around it as he tamped tobacco into the bowl. "Kid, you got nothing." He blatantly stared at my chest. "You're a pretty enough girl. Why don't you go on down to the employment office and get yourself a nice secretary job? Let your husband worry about making money."

"Mr. Johnson, I have a Bachelor of Science degree which I got in three years while working full time at Mercy Hospital," I said, jaw clenched. I stood and gathered my things and what was left of my dignity. "I will make this work. I'm only sorry that you've passed up this opportunity."

Nate Johnson was laughing as I closed the door behind me.

By the time I reached my car, I'd worked up a foul mood. Who did that old fart think he was, telling me I had nothing? My ideas were good; I knew they were. I'd spent the last year perfecting every design. Tonya had been back to the drawing board so many times she'd threatened an artist's strike. But I couldn't squelch the prickle of doubt that crawled up my spine. I'd made a list of twenty potential local investors, started with the most promising, and worked my way down. So far, I'd been politely dismissed, laughed at, and sent packing nineteen times. Number twenty was waiting downtown.

If just one person would believe in me... why was it so hard? Why was I reduced to groveling to the likes of Nate Johnson to get somewhere?

I unlocked the car door, took off my jacket, and tossed it into the passenger seat. It was nearly July, and a wave of heat swam from the car, bathing me in sticky sweat. The old Datsun's air conditioner had blown the summer before, so I couldn't expect to cool off before my last appointment. Oh well, it probably wouldn't matter anyway. If Nate was any indication of what this next one would be like, I might as well skip it.

I climbed into the car, rolled down the window, and cranked the engine. God, it was hot. I looked at myself in the rearview mirror. Fine droplets of perspiration dotted my brow, and I dabbed my face with a napkin from the glove compartment, but there wasn't much hope for my hair. It was plastered to my head like a bathing cap.

Nothing was working out the way I'd planned. The business office at the hospital was already overstaffed, so my chances of moving out of the archive room were slim. Plus, Spring City was the kind of place where people held on to their jobs. Most of the local businesses had an experienced staff, and I was just a snot-nosed kid with nothing but a piece of parchment. In truth, I didn't know beans from apple butter and was no competition for applicants with even a year's experience in any field.

The job placement counselor at State had advised me to relocate and get some marketable experience under my belt. That wasn't an option, though. Lora had years of study ahead of her, and she'd established herself as a star pupil at State. Asking her to break in a new university was out of the question, so I'd have to make my way in Spring City.

It wasn't fair. I had great ideas and was willing to work hard, but I was busting my hump for peanuts. I seemed doomed to failure. Maybe Lora had made a mistake when she'd chosen me over Jock Richardson.

I was fuming. Desperation seeped from my pores. I slammed the gearshift into reverse, backed out of the parking space, and headed toward Highway 17. For ten minutes, I cruised along the four-lane road doing sixty, letting the rushing wind blow-dry my hair. I turned left onto Main Street, cruised past Midtown Office Supply, and parked between a Mercedes and a Honda Civic.

This was my last chance. If I didn't land this son of a bitch, I was looking at failure. The rest of my days would be spent filing death certificates and bandaging paper cuts. I got out of the car, put on my jacket, and grabbed the sketches from the back seat. I marched down the sidewalk, eyes narrow and jaw set. My high heels pinched my aching toes. The pain urged me on.

The windowed storefront of Midtown Office Supply displayed a variety of products: fountain pens, ledger books, adding machines. A handwritten sign on the door advertised three-day delivery on rubber stamps. As I drew near, a bright ray of sunshine reflected off the glass, blinding me with purple and orange spots.

I barged through the door, and a tiny brass bell jingled above my head. A woman in a hot-pink pantsuit stepped around the counter. She had a serious case of helmet-hair and wore enough makeup to last me for three months. She smiled—lipstick on her teeth. Perfect.

"Can I help you?" She clasped her hands in front of her as if in prayer.

"I'm Claire Blevins. I have an appointment with Mr. Ornduff."

"I'll tell him you're here." She looked me up and down before disappearing through an open doorway to her right.

The woman soon returned, followed by a tall, stocky man with too much black hair, but at least he was clean—small favors. The woman retreated behind the counter while he greeted me, hand outstretched.

I pounced before he could speak. "Mr. Ornduff, I'm Claire Blevins, and I've got a proposal that will put you on the map."

He scrutinized me for a moment, then smiled. Turning to the woman, he said, "Hold my calls, will you, Mary?" He looked back at me. "Come on in, Claire. And call me Reggie."

CHAPTER 28

It's Friday night, and despite my reservations about dating Rebecca, I'm excited about seeing her. I've visited her at Choppy's every day for lunch, but she's cautious of what she says in the restaurant. We've talked on the phone till my ears went numb, but hearing her voice isn't like seeing her, watching her eyes flicker and her lips curve into that whimsical grin.

The past week has been an emotional roller coaster. One minute I'm thinking about this fascinating woman I'm coming to know and wondering what the future might hold. The next, I feel the sting of broken promises and swear to put an end to this charade before someone gets hurt.

It would be a lie to say I don't like her, and liking her might be a lot healthier than loving her. With like, you don't sit up nights wondering where she is or what she's doing. You don't worry that a charming stranger will swoop in and take her away. And you sure don't have to put out your heart like a doormat for her to wipe her muddy shoes on.

The doorbell rings and I order Jitterbug to stay in the den, which is as effective as telling the wind not to blow. She hops along beside me to the foyer, ears flapping, tail wagging and nails clicking on the parquet floor.

When I open the door, Rebecca greets the dog first, bending down to scratch her behind the ears. "Hey, little girl," she says. But when I close the door, she turns to me. "Hey, big girl," she whispers, her eyes luring me closer.

When she puts her arms around me and grazes her lips against mine, a surprising lust surges within me. I draw her to me, parting her lips with my tongue, savoring the sugary mint of her mouth, inhaling her breath. This is not a gentle, romantic kiss. It's lusty and sloppy, growing from a need so primitive it defies explanation. Instinct takes over, and my hand inches toward her breast. God, I need to touch her. But somewhere between my gut and my brain, a seed of reason takes over and I return my hand to the small of her back.

I step back a little. "Hey to you," I finally manage to say, wishing that kernel of good sense would mind its own business so I could drag her to the bedroom.

"That's the kind of greeting I could get used to." Rebecca's smile makes me wonder if she wants to skip the formalities of dating and head down the hall, but she says nothing else, and reaches into the pocket of her blue ski jacket. She pulls out a bag of dog treats. "Can she have these?" she asks, keeping the pouch out of Jitterbug's sight.

I nod and take her hand as we go to the kitchen. "What about me? Don't I get a treat?"

"Gee, I don't know if you deserve one." She opens the treat bag and drops a soft dog biscuit onto the floor. With one gulp, Jitterbug scoops it up, swallows it whole, and gazes up at us with doleful brown eyes.

I unzip Rebecca's jacket and slide my arms between its fleece lining and the soft cotton of her sweatshirt. "What do I have to do to deserve a treat?" My lips find the slope of her neck, and I feel my own breath sweeping down between us. A pleasant warmth swells in my groin.

"A little more of this would be nice." She presses closer, hips against mine, breasts against mine.

"Talk me into it."

She pulls back and brushes her hand against my cheek. "I'm starting to like you. Is that okay?"

The warmth in my groin turns to ice, and a knot ties up my guts. "Just don't love me. Remember, it's not our third date yet."

She chuckles as she takes her jacket off and hangs it on the back of the kitchen chair. "I won't love you, if you don't love me. Fair enough?"

"Good deal." I hope she's serious, but I'm afraid she's not. I head for the den, motioning for her to follow. "So you're ready to see this film, huh?"

Rebecca falls in step behind me. "I warn you, this stuff scares the hell out of me."

"Don't worry, I'll protect you."

We sit on the sofa, and I punch a button on the remote. Ten minutes into the movie, the doorbell rings. Assuming it's the pizza I ordered, I stop the tape and dig a bill out of my purse. But when I get to the door, it's Tonya standing on the front steps holding a pizza box. I glance toward the street, but the delivery boy is nowhere in sight.

"Already paid him," she explains as she brushes past me and heads to the kitchen. She shoots a glance toward Rebecca on the way by.

When I follow Tonya into the kitchen, she says, "Why didn't you tell me she was so pretty? When you're through with her, give her my number."

"Go for it," I say, pretending to snarl.

"Maybe I will." Tonya drops the pizza on the stovetop and marches toward the den.

I follow her in time to catch her extending her hand to Rebecca. "Tonya Knight," she says and her gaze lingers too long on my date's bosom.

Rebecca stands and shakes Tonya's hand. "I'm Rebecca Greenway. Nice to meet you."

Tonya sits on the loveseat, blocking my direct access to the sofa. "So, Rebecca, where're you from?"

Rebecca remains standing and shoots me a puzzled look. "I'm from here originally, but I've lived in Hickory and in Charlotte since I was about twelve."

"What brings you back to town?" Tonya leans back and crosses her legs.

"My dad owns Choppy's Restaurant, and I came back to run the place."

Tonya wets her lips, shoots her eyes toward me, and looks back at Rebecca. "So, do you go out with *all* of your customers?"

Rebecca is clearly offended, but recovers quickly. She circles the coffee table and kisses my cheek. "Only the ones I find interesting." She winks at Tonya and saunters to the kitchen.

Tonya scans Rebecca as she rounds the corner. "I like her," she mouths.

I stroll toward the kitchen. "Fly, you want a slice of pizza?" I call over my shoulder, tossing a too-casual glance in Tonya's direction.

"Thanks, but I've got plans."

In the kitchen, Rebecca says, "Who the hell is that? She looked at me like she wanted to rip my clothes off."

"Don't mind her, it's her way of making sure you're on the level. You know, not out to score and run."

Rebecca shakes her head as she flips back the lid on the pizza box. I curl my free arm around her waist and give her a peck on the cheek. "But watch out. She's not the only one thinking about ripping your clothes off."

"Jitterbug, too? I knew there was something about that dog I liked." She snickers as she drops a steaming slice of pizza on each of our paper plates.

"Yeah, Jit made me promise not to tell, but I thought I'd better warn you." I bump my shoulder against hers. "We're going to arm wrestle for you later. Winner take all."

We laugh as we take our dinner to the den and plop back down on the sofa. Tonya is still sitting on the love seat, legs crossed. A threatening smile pushes up the corners of her lips. Her feelers are out. She's like a hundred tiny ants, antennae probing for anything out of the ordinary, for anything signaling Rebecca is not what she seems.

I take a bite and turn to Tonya, speaking with my mouth full and trying not to spit tomato sauce on the carpet. "We're watching *Night of the Living Dead*. Want to stick around?"

She gags and jumps up. "Hell, no. I've seen that stupid movie a hundred times. Don't you ever get tired of it?"

"How can you get tired of the classics?"

Tonya moves toward the door, giving us plenty of opportunity to see her butt. It's a nice view, but I'm more interested in the woman beside me. Rebecca looks away and tears a piece of crust from her pizza.

Tonya snorts as she heads for the foyer. "*Casablanca*, that's a classic. *The African Queen*, that's a classic. Horror movies, yuk."

"She's got a Bogart fetish," I tell Rebecca. "If an old movie doesn't star Bogey or Hepburn, she thinks it's trash."

Rebecca laughs. "I'd be inclined to add Spencer Tracy to that list, and maybe Jimmy Stewart." She looks at Tonya, her subtle peace offering dangling between them.

Tonya stops mid-step and turns around. Her face relaxes, and she flashes a rare genuine smile. "Finally, someone around here has some taste."

"Don't rush off," Rebecca calls after Tonya, who has already spun around and reached the foyer.

"Better be going. Ladies are waiting."

I follow my friend to the door and catch her elbow as she steps onto the front porch. "You could be a little more polite, you know."

"Me? Not polite?" Tonya kisses my cheek. "I'm just a mild-mannered little girl looking out for her friend."

"There's something fundamentally wrong with that statement." I slap her shoulder as she turns away. "But thanks anyway."

Tonya stops and looks back. "I think she's okay," she says, but Tonya doesn't trust Rebecca. I can tell by her final glance into the house, one last bullshit feeler before leaving.

I go back to the den where Rebecca is playing hide-and-seek with Jitterbug. The dog is in heaven, hiding behind the loveseat and peeking out. Rebecca pretends not to see her, then reaches out and pats her head. I sit back down, and Rebecca says, "I don't think your friend likes me."

"Don't pay any attention to Fly. She's a little overprotective."

"Sure it's not jealousy?" she asks, brow cocked.

"She might be a little jealous, but she and I could never be together. It won't happen."

"Why? She's very pretty."

"She's too butch for me."

"Shut up! That woman's not butch at all."

"Not on the outside, but inside she's stone butch all the way."

"A body like that, and she won't let anyone touch her? Oh well, to each her own." Rebecca shakes her head.

I'd hate to think that if Rebecca and I ever do go to bed together, we won't be compatible, so I take the opportunity to do a little fishing. "And you?"

"And me what?"

My face reddens but I try to sound casual. "Well, I guess I'm wondering—"

"What I like in bed?"

Her straightforwardness startles me, and I suck in a ragged breath. "I didn't mean to sound crude, but I guess that's what I mean."

"Don't be embarrassed. I've wondered about you, too. So, if that time ever comes for us, you should know that I like to take advantage of all my options."

When my voice decides to function again, I mutter, "Me, too."

That's enough for now. Tonight, it's dinner and a horror flick, nothing more. We finish our pizza, put away the leftovers, and settle down to watch the rest of the movie. But soon, Rebecca's long week catches up with her, and she starts to yawn. I drop a throw pillow across my lap, and with little protest, she kicks off her sneakers and stretches out. She's asleep before the movie is half over, but that's okay. I turn off the TV and listen to her breathe.

* * *

My lover often visits me in my dreams, but tonight is different, as if she knows there's someone in the house, as if she's aware that the woman curled up on the sofa isn't Tonya or Elizabeth. As I lie on the love seat half asleep, feet dangling over the arm and neck bent at an awkward position, Lora smiles that lopsided grin and opens her arms. She looks younger than the last time I saw her, almost like the cheerleader who made love to me in her parents' house. I long to feel her again. I want her inside me, around me. I want to touch her as I once did.

"I'm coming home," she whispers. "I'll never leave you again."

As I go to her, peace flows through me. It's finally over. But as I reach out, she drifts away, hovering beyond my grasp. I try again, but it's no use. She's gone.

I sit up and call her name, but the sound comes out like air trapped in a drain, burbling toward the surface, making no sense. At first, I think the arms around me are hers, but they're Rebecca's.

"You scared the shit out of me. Are you okay?" Her kindness should be soothing, but I don't want to be comforted. I want to go back to the dream.

I plant my feet on the floor and fall back against the cushions. "Sorry to wake you."

"It's okay." She rubs her eyes and squints toward the DVD clock. "How long have I been asleep?"

"A long time." I force the dream fog away and take her hand. "You looked so comfortable, I didn't have the heart to wake you."

She yawns and squeezes my hand. "Bad dream?"

"Yeah."

"Want to talk about it?"

"No."

Rebecca holds her breath, then lets it out. "Are you still in love with her?"

"Am I that transparent?"

Rebecca's gaze softens. She's reading me again. "Where is she now?"

"I don't know."

It's a lie. I know exactly where she is. I've driven by a hundred times, and each time, I gaze at the hill, wondering if she sees me pass, supposing that she is probably happier now. Once I even pulled over, but being so close and so distant at the same time made me feel worse.

Rebecca rests her head on my shoulder. "I'm sorry she hurt you."

"Anyone with the sense of a grapefruit would've moved on by now."

"But that tells me something about you, Claire. It tells me you don't give your heart away easily, and you don't give up at the first sign of trouble. But from what Elizabeth told me, it's been a long time. If there's no chance to reconcile, you really do need to get on with your life."

"What did Elizabeth tell you?"

"Don't worry, she didn't fill me up with a bunch of gossip. She just said that you've been single for about three years, and she wishes you'd start living again."

I kiss Rebecca's forehead. "I'm trying. Thank you for being so understanding."

"I like you, but I won't push for something you're not ready for."

"How did you get to be so kind?"

"Patient," she says, correcting me. "I think you're worth knowing, and you can't know someone in just a few days."

"I've been coming in the restaurant for months, so we're not exactly strangers." I lean back and stroke her cheek. Her skin is like fine silk beneath my fingers, her eyes tranquil as she watches me, but her poise is astounding. What she sees in a nut like me, I'll never understand.

"We're not exactly lovers either." Rebecca yawns again, turning her head away and covering her mouth.

"Do you want to be lovers?" I ask.

She sits quietly for a moment, her eyes darting from the rumpled blanket on the sofa to the stack of logs by the fireplace, then she looks at me. "I'd like to make love with you, but not till you're ready."

The thought of being intimate with Rebecca makes my heart skip a beat. She's so pretty, so kind. I imagine my hands on her, giving her pleasure. I feel my lips graze her skin, and her body respond to my touch. I picture the desire in her eyes as she enters me, indulging my deepest needs.

"Maybe soon," I whisper.

"Take your time. We don't need to rush." She picks up her sneakers and slides one on. "I'd better be going, I've got a busy day tomorrow."

I watch her put on her other shoe and retrieve her jacket from the kitchen. As we head for the door, she takes my hand and wishes me a good night. I kiss her lips before she leaves.

CHAPTER 29

"Oh, no! It's broken." Lora sat on our brand new king-sized bed, a crumpled piece of newspaper on her lap.

I wound my way through a maze of moving boxes and eased down beside her. "Just the glass?"

"Maybe." Picking up the brass picture frame by its corner, she let the remaining glass fall onto the paper. She inspected the frame's contents and then smiled at me. "The clover is okay."

"If we move again, we'll make sure to hand-carry it." I squeezed her shoulder as she placed the frame on the nightstand. I could almost see the visions dancing behind her eyes as she relived the day we had moved into that ratty apartment.

The clover had been there. It was more than a mutated weed or a simple good-luck charm. It was an odd but beautiful thing—an emblem of our unusual but extraordinary love. Ever since Lora had found it that day outside our first apartment, we'd sworn by its magical powers. From our bedside, it had seen us make love, witnessed hours of study, and watched over us as we slept. We wouldn't dare spend the first night in our new home without it.

Lora stood and dumped the newspaper into the trash. "I'll get a new frame tomorrow."

I watched as she flittered around the room, hanging up clothes, hand dusting the dresser and kicking cardboard boxes out of her way. The house was only a small split-foyer in a middle class neighborhood, but Lora was ecstatic.

All the late nights and road trips had finally paid off. I had lots of potential—my boss had said so, said that after a few years on the road, I could settle into an office job. Then I would be the boss and let underlings spend their weekdays getting doors slammed in their faces. They, not I, would spend night after night on lumpy hotel mattresses watching backwoods local television stations till their eyes blinked shut from utter exhaustion.

I caught Lora's hand as she swept past. "Hey, slow down a minute."

She stopped and sat down on my lap. "Whatcha got in mind, sailor?"

"I've been gone for four nights. Guess I need a little pick-me-up." I cupped her breast in my hand and traced my lips along her throat.

She sighed and pressed her chest against my face. "Jesus, how do you do that?"

"Do what?"

"Turn me on like a water faucet."

Her words were enough to send a throbbing ache to my groin, and when her hands slipped underneath my sweatshirt and stroked my damp skin, there was no stopping.

We'd made the bed, but Lora threw back the cover and with a mischievous push, shoved me down. With her straddling my legs, I tugged off my shirt and pulled her already naked body down on me. God, I loved her.

After an hour of playing follow-the-leader and teasing one another to the point of exhaustion, we rolled apart. The fresh sheets and blankets lay in a clump at the foot of the bed. Spent but fulfilled, we lay on our backs and held hands. We watched the moon rise through the bedroom window and listened to tree frogs sing in the backyard.

Lora rolled onto her side to face me. Throwing one leg across me, she said, "You know, baby, back in high school I used to wonder where I'd be by this time in my life."

"Bet this ain't what you expected." I pulled her hand to my lips and kissed her fingers. My scent lingered on her skin.

"That's for sure." She traced her index finger along my stomach, drawing circles and upside-down triangles. I could generally tell what Lora was thinking, but right now the notions in her head were so distant and vague, I couldn't get a handle on them.

I had to ask. "Are you sorry we ever started this?"

"No, are you crazy? I'm thinking how things can turn out so different than you thought they would. Back in high school, I thought I'd marry Jock and follow him around the country. You know, be a baseball widow. I thought I'd spend nights rubbing his arm down with alcohol or something."

"Is that what you wanted?"

"Stop it. You're being silly." She brushed her moist hair from her eyes. "I'm saying that sometimes life takes a detour, some little thing happens, and you end up somewhere totally different from where you thought you'd be."

"What do you mean?"

"Remember that day in my bedroom at home? The day you told me what you and Matthew had done out by the mill, and I asked you to demonstrate?"

I chuckled. "How could I forget?" The day was as fresh in my memory as what I'd had for lunch a few hours earlier. I could still see her sitting there, afraid but determined. I could smell the scarf getting hot on the lamp and her buttery popcorn breath. With the memories, though we'd just had sex, moistness crept between my legs.

The air conditioning kicked in, showering our damp bodies with a cool breeze, and I shivered.

Lora rolled onto her back and yanked a blanket across us. "I was so confused back then. I knew I wanted you, but I almost lost my nerve and didn't suggest it. Where do you think we'd be now if I hadn't? I might be wasting away, always waiting for Jock to come home, and who knows? You might've ended up with Matthew."

"And right now I'd be married to the most popular history teacher at Franklin High." I shook my head. "Pity Matthew's knees didn't hold out. He had real talent."

She gave me a quizzical look. "You think he's not successful because he never made it to the pros, because he doesn't earn a fortune?"

"Of course not, honey. It's a noble profession, but he's never going to get rich teaching high school. Don't you think he'd rather be playing ball and making serious money?"

"Guess we'll never know. Things didn't happen the way we expected for any of us." Lora looked into my eyes. "That day was a turning point for us. I tried to deny it, but that was the day I realized how much you really meant to me. I knew we'd spend the rest of our lives together, and that felt so much better than imagining a life with anyone else."

I nuzzled into the crook of her arm. "I know it's been hard for us financially and everything, but I hope it's been worth it."

"I wouldn't trade our worst day for anything in the world. I love you more now than ever." She turned her body in to me and caressed my skin with hers.

We lay in silence for hours. Arms wound around each other, we watched the moonlight work its way down the far wall and across the floor.

But in the peaceful darkness, restless thoughts careened through my mind. As I considered what might have been, what could have happened, tears stung in my eyes. What if we'd never been assigned to the same composition class? What if I'd stayed in the locker room with Jill after that first, disastrous basketball game instead of tagging along with Lora to Pizza Oven? What if I'd been more hesitant in Lora's bedroom that afternoon? Was there a master plan, or did our present situation result from dozens of unrelated coincidences?

More important, was our future set or were we at the mercy of random events and twists of fate?

* * *

Moving into our first house was the realization of a dream for Lora and me. Finally, we were acting a little more like grown-ups. But grown-ups have responsibilities, and I was keenly aware of mine.

Leaving Lora every week was bad enough, but hitting the road a day early had put a serious dent in our moving schedule, and our little bedroom jaunt on Friday night had put us even farther behind. By Sunday evening, we were supposed to have done the major unpacking and hung the replacement drywall in the downstairs den. By the time I returned home Thursday night we should have been ready to start painting, but we'd barely started unpacking. The lumber company had delivered the drywall on Friday, and it leaned, untouched, against the cinder block wall in the garage. To beat it all, I had an early appointment scheduled for Monday morning in Alabama, and that meant leaving home on Sunday.

Lora dropped a laundry basket on the bed and emptied its contents across the spread. "Don't forget to take an extra pair of panties." She was miffed and made no bones about it.

"Honey, I've told you a hundred times. I'm sorry, but this guy might be a big fish, and the mortgage won't pay itself, you know."

"Why do you worry about money so much? I'll have my PhD in three weeks, and Debbie is going to give me her overflow at the clinic. Money won't be a problem."

"Money will always be a problem."

Lora folded a pillowcase and threw it too hard into the basket. "Why don't you say what you mean, Claire? Money will be a problem as long as Jock Richardson has more of it than you do."

I shook my head and wandered toward the closet. "That's absurd."

"Is it? You've been jealous of him for years, and for the life of me, I don't understand it."

I returned to the bed with an armload of shoes and found Lora in confrontation mode, one hand on her hip, squinting toward me with blazing eyes.

"I'm not jealous of Jock." I slid the pumps into the garment bag and turned away.

"Don't you see what you're doing? You're working yourself to death in the name of money. You spend most of the week on the road, and when you come home, you're either at the office or passed out on the couch." Her face relaxed, but the fire still burned in her eyes. "All you have to do is hire another sales rep and let someone else do the leg work."

"Honey, I see what you're saying, but you don't understand." I met her stare for an instant before returning to the closet. When she got like that, an instant of her eyes was all I could take. "I designed this equipment, and no one will ever work it the way I do."

With an exasperated sigh, Lora plopped down on the bed. "You mean we're going to have to live like this till you retire?"

I hung three suits in my garment bag and watched her fold a washcloth. She looked tired. Between the move, my absence, and the stress of finishing her degree, she had a lot on her shoulders, but things would be better soon. We'd get settled in, and she'd hang her framed diploma over the mantle. My work schedule, however, was another matter.

I sat on the bed beside her and took her hand. "Give me a little longer. While I'm building the market, I can make enough money to do some heavy investing. Then I can hire a whole team of sales reps and kick back in the office. Be home by dinner every stinking day. You'll get so sick of me, you'll beg me to go back out on the road."

Lora laughed and touched my cheek, but a peculiar sorrow glazed her eyes. "My baby always thinks about our future."

I took the remark as a compliment, but she went on. "Planning for later is okay, but what about now? You're so big on investing, don't you think we should invest some time in ourselves, in our relationship, while we're young enough to enjoy it?"

"Learn that in one of your psychobabble textbooks?" Half of me agreed with her, but the other half was planning my sales pitch for Monday morning.

"I miss you, that's all. I know you're trying to do what's right for us, and I'm proud of what you've accomplished."

I looked into her eyes, commanding her attention. "Honey, one of these days, I'm going to give you everything you deserve."

She leaned in and whispered, "You already do."

CHAPTER 30

I'm a woman with a purpose. In a rare moment of clarity, an *aha!* hit me. I'd been thinking about Tonya and how it looked like she'd never outgrow bar whoring and bed hopping. Then I thought about other friends. Some had a few flings and settled down after college, others waited till they were thirty or so before making a commitment, and still others went for the used-car approach—finding a happy relationship for a few years and then trading in their ride for a newer model.

That's when it came to me: I'm doing things backward. While I was playing house and building a business, my peers were out living it up and passing women around like marijuana cigarettes. Now, here I sit on the brink of forty, and the sum total of my wild oats would fit in the palm of my hand. But it seems this puts me in a powerful position. I've been "pre-broken." I understand the complexities of life and have survived its ups and downs. I've felt pain, but I'll never hurt that way again. It's impossible. Scars have no feeling. Maybe the best part of my life is over, but the worst is in the past, too.

Now it's my turn to kick up my heels. With street smarts and a thick hide, I can do anything. It's better this way, now that I'm not a heart-on-my-sleeve kid with big eyes and a head full of ideas. Women don't stupefy me. Unlike a kid, I'm not held down by a shortage of cash or the lack of social graces. You don't sell as many filing systems as I have without gaining a certain amount of charm and a little finesse. Hell, I could talk Fidel Castro into voting Republican. Seducing Rebecca shouldn't be that hard, and that's exactly what I plan to do.

This newfound wisdom could be an overdose of Tonya, of listening to her prattle on about her weekend fling with the unfulfilled wife, or it could be a midlife crisis. If it is, then bully for me. I'll ride it till I'm sixty.

In preparation for my Sunday evening date with Rebecca, I take a shower and shave everything I can think of. Then I apply an extra dab of body lotion to my legs and a smidgen more eye shadow than usual.

Jitterbug tires of watching me dash about and stretches out at the foot of the bed.

I've picked out a nice pair of silk panties and a matching bra from Victoria's Secret, and I check myself in the mirror before getting dressed. Not too bad for an old woman. Luckily, my nipples haven't found my waistline yet and my butt hasn't started creeping down my legs. Sure, I could stand to lose five pounds around the middle, but the overall package isn't too shabby.

I put on a forest green sweater with a deep V-neck that hints at my cleavage, and a pair of baggy jeans that make my midriff look somewhat smaller. A final makeup check, a subtle dose of Gucci cologne, and I'm out the door, armed and dangerous.

When I arrive at Rebecca's, I bound up the steps and knock hard on the door. She lets me in, kissing my cheek as she closes the door behind me. She's sexy as hell in her black ribbed turtleneck and snug jeans. I could pounce on her now, but that would be too much, even for the new and improved Claire.

"Hey, girl. You're right on time." Rebecca grabs a leather jacket from the back of the kitchen chair. "Hungry?"

"Yeah."

She shakes her finger at me. "You know, that Tonya person surprised me the other night. She looked at me like she wanted to rape me, but she looked at you like a lovesick puppy. I thought for a minute you'd neglected to mention something."

I hold up my hands. "I promise there's nothing between Fly and me. Besides, I wouldn't do that. If I were seeing anyone else, I'd tell you. You'd do the same, right?"

"Of course. As long as we're dating, or whatever it is we're doing, I think you have a right to know if I'm involved with anyone else." She puts on her jacket and opens the door. "I'm not, though. Seeing anyone else, that is." The heat kicks on, and the vent over the door blasts my head with hot air.

"Guess that means we're exclusive by circumstance," I say.

"I could start seeing someone else if that'd make you feel better, but I'm not good at juggling."

As we step out onto the landing, the freezing wind picks up a stray leaf and sends it spinning toward Choppy's roof.

"Don't put yourself out on my account." I thrust my hands into my jacket pockets and bump her shoulder as we descend the steps and hurry to the car.

I left the motor running, and as I slide behind the wheel, the seat feels warm. Rebecca glides into the passenger seat and reaches for my hand. I take it, wondering how it will feel later, when the same hand explores more intimate places.

"You look like the cat who swallowed the canary." She runs her other hand through her hair, settling the effects of the bitter wind.

"I haven't swallowed anything." I reach across my lap and put the car in gear with my left hand.

She wiggles around in the seat and finally settles down. "So what do you want to eat?"

"Entirely up to you." I stop the car at Choppy's exit and look up and down the street. Dozens of restaurant signs line both sides of the four-lane road. There's everything from tacos to prime rib.

Rebecca purses her lips. "Haven't thought about it, really. We were swamped at lunch, and I didn't have time to think about much of anything."

"I'm hurt. You didn't think about me once?" I fake a pout.

"Oh, I might have let you cross my mind a couple of times... a couple of *dozen* times."

An old red pickup passes, belching gray smoke from its tailpipe.

I lean close to the steering wheel and look in each direction. "You'd better tell me which way to go or we'll sit here all night."

"Surprise me."

I think a minute, then punch the gas and swerve to the left. It'll be a surprise, all right. It's quirky, unusual, and not like me at all. A smile tickles my insides before finding my lips. I *like* not being me.

"So where're we going?" she asks as she grabs the armrest.

"It's a surprise, like you wanted." I drive too fast down Freedom Drive whizzing by vacant car washes, discount stores with big red sale signs in the windows, and the super grocery store at the corner of Freedom and Winchester. It's all a blur—even Rebecca seems indistinct, an obscure visage not two feet away.

When I wheel into the parking lot of Belmore Lanes, she shoots me a puzzled look. "We're going bowling?"

I grin. "Come on."

She lets go of my hand and we get out. The sky has been clear blue all day, but the winter sun is about to set. The heavens seem dreary and gray, a depressing vise pushing us down into the cold earth.

Belmore Lanes is not exactly a family establishment. This is a hardcore bowling alley: no video games, no air hockey, just pins, balls, and plenty of beer on tap.

We go in and see league bowlers in team shirts with their names stitched on their chests—people called Buster, Ned, Pinkie, and Vie— milling around, high-fiving and slapping one another's backsides. Rebecca and I are trespassers here in the bowling underground, where the sun never shines and the thunder never stops. The regulars sense the intrusion and eye us with caution.

A fog of cigarette smoke lingers around the snack bar, and a heavy metal song blares on the jukebox. I point to the snack bar and try to tell Rebecca to find a seat, but the screeching guitars drown me out, and I end up leading the way through a wave of beer breath and talk of strikes and spares. The song ends as we find two stools at the counter.

"Are we going to get killed?" Rebecca slips up onto the seat and clutches her purse to her chest.

"Nah, they're a tight-knit group, but they've seen me around. If you want the best hot dog in town, you have to come here." I snatch a napkin from the dispenser and wipe up a greasy spot on the counter in front of me.

A burly gray-haired woman wearing a Dale Earnhardt baseball cap and a white apron stained with mustard comes toward us. When she sees me, her eyes widen and she grins. Her teeth are as yellow as the smoke film covering the walls. "Well, howdy, stranger. I thought you'd left the country."

"Hi, Maude. Guess it has been a while. My lunch hours have been pretty busy lately, but I just couldn't wait another day for one of your chili dogs."

"I hear they're the best in town," Rebecca says.

Maude shrugs, but her modesty is skin deep. "It's my chili that does it. I've had folks from New York City offer to buy the recipe, but I won't sell. Not till I win the lottery, that is." She gives a belly laugh, sidles up to the counter, and juts an elbow toward me.

Rebecca smiles, but seems more entertained by Maude than by the comedy. "Then put a little extra chili on my dog, please, and a side of jalapenos if you've got some."

Maude jots a note on her order pad before looking at me. "Usual for you, blondie?"

I nod and watch her lumber toward the grill. "How's this for a surprise?" I ask Rebecca.

"Wonderful. You don't know how I've learned to hate restaurants over the years." She tucks a stray strand of hair behind her ear and glances around. "Everything's gotten so mass-market and franchised. Places like this are hard to find."

"Choppy's isn't a franchise, is it?"

"No, and that's the reason I'm there. The one thing that's worse than answering to my dad is answering to a corporate office." She glances toward the coin-operated pool table in the corner. "Enough restaurant talk. Five bucks on a game of eight ball?" That twinkle in her eye tells me I'm about to say goodbye to a five spot.

"Why, Miss Greenway, is that a challenge?"

"If you're up to it." Her eyes linger on me as she smiles.

Fifteen years ago, it could've been dangerous for her to look at me that way in public, but the crowd is caught up in its own world, and perhaps time has softened its fear of us, so no one notices the ripple passing between the two women at the lunch counter. We recognize it, though.

The food arrives, so we thank Maude and dig in like death-row inmates. Between bites of scorching chili, Rebecca tells me about the time she almost got arrested for hustling darts at a bar in Charlotte.

"But those days are behind me." She wipes a dollop of ketchup off her lower lip. "I'm straight and narrow all the way."

"All the way?"

She glances over her shoulder. "Not *all* the way."

"I'm not sure I understand. Maybe you could explain it to me later."

She leans in and whispers, "Promise."

After we eat, Rebecca and her sledgehammer stick make quick sushi out of me at the pool table. As I feared, she is merciless, slamming one ball after another into the pockets. She leans over the table and calls each shot with confidence. Some guy named Boozer, sporting a mullet haircut, appears to be enjoying every opportunity to gaze at her wonderful butt and watch her breasts sway as she bends down to line up a shot. Got to give him credit—he has good taste. I can't take my eyes off her, either. When she's drilled the eight ball into the side, she saunters up to me with her hand out.

"All I've got is a ten." I hold the bill up between my fingers.

She snatches it away. "I'll make change." She tucks the cash into her back pocket and puts the house cue back into the rack.

My safe little fantasy of Rebecca Greenway is over. The prim restaurant manager has been replaced by a real person, a woman who likes hot peppers and just fleeced me in a game of pool. Versatile, that's what she is, and I like that. But before I start liking her too much, I remind myself that this is nothing more than lust.

As we ramble out into the night, I breathe in the crisp air. It feels good. The stars are out, and the rising moon casts an eerie glow on the parking lot. It's a perfect night for a vampire movie.

We're quiet on the drive back to Rebecca's apartment. I take my time pulling into the parking space beside her Mercedes. Rebecca leans back in her seat and bites her lip, not quite looking at me. "I've got a bottle of Merlot upstairs that's dying to be tasted. Interested?"

This is it, my moment of truth. Can I go up those stairs and do things with Rebecca that I've done with only one other woman? Can I touch her without feeling someone else?

Determined to find out, I unsnap my safety belt. All this thinking about liking people, loving people, and caring about people is giving me a headache. I need sex, and there's nothing wrong with that. "I wouldn't want to disappoint a lonely bottle of wine," I tell her.

We don't speak on the way up the steps, and Rebecca fumbles with the keys as she unlocks the door. She gives me a tense smile. "My hands don't seem to want to work."

By the time we make it into the studio, we've resorted to nervous laughter.

She finds the Merlot in the top cabinet, struggles with the corkscrew before popping the cork, and leaves the open bottle on the counter. After another uncertain smile, she excuses herself and disappears into the bathroom.

I slip out of my jacket and check my breath against my hand. Fly taught me one thing—always have mints in your purse, just in case. A burning thought hits me. Am I turning into Tonya? Will I get to the point where I don't care about anyone or anything, as long as I get laid? Doubtful. I've got mints in my purse; she carries a whole bag of travel-size toiletries in her trunk.

I sit down on the sofa as Rebecca comes back from the bathroom. When she sits down close to me, I'm so keyed up I can't think of anything but dragging her to the bed and having my way with her till the sun comes up. We'd better get this show on the road before I lose my gumption.

"What's the matter?" she asks. "You look a little green."

"I feel fine. A little nervous, maybe."

"You don't have to be nervous with me." When she strokes my cheek, I'm past the point of conversation. I pull her to me, rougher than I intended to be. I'm out of practice with this sort of thing, but she doesn't seem to mind. She meets my mouth with the same kind of determination that's rumbled around inside me all day.

She moves her lips to my ear. "I'm having trouble controlling myself with you."

My sex fires up and my brain goes dull. "You don't have to control yourself. We can do anything you want. I'm ready to be with you tonight."

She pulls back and studies me for a second. "If you're sure, I mean really sure..."

Reading her words as an invitation, I stand up and guide her to the bed. She sits on the edge, and I drop to my knees in front of her and bury my face in her chest. She wraps her legs around me and runs her hands through my hair and along my back. Without asking, I pull her sweater up over her breasts, kissing them through her bra.

She pulls her sweater over her head and strips off her bra. When it falls away, I close my eyes. I don't want to see the woman. I want to feel her sex. But when her flesh goes hard against my tongue, my eyes fly open and my brain wakes up. I haven't been thinking of Rebecca. All I've been caring about is the physical release, enjoying what I feel without regard for her. Who the hell do I think I am? This is not the dream woman I've been watching from a distance for months. This isn't a safe little fantasy where I get my jollies and forget about it like it never happened. This is real, and it affects us both. Rebecca is a living person, not a toy. I can't just buy her a cheap dinner, then take her home and maul her before she even pours the wine. I'm treating a funny, kind, beautiful woman like a two-dollar whore.

I fold my arms around her waist. My body trembles. "I can't do this."

She lifts my chin and forces me to look at her. "Hey, take it easy. Everything's fine."

Rebecca tries to hug me, but I turn away and sit on the floor. I can't stand to see her there, only half-dressed. She's opening herself up to me and expecting me to do the same. I can share my body, but I have nothing else to give. Maybe *I'm* the two-dollar whore.

She slides off the bed and scoots up against my back. Her knees frame me and her arms circle my waist. "We don't have to do this."

"Jesus, I didn't even let you take your shoes off."

She peeks over my shoulder to her feet. "Let me? I don't recall feeling any particular need to take them off yet."

"I can't use you like this." I lean in to her embrace. The downstairs music reverberates against the floor, sending a shiver along the backs of my legs.

She rests her chin on my shoulder, and her voice softens. "How are you using me?"

I don't respond, and she squeezes her arms tighter, as if she's insisting that I elaborate. I guess I owe her that much—after all, I had half of her breast in my mouth. "I don't know. It's like I need something, but I don't know what."

"Claire, I do care about you, but I don't demand anything. If we've gotten a little carried away this evening, I'm sorry."

I clutch her hand to my chest. "No. It's not that. It's just..."

"How long has it been since you've done this?"

"About three years."

"That's a pretty long time." She brushes her fingers through my hair. The compassion of her touch comforts me. "What's her name?"

"Who?"

"The one who did this to you." She speaks as though my scars are visible, like she can touch them and somehow feel the remnants of my misery.

"Doesn't matter."

Rebecca's warmth flows into me like soothing milk. If she asks my lover's name again, I'll say it, but instead, she says, "How long were you together?"

"Eighteen years. We got together in high school."

"No wonder you're having a hard time. Best I've ever managed is five years, and that one almost killed me when it was over. Trust me, you'll be okay." She kisses my shoulder.

The evening isn't going as planned. Should've known my burst of inspiration wouldn't last. Should've known Rebecca would become a person to me instead of an object, and I'd back out. I'm aware of her breasts pressing against my back.

"I'm sorry for freaking out. I guess it's just that I've never been intimate with anyone but her."

"Talk to me. Tell me what's on your mind." Her hug feels safe, protective.

"Did you ever wish you were one of those people in the movies or in a book? The kind who always knows what's right, who never doubts or second-guesses?"

"Yeah, that might be nice, but those people don't exist in real life. Everyone gets scared. Everyone wonders if they're doing the right thing, sometimes."

"Guess I spent too many years with a psychologist. When I feel something, I end up trying to figure it out, break it down, and see where it really comes from. I'd be way better off if I could stop thinking so much."

"You don't have to get so uptight about this—just feel it. Let go with someone else, so you can get her out of your system. I'm not talking about sex, now. It's more than that. It's about letting your guard down and being really intimate. You know, putting yourself out there."

Without questioning my own motives, I reach down and untie her left shoe. I slip it off, then the right.

She stands up and helps me to my feet. "Come here, you." She hugs me tight, then folds back the bedspread. "One step at a time," she whispers, unbuttoning her jeans. She wiggles out of the denim, and her pants fall to the floor.

I'm sweating down to the bone, but I'm not focused on her breasts or that sexy pair of black panties covering her hips. I'm watching her eyes, patient and gentle, knowing the things I can't say. She's like a mirage, and I worry that she'll disappear if I reach for her, taking the deep understanding in her gaze with her.

"Now you," she says. She eases my sweater over my head, then helps me out of my jeans. Rebecca never takes her eyes off mine, doesn't look at my body or cop a cheap feel. She backs up to the bed and pulls me between the sheets with her. The linens are fresh from the dryer and still smell of fabric softener.

She traces her finger along my bra strap. "Can we take this off?" I nod, and with one hand, she unhooks the back fastener.

We're lying face-to-face, our bodies barely touching. She takes my chin and guides my lips to hers. Her kiss is tender and light, the kind of kiss you need after a hard day at work, giving everything and demanding nothing.

Then she lies back and pulls my head to her shoulder. "Let's just sleep tonight, okay?"

I snuggle up, one arm across her stomach, one leg draped over her thighs. I haven't felt a woman's naked skin against me in forever. My sex drive should be kicking into high gear, but this is different. Rebecca is giving me more than sex. She's soothing my heart in a way no one else has—not Tonya, not even Elizabeth. In their arms, I'm a child. In Rebecca's, I'm a woman. As I drift off to sleep, I realize that she knows what I need better than I do.

* * *

I wake a little after midnight. Disoriented and confused, I can't figure out where my dreams ended and reality began. A stream of red light flashing from a billboard across the street illuminates the room in spurts. The paintings on the brick walls are there, then they're gone. The TV screen stares at me with one huge eye, then blinks shut. Rebecca's slow breathing is the only constant, the one reliable stimulus my senses can relate to. I snuggle against her back, and she murmurs as she holds my hand tight against her chest.

I untangle my fingers from her grasp and slip away. I find my clothes by the blinking light and step into my jeans. By the time I reach the sofa, I've pulled my sweater over my head, but as I sneak toward the door in my sock feet, she says, "Claire? You don't have to go." Her voice is filled with sleep, raspy and low.

I thought I wanted a clean getaway, but when she says my name, I'm tempted to slide back into bed. I go back to the bed and sit down beside her. "Sorry I woke you."

"I sleep like a cat," she mumbles as she takes my hand.

In the glow of strobing neon, she half sits up. The sheet falls to her waist, exposing her breasts, but she doesn't rush to cover herself. She's as comfortable with me now as she was a few hours ago. I'm tempted to stare, but don't. What's passed between us is good and pure. I won't ruin it.

"Thank you for last night. I had a great time," I tell her, brushing my fingers against her cheek

"No, thank *you*. It was great. I can't remember the last time I had a hot dog." She wipes her eyes and hugs her knees to her chest.

"I'd better be going. Poor Jitterbug must think I've gotten lost." I slip on my shoes and kiss her cheek before standing up.

"See you tomorrow?" she asks as I bump into a kitchen chair.

"Lunch? Sure, I'll be there." I take a last look over my shoulder before stepping out into the freezing night air.

It looks like snow. Ominous clouds block any light the moon might be trying to shed. I grab the handrail and ease down the steps. All the way home, I'm whistling *Close to You,* by the Carpenters.

CHAPTER 31

I was pretty proud of myself. Lora and I had lived in our first house for five years, and the mortgage was over half-paid. Yep, I'd worked my ass off, but look what I'd done.

Good old Claire deserved a break, so I'd taken a rare day off to do something I'd been putting off for ages, something just for me. I'd spent the whole day measuring, nailing, and climbing up and down a stepladder to make sure the basketball hoop above the garage door was installed to the manufacturer's specifications. After spending five hours in the muggy summer heat, I wasn't about to quit till I tried it out.

I stood before the hoop and wondered whether I still had it in me to lob the ball far enough to hit the rim. Time for truth. Could my thirty-year-old body still cut the mustard? I'd barely handled a basketball since high school, and it felt odd and large in my grip, like a huge orange cantaloupe.

I spun it between my hands, dribbled once, dribbled again, lined up the shot, and tossed it toward the basket. Nothing but net. Ha! I still had it. I skipped up and grabbed the rebound. A trickle of sweat soaked into my collar. Another quick hook shot. The ball ricocheted off the backboard and tumbled through the hoop.

And the crowd goes wild! Blevins charges the basket again, feints left, pivots right. And again finds the hole. I was standing in the middle of the driveway, arms above my head in a Rocky Balboa victory dance, when a car horn sounded behind me. I turned to see Lora pulling in, all smiles as she watched me make a complete fool of myself. When I moved aside, breathless but exhilarated, she stopped her black Camry beside me and rolled down the window.

"Who are you today? Annie Meyers? Nancy Lieberman?" She tossed her sunglasses into the passenger seat and shaded her eyes with her hand.

She looked so pretty. Sure, I'd seen that navy linen suit before. I'd watched her thousands of times as her dark hair caressed her cheek when she tilted her head and smiled, but I lived for the moment of recognition, that split second when she realized it was me dancing around the driveway like a fifteen-year-old boy, the instant when her heart sprang up from her chest and kindled a flame behind her eyes. Coming home made it all worthwhile—the time away, the long distance calls, the loneliness of the road.

When I'd made it home from a late meeting in Nashville Thursday night, Lora had been in bed for hours. I'd been a sleep-deprived space cadet when she'd left for the office early that morning, so we'd hardly seen each other in five days. When our eyes met, we both broke out in silly grins. If anyone had seen us, they'd have thought we'd been smoking something very good.

I bounded across the concrete and picked up the ball, which had landed beneath a pink rhododendron by the driveway. "Think I've got any college eligibility left? I might call Pat Summit and see if the Lady Vols need any help this year."

"Gee, I don't know. I hear she's got a six-foot-two forward who's slippery as an eel. She might manage this season without you." Lora pursed her lips, mocking my enthusiasm with a roll of her eyes.

"Maybe next year." I tried to spin the basketball on my index finger, but as usual, it careened away and bounced toward the street. "Up for a little one-on-one?" I skittered after the ball.

"Sure. Let me change first."

In a few minutes she returned wearing sneakers, baggy shorts, and one of my old Lady Warriors T-shirts. She'd pulled her hair back into a ponytail and looked as energetic as when she'd donned her cheerleading uniform so many years before to coax the Warrior football team to victory.

"Let's have it, hotshot." She bolted toward me and snatched the basketball from my grasp.

"Hey! I wasn't ready." But she'd already done a quick layup and was passing the ball back.

During our game we indulged in plenty of spirited hand-checking, and I took a couple of charges on purpose, letting her body shove against me and then slide away as she made her shot.

Lora had taken care of herself over the years, exercising regularly and watching what she ate. I, on the other hand, had become sedentary, spending too much time behind the wheel of a car and foregoing salad bars for fast food. So, with minimal effort, she trounced me in a game of twenty-one, but I didn't mind. It was worth the humiliation to watch her breasts swaying as she dodged around me and drove the baseline.

Exhausted after her final basket, I grabbed the rebound and parked myself on the red-brick retaining wall between the driveway and the front yard. The sun was beginning to dip behind a huge oak tree in the neighbor's yard, but it wouldn't be dark for hours. It was my favorite time of year—when the evenings drew on like lazy ballads.

"Uncle!" I moaned between gasps.

Lora sat down beside me and elbowed my ribs. "What's the matter, old-timer? Not enough visits to the gym?"

"Too much time in cheap motels and too many passes through McDonald's drive in," I said, lungs still heaving. "Besides, I've been out here working all day while you've been sitting on your ass."

"Saving the world is mentally exhausting." She grinned and snatched the ball from my lap. Adding insult to injury, she spun the ball on her index finger for a full fifteen seconds before letting it drop to the pavement.

"Show-off! I never did understand why you didn't play ball in high school."

Lora snickered and shot me a lusty glance. "If I'd been on the court, I wouldn't have had such a great view of your ass. Looked pretty good from the bleachers."

"You watched my ass from the bleachers?"

She dribbled the ball first with her left hand, then with her right. "I've told you that a hundred times."

"I know, but I never get tired of hearing it." I stood up and wiggled my butt on the way into the house. "How's it look up-close?"

She skipped up behind me, and once we were shielded from the neighbor's sensitive eyes, wrapped her arms around my middle. "Looks even better now than it did then."

"Never get tired of hearing that either. You've always been good for my ego, you little shit."

She sniffed the air between us—we smelled like a couple of wet dogs in a locker room. "Well, I've always been honest. And honestly, right now you smell bad."

"Whaddaya mean, bad? This is a great smell. They make cologne out of sweat, you know that? A guy at that place in Birmingham told me." I tugged my wet shirt over my head and shoved it in her face. "We could bottle this and sell it."

"Oh, no. No more inventions for you, hotshot. You're away from home enough as it is." She pushed away and scampered toward the bedroom, the swish in her own backside teasing me to follow. "No hanky panky till we shower," she yelled.

* * *

After a luxurious hot shower, Lora and I settled down at opposite ends of the sofa sipping frozen strawberry daiquiris as we talked about our respective weeks. Sadness crept into her eyes as she told me about a young male client—not *patient*, but *client*—whose mother had caught him "messing around" with another boy. Lora wasn't sure if the boy was gay or just testing the waters of adolescence, and from what she could tell, neither was he, but the mother had gone off like a hand grenade in a bomb factory, spouting Scriptures and smacking her son's head during their initial consultation.

"When I got him alone, he would hardly speak, just nodded and looked at his shoes." Lora took a long pull on her drink. "After I talked with him, I spoke with the mother. You should've seen the look on her face when I told her that if her son is homosexual, I can't and won't try to make him straight. She acted like I'd set fire to her family Bible."

I shook my head. Who knew what my own parents would've done if they'd caught us all those years ago? But by the time they'd found out about my relationship with Lora, I was earning more money in a month than they'd paid for their first house, and although they didn't like it, there was little they could do about it. So we managed a head-in-the-sand coexistence. I pretended I didn't have a bedroom, and they pretended they didn't have eyes. My brother had been great, though. Robert treated Lora better than his own wife, and I was more than a little cocky about the fact that my girl was prettier.

As the evening waned and darkness fell, Lora and I crept closer to each other till we were sitting Indian-style, knee-to-knee, forehead-to-forehead. The gentle breeze carried the mournful call of a screech owl through the open windows.

"Claire, I was thinking about your trip to Los Angeles. Why don't I fly out with you? We can drive to Las Vegas for a few days, the two of us." Lora's strawberry breath flooded my face.

"I didn't know I'd gotten involved with a gambler." I sipped the last of my drink and made a rude sucking noise with my straw.

"I'd never ask you to gamble away any of your precious money, but I thought it might be fun to see the sights, take in a show or something. You know, just be together for a while."

"That sounds great." I envisioned us strolling down the Las Vegas strip, surrounded by twinkling lights, taking in everything from pirate ships to pyramids. I shook my head. "But I can't do it, honey. I've got four interviews in L.A. on Monday, and I want to take my time with them. The West Coast is a brand new territory for us, so we have to be very careful who we hire. After that, I'm back here on Tuesday afternoon to train Bob Carlisle."

She leaned back and stretched her legs across my lap. "Bob can wait a day or two, can't he? You said yourself he's going to need some time to learn the ropes before he can take over your sales territory."

"The sooner I get him trained, the sooner I can get off the road. That's what we want, right?"

"Yes, that's what we want." Lora laid her arm across her face in a feeble attempt at hiding her disappointment.

She'd been begging me to take a vacation for two years. Just a few days in the sun, she'd say. Stop and smell the roses for a change. But I was so freaking stubborn, so blinded by insecurity.

I rubbed her feet, pressing my thumbs along her arch. "Baby, don't worry about it. Besides, you know what they say, 'Absence makes the heart grow fonder.'"

She raised her head and glared at me. "They also say, 'Out of sight, out of mind.'"

"When I get Bob trained, we'll have all kinds of time. I promise, we'll go anywhere you want."

Lora's thigh muscles tensed. "Jesus, Claire, when are you going to stop wasting today worrying about tomorrow? Anything could happen. We could die on the way to work Monday morning, and then what? Then how important would the business be?"

"Come on, don't be dramatic. Let's not get into this again, okay? We've had a good day, right? Let's enjoy the rest of it." I ran my hand up her leg and squeezed that ticklish spot behind her knee.

"Stop it." She giggled as she sat up and poked my ribs. "Don't make me feel bad for wanting to spend some time with your tired old ass."

"I'll show you how tired and old my ass is." I lunged forward and fell on top of her. "Kiss me, you hateful hag."

She relaxed and planted her hands on my hips. When she kissed me, I forgot about everything—money, business proposals, hiring new sales reps. All I wanted was Lora, and for the moment, I had her.

CHAPTER 32

"The key to horseback riding is not to be intimidated." Rebecca glances over her shoulder as she cinches the girth on a chestnut mare. The mare eyes me but is more interested in the carrot in Rebecca's pocket.

"I'll remember that." I lean against a stall door and watch her drop the stirrup into place and pat the mare's muscular chest.

When Rebecca told me that her father kept two horses boarded at Morningside Stables, she seemed excited about introducing me to riding. I didn't have the heart to tell her that I'd grown up around horses and had once entertained the notion of becoming a professional rider. But she has to find out some time.

I nod toward the mare. "She's holding her breath."

Rebecca smacks the horse's rump. "What are you trying to do to me you old nag, make me break my neck?" She tosses the stirrup back over the seat and gives the mare a quick knee to the midsection. The horse exhales, and Rebecca tightens the girth again. She pauses and turns to me, looking flustered. "You've been holding out on me, haven't you?"

"Not really. I honestly haven't been on a horse in at least fifteen years. It's almost like starting over."

Rebecca gives me a dirty look and holds up a shiny metal instrument with a crooked end. "Okay, missy, know what this is?"

"Hoof pick."

She tosses it to me. "Then make yourself useful." She snatches a halter off the tack hook and saunters down the hall. "Just let me stand there and make a fool of myself. I don't care. I'm used to looking stupid." She glances over her shoulder and tries to hide the smile spreading across her lips.

Rebecca's the kind of person who can take a joke with the best of them. I like that. I also like the way her faded Levis and flannel shirt accent her curves. She's one of those women who can look good wearing anything and seems comfortable in everything, and I like that, too.

Smiling, I go to the mare and run my hand along the back of her foreleg. As she raises her hoof, I watch Rebecca unlatch the last stall on the left. This barn isn't so different from the stables I knew as a teenager. Sixteen stalls, eight on each side, facing a wide hallway. It has a tack room with lockers and a wash stall with hot and cold running water, and rubber matting covering the concrete floor. The aromas of hay, sweet feed, and manure create a pungent, sugary smell that sends me back to a time when I didn't know about women and sex and how you could go crazy trying to get one or the other. Back then, it was all about mountain trails and the solid thud of my gelding's hooves as we rode across fields of buttercups and knee-high alfalfa. Back then, it was me and a bay quarter horse named Buster—the world before us, the opportunities endless.

But time limits us. Each choice narrows the field and gives us fewer options, and before we know it, we've furrowed out a considerable rut with little opportunity to alter our path. I'm at one of those rare intersections now, and the choices are bewildering. Should I take the high road and tell Rebecca that we'll never have a serious relationship, that I just can't do it, or should I hang back and get what I can while I can? Would she care either way?

"How are you doing?" Rebecca asks before disappearing into the stall.

I'm scraping manure and sawdust from inside the mare's hoof and don't look up. "Marvelous, simply fantastic," I reply in a phony British accent. "Are the hounds ready?"

"Not quite." She exits the stall, leading a huge bay gelding. He has a strong jaw, and a white blaze running from his forelock to his muzzle. If it weren't for one white stocking on his rear leg, he'd look just like Buster. I love him immediately.

"Here you go, Dale Evans." Rebecca hands me the lead line and points toward the tack stand. "Know how to saddle him up?"

"I think I can fake it."

After I groom and saddle the gelding, we lead our horses into the bright March sun. The air is so clear. It's like your first look through a freshly-cleaned windshield when all the bugs and road scum are gone.

Rebecca steps into the left stirrup and swings into the saddle. She sits like she was born there, heels down and toes barely touching the stirrups. Rusty as I am, I have a little trouble hiking my leg up high enough to heave myself into the saddle, but with a groan and a few curses, I manage it, and thread the reins through my left hand.

"You'll have to work on those thigh muscles if you want to ride." Rebecca nudges her heel into the mare's ribs and guides her through the paddock gate.

"My thigh muscles might surprise you," I call out, still trying to remember how to sit back in the saddle while keeping my weight in my heels. Perhaps I was a bit too cocky in the barn.

Heading off side by side toward a wooded hill at the end of the pasture, we pass a pond where dozens of geese barely notice our intrusion. The warm breeze caresses my face, and I settle into the gelding's rhythm, rocking with him as he navigates the worn path.

Closer to the tree line, a lone sycamore stands, its naked white branches splayed like gnarled witch's fingers. There's an almost rebellious air about the tree, as if it's saying, "I will live again."

Rebecca points toward the tree and tells me that's where the trails begin. We pause, and as our horses nip at each other's muzzles, Rebecca says, "I know a path that leads to Thatcher's Creek. It's a little rougher than the others, but it's very private. Think you're up to it?"

"I was born up to it, kiddo. Lead the way."

She nudges the mare with her heels and makes a clicking sound with her tongue. Pure cowgirl.

The gelding seems to know the way. He picks though a briar patch, unconcerned with me or the creaking of the western style saddle on his back. I keep thinking his name is Buster, but when I call him that, Rebecca reminds me his name is Nick.

We follow a worn path into the woods. The trees are still naked, waiting with solemn patience for their sap to rise, but the beginnings of spring are obvious. Tiny wildflowers of purple and crimson weave between fern groves where the foliage is beginning to ripen, and orange-breasted robins dart among the trees carrying twigs and brown grasses in their beaks. It won't be long before hatchlings warble from the nests their parents are building today.

Rebecca and I talk about things we've never discussed. She admits that she does sweat the small stuff, doesn't much care if all men are from Mars, and is pretty sure Dr. Phil is from a planet she calls Hateful. She's allergic to shellfish and almost died once when she ate a shrimp egg roll. She wet the bed until she was eleven, but the problem stopped as soon as her parents divorced and she moved with her mother to Hickory, North Carolina. It takes a lot of guts to tell me stuff that personal. I wish I could hold her hand, but the path is too narrow for me to ride next to her.

In a low voice, she describes her first relationship with a woman who loved her like heaven but hated her like hell. Rebecca has been hurt, too, left to lick her wounds and piece together the ruins that once were her life. But she's done something I haven't. She's moved on.

Her candor rubs off on me, and despite my need to keep her at arm's length, I find myself spewing stories of my own childhood and early teenage years. I tell her about the time I was six and Mom caught me trying to shoplift a pack of Dentyne gum because she'd refused to buy it, and the day my brother talked me into peeing on an electric fence at our grandfather's farm. I describe straddling the wire and pulling my shorts leg aside, and she laughs till her eyes fill with tears.

I tell her about my horseback riding days, and how I'd once wanted to tour the rodeo circuit and make my living barrel racing. She seems impressed and challenges me to a race next week. Next week? Will we still be speaking then?

A brick wall separates my childhood from the rest of my life. I'm unable to tell her anything after I turned seventeen, after that rainy day in my best friend's bedroom. There are no stories about how our basement flooded and we didn't have sense enough to uncover the floor drain, opting instead to rent a pump and drain the water right back into the wet-weather spring that caused the flood in the first place. I don't tell her about the time I kindled a fire with the fireplace damper closed and the neighbors called 911 because of all the smoke.

We've talked nonstop for two hours by the time we reach the clearing along the bank of Thatcher's Creek. At the creek's center, deep murky water lazes along in no particular hurry, but closer to shore, jagged rocks and fallen logs create miniature rapids full of whitecaps and gurgling foam.

Evergreens, elms, and weeping willows line both sides of the water, their branches spanning the narrows to create a canopy of knotty boughs. There's a grassy plot to our left, where we dismount and let our horses drink from the stream.

Rebecca squints toward the afternoon sun. "We can't stay long. Sun will be down in about three hours."

"It's nice here." I take her hand in mine. She leans in and gives me a quick kiss before she lets go and tugs the mare away from the stream.

I drape Nick's lead across a nearby blackberry bush and sit down on a low rock near the water. My muscles twitch. The sun is warm, the breeze gentle as it tosses my hair first one way, then the other.

Rebecca wanders along the water's edge and stops to skip a flat stone across the surface. The rock makes three distinct hops before sinking. She turns to me. "No worries, no hassles. Doesn't get much better than this, huh?"

"Sit with me." I extend my hand, and she sits between my legs with her back to me. I wrap my arms around her middle and rest my chin on her shoulder. Her hair blows across my face. It smells of earth and apples. I don't brush it away.

"I remember the first time I saw you," she says. "Never dreamed we'd end up here."

Grinning as I recall the day I ambled into Choppy's and she approached me, I say, "Who would've guessed? Must've been fate that I came in on the day you were doing that promotional survey."

Rebecca shakes her head. "That wasn't the first time."

"Sure it was."

"The first time was about a month before. You came in and picked up baked potato soup and a chef salad. The order was under the name Kingsley."

"What? I never saw you before you came up to my table that day and asked if I'd like a complimentary gift certificate. You said all I had to do was answer a few questions and sign up for future promotions."

A single powder-puff cloud drifts across the sun and briefly shades us before moving on toward the eastern sky.

"I can't believe you fell for that crap." She laughs and settles back against me.

"Do I sense a confession coming on?"

"I saw you come in that day for the pickup order and flipped. You had on a navy pantsuit with a silk blouse. But the way you smiled at the hostess—I knew right then I wanted to meet you."

She takes my hand. "Every day after that, I'd watch for you to come back, but you didn't for almost a month. So when I saw you in the booth that day, I went back to my office and found some old gift certificates. I figured it was the best way to introduce myself and, you know, see if you were on my team."

I'd thought it was my imagination or wishful thinking, but Rebecca hadn't been scanning the crowd, she'd been checking me out. When she stopped by to say hello and turned on the charm, she wasn't being a good manager, she was flirting with me. With me, Claire Blevins, who was too dense to know a come-on if it bit her on the ass.

My face goes bright pink. I'm glad she can't see. "Did you peg me from the start?"

"Kind of. My gaydar is about ninety percent accurate, and I noticed the way you looked at me. But there was something I couldn't put my finger on, something that kept you distant. I thought you were probably in a relationship, so I decided to play it cool. Wouldn't do me any good to get too close if you had someone waiting at home, would it?"

I nod, and even though she's looking at something across the water, she seems to sense my agreement. A small bass jumps from the shallows, breaks the surface with a splash, then disappears beneath the creek's cloudy surface.

Rebecca goes on. "But after a while, you kind of started flirting with me."

"I'm not much of a flirt. Never had any practice. Like I told you before, I met my lover in high school."

Rebecca wiggles around to half-face me. "This is all new to you isn't it? Dating, I mean, getting to know someone?"

"Yeah. Most of the time I feel like I'm twelve going on ninety."

"That's what I like about you, Claire. You're experienced, but you're almost naive when it comes to some things."

"Like what?"

"Like when a woman is trying to hit on you." She pokes a finger into my ribs. "I swear to God, I thought I'd never get you alone long enough to find out if you were interested."

"Okay, hold the phone. Didn't it tell you something when I started coming in for lunch almost every day? Hell, I've already told you that I hadn't been in Choppy's more than four or five times over the last five years. No offense, but it wasn't the salad dressing that kept me coming back."

Rebecca sighs, I sigh, then we sit quietly for a long time. Water thrashes against the rocks, and blue jays caw in the distance. It's peaceful here, close to this woman, far from my routine, my prison. For a minute, I forget the gloom and the self-hate. All I feel is Rebecca, and it seems natural when I bury my face in the slope of her neck. She doesn't speak, but leans into me.

Her flesh tightens at my touch, and she whispers, "What are you doing?"

"Want me to stop?"

She puts her hands on my knees. "When I told you I'd be patient, I wasn't giving you license to tease me."

"Who says I'm teasing?" I trace her neck with my lips and nibble her earlobe. An easy breeze blows in from across the water.

She shivers and glances toward the sun. "We'd better head back now, but if you're in the same mood later, we'll talk about it."

Uh-oh. I could be in serious trouble, here. But on the other hand, maybe it wouldn't kill me. I trust Rebecca not to take advantage of me, or force something I don't want to do. So maybe later, when the lights are low and the mood is right, we'll move on with this thing.

CHAPTER 33

It never occurred to me not to trust Lora. Sure, I wasn't self-confident, never did feel good enough for her, and definitely never understood what she saw in me. But I was confident in my lover. True-blue as they come, my Lora was. A lot of women hit on her. Pretty women, women with plenty of cash, women with style to spare. She brushed each one of them off with a firm smile. For some crazy reason, I was her choice.

It didn't happen all at once—the paranoia, the suspicion. It crept up on me, like a cold, where first you get a tickle in your throat, then your nose stops up, and before you know it, you're miserable. But with a cold, you know you'll get over it. My mistrust was incurable. It stayed with me constantly, draining my energy and making me short-tempered. By the end, I'd turned into a pure bitch.

I didn't handle it well, right from the beginning. Things might have turned out okay if I'd talked to her. Maybe we could've avoided the catastrophe if I'd confronted her and given her a chance to come clean. But I hid my fears and let them fester into resentment and eventually tear me apart.

I wasn't trying to snoop through her purse the first time, but that's what I ended up doing. After that, it became an obsession. I looked for anything that might be evidence of her betrayal—a long lunch hour, an odd phone call, a strange expression—and I found just enough.

It started when we'd been in the new house, the one I live in now, for about two years. I'd turned my sales territory over to Bob Carlisle, and other than the occasional out-of-town meeting or trade show, I spent most nights at home. Lora's practice had grown to the point where she was turning new patients away. We were where I thought we wanted to be.

It was late spring. Lora and I had spent all day that Saturday working in the backyard. We'd fashioned a rambling flower bed along the back fence, edged it with clay bricks from an old farmhouse, and planted it full of purple coneflower, hosta, Dutch iris, and at least ten other types of flowering perennials. I'd even agreed to put a concrete statue of a naked Greek lady square in the middle of the bed. Lora had promised to put clothes on it when my parents came over.

We'd gotten up early that day, grabbed bowls of Cheerios for breakfast, and started working by seven. By noon, we must have carted a hundred wheelbarrow loads of supplies from the driveway to the back fence. The day was hot, and a hazy dampness lingered in the air, making our sweat cling to us like sticky cobwebs. Between the dirt and the sweat, we looked like two mud pies with legs.

When we finished up around five, Lora swore we'd dug up enough dirt to sod the Astrodome. I mentioned that the Astrodome didn't have real dirt and grass—not a good point to make at the time. She'd shot me a don't-be-a-smart-ass look.

All in all, it had been a good day. We'd worked well together, as we always did. We'd been planning the landscaping project since Christmas, so getting into it was kind of a relief and gave us a real sense of accomplishment.

When we'd cleaned and put away our tools and staggered into the house, exhausted and filthy, Lora headed straight for the shower.

"Shotgun," she shouted on her way down the hall, already peeling her T-shirt over her head and using it to mop the sweat from under her arms.

I went back outside. Who knew what I might drop on the carpet or furniture? Jitterbug, just a puppy and not weighing more than five pounds, was scampering around the yard like a fuzz ball in the wind. She was a sight, checking out the freshly turned earth and trying to paw the plants. Tired of scolding her, I picked her up, tucked her under my arm, and went inside.

The shower was still running, so I got a bottle of water from the refrigerator, sat down at the kitchen table, and lifted Jitterbug into my lap. Lora's Claiborne handbag lay half-spilled on the table, and I noticed a lipstick had rolled out and ended up behind the napkin holder. I picked up the tube, set the purse upright, and as I tossed its scattered contents inside, I noticed a credit card receipt.

Thinking it might be important, I straightened out the crumpled scrap of paper. It was a Visa receipt, which struck me as odd because Lora didn't have a Visa. I looked closer—forty-three dollars from Damron's Pub. Also odd. Damron's was a dark, cozy place where people went when they didn't want to be seen. Why would Lora go there? I put Jitterbug down and she scampered to her water bowl.

I took a closer look at the receipt. It was for four Bloody Marys, which was Lora's drink of choice, two gin Collinses, and an order of breadsticks. The cardholder's name had been ripped off, and the remaining partial signature was illegible. The receipt was three days old. That would've been Wednesday, the night I worked late with Reggie to troubleshoot the bugs in our new rail system. But I'd been home by eight, and Lora had been stretched out on the couch watching CNN. She hadn't mentioned anything about going out after work, and nothing in her demeanor had indicated she'd been drinking. I'd been tired, though, and might have missed it.

Lora sauntered into the den, wearing her pastel blue bathrobe and towel-drying her hair. She groaned and stretched her arms above her head.

"What's this?" I asked and held up the receipt.

"What?" She snatched the paper from my hand but didn't look at it. "Oh, I forgot. I went out with June the other night. Her husband isn't doing much better, and she needed to get some things off her chest." She tossed the receipt in the trash and twirled toward the refrigerator for a bottle of water.

The excuse didn't make sense. I'd known June, the counseling center's secretary, for over five years and had never seen her drink anything other than white wine. True, her husband was very ill, probably terminal, but she wasn't the kind of woman to go out for drinks while he was suffering in the hospital.

Once I thought about it, Lora had been a little distant all day. She'd wandered off to the garage, only to return a half hour later without whatever tool she'd gone after in the first place. Then she had stopped for a drink of water and ended up sitting on the patio for fifteen minutes, looking at nothing. Something was distracting her, and I hoped it didn't have anything to do with the person who drank gin Collinses, so when I mentioned the gin on the bar tab, it didn't surprise me when she said, "What?" Still off in her own little world.

I stood in the doorway between the kitchen and den trying to act nonchalant, but red flags were popping up in my head. "The bill. I've never known June to drink gin."

"What? Oh yeah, surprised me, too." Lora walked past me into the den and fell on the sofa, still in a muddle. Only when Jitterbug followed along and jumped into her lap did she notice she wasn't alone. She gave the puppy a loving pat on the head.

"How's he doing, anyway?"

"Who?" Lora picked up the TV remote and punched the power button.

I hadn't lived with her for almost eighteen years without learning a thing or two. This wasn't one of her I-can't-give-details-about-a-client routines. Lora was avoiding the subject.

"Carter. You know, June's husband. We were talking about him," I shouted. I wasn't going to be drowned out by a re-run of *Alice*, no matter how high Lora turned the volume. She would acknowledge my presence or else.

Or else, what? She might have asked, if I'd said those words aloud. But I kept my barbs to myself. I wasn't interested in a confrontation, just her attention.

Lora muted the television and dropped the remote beside her on the sofa as she cuddled Jitterbug to her chest. "It's a sad situation. His chances of survival are almost none. She can't bear the thought of letting him go, but watching him suffer is killing her right along with him. What's she supposed to do?"

I imagined Lora lying in a hospital bed, death looming in the shadows, and an unspeakable horror coursed through me. "I don't know."

"What would you do?"

Looking up, I caught her eye. "Why? Are you sick?"

"Don't be silly." She paused as if not sure what to say, but after a moment, she went on. "What would you do if you thought you were losing me after all these years?"

I shivered in the heat. "I know what I wouldn't do. If it were you, I'd never give up hope. I'd never quit believing in you."

Her lower lip trembled. Tears spilled over her lashes and down her cheeks. She moved Jitterbug from her lap and reached out to me. "I know you wouldn't give up on me, honey."

I went to her and, dirty as I was, got down on my knees and hugged her. When she wrapped her arms around me, she said the strangest thing. She said, "I really *do* love you." As if there was a reason to doubt, as if somewhere along the line, she'd started to re-examine her feelings and had found them lacking. But I refused to believe her love would ever waver, and I dismissed the idea as a result of her concern for June and Carter. After all, her compassion and empathy were two of her best assets. They made Lora tick.

I held her close for a few minutes. The fresh-shower scent of her damp skin and hair comforted whatever dread I might have felt about the credit card receipt.

Don't be silly, I told myself. This is Lora, not some bimbo I picked up off the street. We've spent half our lives together. And we'll spend the other half just the same.

But the seed was planted, and like an oyster turns a grain of sand into a pearl, I would worry my speck of doubt into full-fledged torment.

CHAPTER 34

My muscles ache, muscles I forgot I had. My thighs tingle as I step into the shower, and some kind of knot has worked its way into the small of my back, but it's a pleasant soreness. Getting out and doing something different has invigorated me.

I work up a good lather with the shampoo, and as I rinse my hair, I watch the foam swirl about my feet. The shower's steamy warmth soothes my body and my thoughts. Strange as it sounds, I've gotten used to being morose. There's a certain comfort in steady grief, in knowing the next day will be the same as the last, but lately things have become confusing. I don't know what tomorrow might bring. Conflicting thoughts boomerang through my head. As one notion prods me to take my relationship with Rebecca to a physical level, another springs from the depths of my psyche and reminds me that someone's bound to get hurt. Real life doesn't play out that easy. It didn't before and it won't now.

One thing for sure, Rebecca Greenway intrigues me. She's got so many of the qualities that attract me to a woman, not the least of which is a warm body, and ever since she took me to her bed last Sunday, I've thought of little else.

So maybe my midlife crisis isn't going to be as liberating as I thought. I might sleep with Rebecca, I might not, but I'll try my best not to mislead her, not to let her believe this situation is more than it is.

Here in the shower, as steam billows over the plaid curtain and the nearly-scalding water pounds my skin, these opposing ideas seem softened, less at odds with one another. It's as if the very steam that relaxes my muscles forces the speculations together and whips them into a huge meringue—all fluff and no substance. From here, it looks as though I could blow them away as easily as blowing out birthday candles.

Birthday candles. Good God. It hits me like a ton of bricks. My fortieth birthday is less than a year away. Visions of egg whites and sugar are replaced with images of wrinkle cream and Depends undergarments. Life sucks.

I want to stay in the shower, suspended in time, never to age, never to face whatever might be in store, but I can't. Rebecca is on her way, and the future is barreling at me with sickening speed. I turn off the tap and stand still for a moment. Then I yank back the shower curtain. On the other side, life waits and will go on whether I'm ready or not.

As I step out of the stall, a sudden pain stabs my groin. I steady myself on the vanity. Looking down, I see a tiny crimson trickle of blood running along my thigh. Wonderful. I'm seriously considering sleeping with Rebecca, and what do I do? I get my period.

The worst part is that my cycle isn't like it used to be when I could take a couple of Tylenol and go about my business. With age, my period has turned into a three-day bloodbath, but in seventy-two hours, it'll be over.

Crap. So much for sexy underwear tonight. I'll have to wear my grannies, which resemble something my mother might have worn while she was pregnant. Very attractive. Oh well, maybe it's a blessing in disguise.

I finish dressing, and as Jitterbug follows me into the den, the bell rings. Another thing about Rebecca, she's reliable. I open the door and invite her in. One look at her in those snug jeans and that ivory cotton blouse makes the whole situation seem like a cruel joke.

She scratches Jitterbug's head as I close the door. "So what's the plan for the evening?" she asks, with no particular undertone.

I shrug and follow her into the den. "I'm flexible. Got anything in mind?"

"I was thinking maybe we could turn down the lights, kick off our shoes, and chill for a while." She pulls me close, and her eyes flicker, gold and green fireflies.

"Thought you'd be sick of listening to me talk after today." My breath mingles with hers and rushes back into my face. The aroma of mint and wintergreen is at once familiar and strange.

Rebecca looks into my eyes, apparently measuring my interest. "We can be quiet, if you'd like."

"How are you so nice all the time? I keep waiting for your inner bitch to come out and rip me to shreds."

"Never." Rebecca's lips find mine. It's one of those kisses that makes me forget all the ugliness of the past and sweeps me to where all is well. I could let her kiss me like this for a week and never come up for air.

But she's still company, and I'm still playing hostess, so I pry myself away and take her jacket. I hang it in the hall closet and return to the den.

Rebecca gets comfortable on the sofa while I make a haphazard pile of kindling and wadded newspapers in the fireplace. In a moment, flames flicker and dance and gradually settle down to a steady crackling fire. I find two cinnamon-scented candles in the pantry and put them on the coffee table. I glance at Rebecca. "Music?"

"Yeah, something soft." She closes her eyes and stretches her arms over her head.

"Coming right up." I open the stereo cabinet and flip through the alphabetized CDs. What am I looking for to set the right atmosphere? After a moment, I stop at Enya's *Paint The Sky With Stars.* Perfect. I slide the disc into the changer and turn the volume down. The first track is *Orinoco Flow.*

I light the candles with a fireplace match and sit down beside Rebecca. "How's this for chilling out?"

She hooks her arm through mine and smiles. "Nice."

We kick off our shoes and prop our feet on the coffee table. The mood is mellow and romantic, but a cramp in my lower back says I won't be doing exactly what I'd hoped, not tonight anyway.

Rebecca drapes her arm around my shoulder. "Did you have fun today?"

"Oh, yeah. I haven't been on a horse in so long, I almost forgot how nice it is to take off through the woods." I lay my arm across her waist and am amazed at how natural it feels to sit here like this, watching the amber firelight cast odd prancing shadows across the room, feeling human contact. It's almost as if the past never happened. Almost.

All is quiet except for Enya's soothing voice and Jitterbug's soft snoring. I absently wonder what the dog dreams about. Is she hip deep in Alpo or scampering through a field of Milk Bonz? Does she really dream or are her whines only reflex?

Rebecca, as if reading my thoughts, says, "Wonder what she's dreaming about."

I chuckle and sit up straighter till I'm eye to eye with her. Rebecca's cheeks are flushed, her eyes dreamy but intent. She's only been here fifteen minutes, but it feels like we've wanted to touch each other for years, like we've already waited too long and don't want to wait anymore. I need to touch her, connect with her.

As if entranced by the same desire, she strokes my leg, and lets her hand linger on my thigh. "Are your muscles sore from the ride? Maybe I should give you a massage."

With a nervous cough, I'm on my feet and on the way to the kitchen. "How about a glass of wine?"

"Sounds good."

"White or red?"

"Whatever you're having."

I grab a bottle of cheap white Zinfandel from the refrigerator. My hands are slippery and I almost drop the bottle. Some player I'm turning out to be. Finally, the cork pops out and I pour myself a full glass, guzzling it down in one gulp. Somewhat buzzed from the quick shot, I make my way back to Rebecca with two filled glasses. She thanks me, takes a polite sip, and puts her glass on the coffee table.

"You seem nervous," she says.

"Me? Nervous? No, I'm not nervous." I drum my fingers on the sofa and take another long pull from my glass. "Why would I be nervous?"

"I don't know." She's infuriatingly nonchalant, taking another sip like she doesn't know what's going on.

I turn sideways to face her, but can't look at her face. "Did you catch the evening news? Someone in Georgia hit that big lottery."

"I missed it." She snuggles down into the cushions. "I took a very long shower after we got back. Horseback riding makes me feel nasty."

"Are you?"

"What?"

"Nasty." Amazing how a big glass of wine can embolden me.

"I did need some help scrubbing my back. Know anyone who might be interested?" With a wicked grin, she puts her hand back on my thigh, this time much closer to my groin. Despite the period discomfort, I ache for her.

"Maybe." I slide closer and finger her ribs. "Are you ticklish?"

Rebecca flinches and curls against me. "My ticklish spots are for me to know and for you to find out."

"Is that an invitation?"

"I've tried to fix the problems we ran into last time." She nods toward the coffee table. "See, we've opened the wine and I've taken my shoes off. Is that better?"

I laugh and hug her. She's making this way too easy, way too much fun, but if I touch her tonight, tomorrow will be one hell of a morning after. Am I ready to deal with the consequences, face the depression and guilt? And what about Rebecca? Is it right to subject her to my neurosis?

That's always been my problem, worrying what might come, wondering if I'm prepared. Didn't Lora always tell me to live more for today, to stop wasting the time I have worrying about what may never happen? Have I learned nothing?

Forget tomorrow, I think, guiding Rebecca's lips to mine. I'm starving for her. Our tongues wrestle, wild and wet. My hands move on their own, and I make no effort to stop them. I'm touching her face, her hair, but as I trace my index finger toward her cleavage, I pause. "Do you want..."

Her reply is low and throaty. "Just don't start something you aren't prepared to finish."

I withdraw my hand and cool down a couple of degrees. Time for truth. "I've got this little problem. I started my period and was hoping we could work around it. You know, stay in the safe zones."

A flash of disappointment registers in her expression but is replaced by a smile. "All my zones are safe."

Sweat pops out on my forehead. Is this really going to happen? Am I going to give in and let my sex take over? If the look in Rebecca's eyes is any indication, the answer is a resounding yes.

She takes my hand and guides it back to her chest. "All we need is a little patience and a lot of trust. I trust you to respect my body. Do you trust me?"

I nod as I fumble with her top button and stammer, "I... I'm not sure... I haven't done this in a while."

"Shhh, don't worry. We can figure it out together." She helps me unbutton her blouse and slip it off her shoulders. I trail my fingertips along her breasts, stopping at her bra's front fastener. Her bra comes off easily and falls to our feet.

"Everything okay?" she asks.

I nod.

Silently, she tugs my sweater over my head and before I realize it, she's reaching behind my back. "Can I take this off?"

I nod again, and as she unhooks my bra, I slip the straps off my shoulders. Rebecca leans in as if to tell me a secret, but instead nibbles at my earlobe. Her hot breath sends me into orbit as she kisses her way down my neck, all the while pressing her body against mine.

Despite my cramping muscles, I'm excited. It's been forever since anyone touched me this way, and I was beginning to wonder if it would feel as good as it used to. It does.

She pulls away. "Want me to stop?"

"No."

I'm mesmerized by her eyes. She moves in again, kisses my throat, eases toward my breasts, her pretty pink tongue slithering along my skin. My insides squirm.

She says, "You have a beautiful body."

Rebecca's the one who's beautiful, sitting there with her rounded, sensual breasts begging to be kissed. I'm not embarrassed, but I flush.

She leans in and touches her cheek to mine, and we kiss again, heat rising between us. As I cup her breast in my hand, she presses her hips against my thigh.

I should suggest we go to the bedroom, but it might be a mood-breaker and she seems okay with staying here. Besides, taking her to my lover's bed might be a bit much for me right now.

Rebecca sighs. "I can't believe we're doing this."

"What do you want?" I whisper.

"I want what you want." She pulls my hand to her lips and kisses my palm, then guides it along her body. She moves my fingers across her cheek, along the valley between her breasts, past her flat stomach, and stops at the top button of her jeans.

Her voice is erotic, teasing. "Tell me what you want, Claire."

Our faces touch, our eyes millimeters apart, unblinking. I slide my hand between her thighs. The denim is warm, and when she moves against me, I can almost feel her excitement through the heavy material.

Rebecca unbuttons her fly, and I help her slip out of her jeans. I'm almost there, only a thin layer of silk between me and her luxurious flesh. I hook my fingers around the waistband of her panties and tug them down over her hips. There she is—Rebecca Greenway, the star of my nighttime fantasies, the lead in my daydreams, the object of my lust. For a moment, I can only stare. She's stunning, but a shred of fear lingers. What if I disappoint her?

She murmurs into my ear, but the words aren't important. It's the intensity of her voice, the heat of her breath, spurring me on. My hands rove her body, lingering on her stomach, then on her firm thighs, and back to her breasts.

I tamp out that last spark of doubt and slide my hand between her legs. Rebecca isn't pretending—she's as excited as I am. Feeling her passion, touching her as a lover, my pent-up lust surges and escapes me in a gasp. "My God, you feel good."

She breathes hard into my ear. "Are you still okay?"

Unable to find my voice, I nod.

"I like the way you touch me." She cups my breasts with her hands. "I like the way you feel."

I'm past the point of thinking. Instinct guides me as I explore her, finding the places that bring her to life, the private spaces that she wants to share with me. That same instinct tells me it's time to move on. As I move inside her, she wraps her arms around me and shudders.

I hold her close with my free arm. "Okay?"

"Oh, yeah."

We move in slow rhythm, relishing the new, but familiar sensation of touching and being touched. In this dance, she's the leader and I'm a puppet surrendering to her pleasure.

Her voice is low and throaty. "Look at me."

I open my eyes and meet her stare. She seems so relaxed, as if we've done this a hundred times and will do it a hundred more. Rebecca closes her eyes. As we continue moving together, her expression changes, softens even more as she clenches around me. Her breath tickles my ear. "Wait."

I freeze. "What's wrong?"

She puts her hand on mine, holding me steady. "I don't want to come yet."

We are still, joined for the first time, drinking each sensation. I inhale her scent, study the curve of her cheek and the way her hair falls into her eyes. I record every subtle gasp, every husky moan.

"I'm sorry," she says, "but I can't stay still." Her hips begin to move against me.

"I want to please you." I press my cheek against hers, and we move faster until she arches against me. Her nails scratch my shoulder as she goes breathless. It seems to last forever, muscles tense, lungs heaving. She collapses into my embrace, clinging to me as I ease my hand away.

We don't talk for a long while. She kisses my lips, my face, my neck. Her breasts press against mine, torturing me with thoughts of what we might be doing if I hadn't gotten my damn period. I want her to touch me so much it hurts, but I can't let her. Not right now.

"Sorry that was so fast," she finally says. "I guess... well it's been awhile, and I've wanted you..."

I press my finger against her lips, and her sexy sweet smell drifts into me. "You've got nothing to be sorry for. I should be the one apologizing for not being, you know, more creative."

"Nothing wrong with the basics." For the first time, a real blush reddens her cheeks. She snuggles closer and shivers.

I pull a fleece throw from under the sofa and drape it over us. "How's that? Better?"

"Always prepared, huh? You must've been a Girl Scout."

"No, I just fall asleep on the couch a lot."

Rebecca looks at me, a hard yet tender stare, and touches my cheek. "I want you to know something. I don't... you know... I don't..."

"Why, Miss Greenway, I don't believe I've ever seen you speechless."

She slaps my shoulder but doesn't go on. Just as well. I'm not sure I want to know what she was going to say.

I giggle and pull her close. This is a wonderful feeling, and I don't want to let it go. Who knows what tomorrow will bring?

CHAPTER 35

The phone rang three times before someone said, "Greenbriar Counseling Center. May I help you?"

"Hi, June. It's Claire."

"Hello there, how're you doing?" June's usually chipper voice seemed subdued.

"I'm good, but how are you? Is Carter feeling any better?"

She took her time answering. "Some days he does pretty good, others I just want to go out and get drunk."

"Should I reserve a space for you in the alcoholics support group?" I slapped my hand to my forehead. "Sorry, I didn't mean that the way it sounded. I just..."

"Don't worry about it. Besides, I haven't had so much as a glass of wine in months. Wouldn't solve anything anyway, would it?"

A shudder prickled up the back of my neck. When I'd found the receipt from Damron's Pub two weeks before, Lora had told me she'd been with June. Why would she lie? Better yet, whom had Lora really been with?

"I wish there were something I could do, June. You know I've always thought a lot of you and Carter."

She sniffled. "Thank you, Claire. I appreciate your concern, but there's nothing we can do. It's in the good Lord's hands now."

"If you need anything..."

"I know. Lora's been a great comfort. You've got a winner there."

"Speaking of Lora, is she available? I thought we might meet for lunch."

"No, she's already gone."

I glanced at the clock and realized it was already after noon. "Guess the day has gotten away from me. When she gets back, will you ask her to give me a call?"

"She's taking the afternoon off. Didn't you know?"

"Uh... oh yeah, I forgot. Well, thanks anyway, June. Give Carter my best, and we'll be praying for you."

I hung up the phone and stared at Lora's photograph. She hadn't mentioned taking the afternoon off. Maybe she was planning something, a surprise of some sort. Could it be one of her no-special-occasion dinners? She hadn't done that in ages. Yes, that had to be it—a mouthwatering dinner with champagne bubbling in those fancy crystal glasses she was so proud of, fresh fragrant roses, and a romantic, candlelit bubble bath. Thinking about it made me hot.

Absently, I muttered, "You little devil."

But what if that wasn't it? What if there was something going on that I needed to know about, something bad? I picked up the phone to try Lora's cell, but hung up without dialing.

I rocked back in my chair and stared at the ceiling. As hard as I tried to come up with an innocent explanation, it just wouldn't fit. Lora had lied to me about being with June at Damron's. And what was up with taking the afternoon off without mentioning it to me? Even when I was traveling, she would tell me every detail of her daily routines, so why not now? Where was she going? Who was she going to see?

All the little oddities were starting to come together to spell something other than coincidence or simple misunderstandings. Over the past few weeks, she'd gotten phone calls at odd hours from people I'd never heard of, after which she'd be distracted and aloof. She'd been having trouble sleeping and often wandered to the guestroom in the middle of the night, claiming she could rest better in the other bed.

At first, I'd blamed fatigue. Lora had made a shift in her practice, seeing only her regular adult clients and accepting disturbed children as new patients. After a while, she'd complained it was too much. On those now infrequent occasions when she did open up to me, she'd cry for the kids, for the sexual and physical abuse they endured, the verbal torment. Many came from the foster care system where they'd been passed around, never knowing a real home, or if they found a good, loving place, they'd soon be uprooted again.

She worried herself to death, growing pale and losing weight. More than once she'd said if something didn't change, she didn't know how she'd make it, so I'd encouraged her to go back to adult therapy full-time, where her clients would at least have some power to overcome their problems, but she'd brushed me off. If she didn't help the kids, who would?

But these other things, the phone calls, the lying, pointed to one thing, and I began to suspect the unthinkable. Lora was having an affair. Why else would she lie about being with June? Why else would she take the afternoon off and not tell me? What else would cause her to be so distant?

A sickness whirled in my stomach. I choked down a swallow of strong coffee and tried to collect myself. Jumping to conclusions wouldn't solve anything. I couldn't convict Lora of infidelity without real proof, so that's exactly what I set out to get.

* * *

I left the office at two o'clock in case Lora came home early. Visions of her meeting me at the door with a chilled glass of champagne had been replaced with horrible images of her sneaking out of town to meet some moneyed-up elitist lesbian in a limo. Thanks to that mental picture, my turkey-on-rye from the deli across the street hadn't settled well.

But the drive home calmed me down. Things were like they'd always been. The red light on Commerce Street caught me, just like usual. And before I could cross the tracks on Industrial Drive, I had to wait for a locomotive pulling carloads of coal to pass. At East Side Elementary, kids played on the swings while they waited for big yellow busses to cart them home.

Things began to feel more normal. I had decided to give her a chance to tell me on her own about taking the afternoon off, but when I pulled into the garage and her car wasn't there, I almost lost it. Where the hell was she?

I went into the house, and an emptiness swept over me as if Lora were already gone. I dropped my briefcase and purse by the kitchen door and collapsed on the sofa. What was I going to do? I couldn't breathe without her, couldn't feel my own heartbeat, but if my suppositions were correct, did I have the power to keep her? Had a stranger taken my place?

I went to the kitchen and downed three glasses of ice water, but still couldn't cool off, so I opened the freezer door and stood as close as possible to shelves full of Lean Cuisine and Banquet TV dinners. After a minute, I headed toward the bedroom and let Jitterbug out of the guestroom as I passed. She darted down the hall in front of me, into our bedroom, and back out. I changed clothes, and as I hung my suit in the closet, a sudden urge overcame me. I went straight to Lora's jewelry box and opened the lid.

I rifled through her pins and brooches and earrings. Everything I touched held a memory, a piece of her. The gold hoops I'd given her for

Christmas ten years before, the pearl studs she'd had mounted from her grandmother's antique choker, the one-carat diamonds she wore on special occasions. They all said *Lora,* all reminded me of what I was doing: digging through her things to justify not trusting her.

I looked into the dresser mirror, but the reflection wasn't me, not level-headed Claire. The woman staring back was a crazed hag.

I spoke out loud. "God, Claire. Get a hold of yourself."

But as I started to close the lid, something caught my eye. It was a neatly-folded slip of paper tucked in the back corner of the velvet-lined box. I pulled it from its hiding place and straightened it out. Scratched in handwriting I didn't recognize was the letter Z, followed by a drawn heart. Below that was a phone number, and I recognized the exchange right away. It was for an exclusive gated community tucked among the western hills of town.

Lora and I lived in one of Spring City's better neighborhoods, among doctors, lawyers, and Indian chiefs, but Forest Hills was a whole different ball game. If you weren't worth at least five million, you couldn't even get in the gates.

My blood froze. So that was it. Despite all my hard work, I hadn't done enough. My lack of real money had come to haunt me. Lora, who always said that having me was worth all the gold in Fort Knox, had been swayed by the mighty dollar. I had to give her credit, though. She'd landed a whale. A guppy like me could never compete with the Forest Hills set.

I tucked the paper back where I found it and sat down on the bed. I could've sworn the framed four-leaf clover on the nightstand blew me a raspberry. I was first hurt, then mad. I jumped up and paced through the house. Lora was everywhere, her grandmother's handmade rag quilt on the bed in the guestroom, her mahogany-framed diplomas hanging on the wall in the study, our pen-and-ink portrait done by a local artist in the hallway—it all reminded me of what I stood to lose. That lopsided grin, those knowing eyes, her gentle hands.

I fell onto the sofa in the den, numb from pain and disbelief. I must have sat there for three hours before I started to cry. I wept for the sting of betrayal and the agony of imagining her with someone else, but the real hurt came at the thought of her leaving, of watching her pack up her things and walk away.

I couldn't bear it.

When the sound of the garage door opening startled me, I forced myself to stop crying. I would pretend nothing had happened. If she wanted to play me for a fool, I'd let her. It was better than living without her.

Lora sauntered into the room, Jitterbug dancing around her heels. She stopped and stared at me. "What are you doing home so early?"

She looked different. The color had returned to her cheeks, and when she smiled, it was the famous Lora Tyler smile that had won my heart so many years before.

I sniffed back the remnants of my tears. "I had a sinus headache, so I came home a little early."

"You don't look so good. Did you take something?" Lora slipped out of her linen jacket before coming to me and touching my forehead with the back of her hand. "You don't seem to have a fever."

"I'm okay now." And I was. Lora was home where she belonged. "How was your day?"

"Nothing special. Yours?"

"The usual."

Lora sat down close to me and slipped off her shoes. "When did this headache start?"

"I don't know, a little after lunch maybe." I pinched the bridge of my nose. My sinuses really were clogged from crying.

Lora put her hand on my thigh and leaned back as she closed her eyes. After a long silence, she said, "Do you think it's possible to be in love with two people at the same time?"

"What?" Tears returned to my eyes, but Lora wasn't looking.

"Being in love with two people at once. Do you think it's possible?"

"Why?"

"One of my adult clients is having an affair. Claims she's in love with both men."

"Does she love them both?"

"I suspect she loves her husband because he's always been there for her. They have a history and all that." She took a deep breath and released it slowly. "But this new guy, he's different. He gives her things her husband can't anymore—excitement and passion."

"What do you think about it?"

"I don't know. Love is a chemical thing, like a drug. After you get used to it, it takes more to get the same high. Remember when we first started out, how exciting it was? We don't feel that anymore. We probably never will again, not with each other anyway."

"I still love you."

She patted my hand, but didn't look at me. "I know you do, but it's not the same. Love changes over time. The initial thrill doesn't last forever, but it's not to say you don't still love the person."

"So just because you don't get a buzz, you have to go out and find someone new?"

"It's not up to me to judge the right or wrong of it, just to help her get through it." Lora stood, picked up her shoes, and headed down the hall.

I jumped up and followed her. "So what do you think? Can someone love two people at the same time?"

Lora turned her back to me as she unbuttoned her blouse. "I guess it's possible. People are complex and we all have a lot of different needs. Maybe it's too much to expect one person to fulfill all of them."

"So every time we get a little bored, we should go off and have an affair?"

"I didn't say that." She went into the closet and returned a moment later, wearing a pair of loose shorts and a tee shirt. "What's for dinner?"

I plopped down on the bed. "What about you? You said our spark is gone. Does that mean you want to have an affair?"

She whirled on me, looking cornered. "Where the hell did that come from?"

"You're the one who brought it up. I'm just wondering how you feel about it."

"Honey, I've had a long day. Can't we drop it and get some dinner?" Lora took my hand and tried to make me stand up. I pulled her toward me, wrapped my arms around her waist, and buried my face in her stomach. I needed her worse than I ever had, needed to touch her, to know she was mine.

She squirmed away and turned toward the door. "Don't we have some steaks in the freezer?"

"Lora..." I couldn't ask the questions that were pounding away at my sanity. All I wanted was for her to stay with me. This time, I couldn't stop the tears.

Her eyes narrowed as she sat beside me and wrapped her arm around my shoulders. "Honey, what's wrong? You look like you've lost your best friend."

Still no words came, blocked by the knot in my throat. I fell into her embrace.

"Honey, please talk to me. I've never seen you like this. Did something happen at work?" Her hands found my neck, and she did that little massaging thing that got rid of my worst headaches.

I kept sobbing. How would I get rid of those migraines when she was gone? How would I do anything without her?

But she wasn't gone yet, and I still had a chance. In desperation, I latched my lips onto her neck, suckling too hard as my hands pawed her body.

She pushed me away. "What are you doing?"

I finally managed one word. "Please."

The look on my face must have been pitiful because she wiped the tears from my cheeks and smiled. "Easy." Kneeling between my legs, she unbuttoned my blouse and unhooked my bra. "Isn't this better?" Her tongue circled my nipple.

Better yes, but not enough. I had to have her, had to show her what she'd be missing without me. I pulled her to her feet and shucked her shorts down to her ankles. She stepped out of them and straddled my lap.

"What's gotten into you?" she gasped as I pulled her closer, teasing her from behind with my fingers.

I growled the words into her ear. "You're wet. You want me, don't you?"

"Yes."

"Tell me."

"I want you."

"Make me believe it."

Her hair fell in my face as she pressed her lips on mine. We fell backward onto the bed, and she tugged my pants down to my knees.

"Touch me," she said as her hand moved between my thighs.

Then I touched her, every inch of her. I touched her with my hands, with my lips, with my body. A strange lust raged between us, something we hadn't shared in years. Long-forgotten needs somehow resurfaced and demanded satisfaction. Two hours, three orgasms, and about a gallon of sweat later, we lay spent and ravenous. Let some rich bitch from Forest Hills beat that.

Lora's head was on my stomach, her still-damp fingers tickling my skin. I stroked her hair. "I was beginning to think we'd forgotten how to do that."

"Guess it's been awhile."

"It's not my fault. Every time I look at you lately, you make up some excuse to get away."

Lora's body tensed. "Stress," she said, rolling over and picking her clothes up off the floor. She didn't look at me as she dressed. "I'm starving. What's for dinner?"

Watching her walk away, I wondered if the other woman knew her like I did. Did her new lover know how she snored in winter but not in summer? Did she understand what Lora meant when she cocked her right eyebrow and frowned? Could that woman ever know the cheerleader, the pizza parlor waitress, the tireless student?

Maybe she couldn't. Maybe that was the attraction.

CHAPTER 36

I wake to the smell of coffee brewing in the kitchen. I expected to feel guilty after sleeping with Rebecca, but the morning-after blues have ambushed me harder than I ever dreamed.

Lora knows. Wherever she is right now, she knows. It's as if she's sitting here, giving me that I-told-you-so look and saying, "Ha! I knew you couldn't hold out. I knew you'd fuck up."

Now I'm mortified, almost the way I felt the morning after swilling nine margaritas at a party and making a complete ass of myself in front of our friends. It wasn't me, I kept thinking, it was the liquor. I'd never behave that way.

This whole charade with Rebecca hasn't been so different from that drunken fiasco. Just like the tequila, the more I had of her, the more I wanted, and before I knew it, I was drunk.

But this time alcohol isn't to blame. I was stone cold sober when I invited Rebecca to spend the night. To sleep with me in *our* bed on the linens my lover paid for. It wasn't my intent to have sex with her the second or third time, but once we got here, I couldn't stop myself. Good God, I even went down on her, something I thought I'd never do with anyone else.

I allowed my weakness to take over, talked myself into it, let myself believe it would mean nothing, but now that I've tasted her wine, it's time to sober up and face the inevitable hangover. It's going to be a bad one. It would be so much easier if I *had* gotten drunk on alcohol and danced on a table or something. A public spectacle is one thing, but what I've done is my own private shame, another scarlet letter emblazoned upon my flesh.

Three years ago, I meant it when I said there'd never be anyone else, begging Lora to stay, pleading for her to come back. I'd never touch anyone else, never consider it. My pledge didn't make any difference, didn't absolve me of my crimes, or commute their unbearable consequences. I swore to God, and now the vow is broken. A disgrace, that's what I am, an out-and-out liar.

I roll over and wipe the sleep from my eyes. The framed clover scowls at me. It knows the truth, a secret shared by the three of us—Lora, the clover, and me. At times, I long to confess, to wear that scarlet letter on the outside for the whole world to see, but I won't. I'm too much of a coward.

"Good morning." Rebecca comes in and hands me a cup of coffee. "Light cream, right?"

"Yeah." I struggle to sit up. She's adorable, wearing nothing but her cotton blouse from last night, its hem bouncing against her bare thighs. The top buttons are open, and I peek at her barely-hidden breasts. Another pang of guilt assaults me. "How long have you been up?"

"A few minutes. Did I wake you?" She sits on the edge of the bed and scans my face.

"No."

"I watched you sleep for a long time. You sure do frown a lot." She sips her coffee and stares at the picture lying facedown on the nightstand, but says nothing.

I glance at the clock. "Lord, look at the time! Guess you have to get to work soon, huh?"

"No, I'm not on till this afternoon. I thought we might go out for breakfast."

"Uh, not this morning. I've got sales meetings all day tomorrow, and I need to get down to the office and get my shit together. I've been letting things slide for the past few weeks." I take a long drink of coffee, scalding my tongue.

"Okay, maybe we can catch up later?" She's reading me, sensing my uneasiness, not pressing too hard. It would be easier to blow her off if she'd make demands of me, or push for something, anything, but she doesn't. She kisses my cheek. "I wanted to tell you something last night, but somehow I couldn't." Rebecca hooks my eyes. "I just want you to know that I don't sleep around... I mean, I have to care for someone before... "

"I'm flattered." I look down into my cup, already dreading the look on her face when I work up the nerve to call it quits between us.

She gives me a sad-eyed smile. "Don't be too hard on yourself. I'm irresistible, remember?"

"That you are, Miss Greenway, that you are." I take her hand and graze my lips across her fingers. She smells of aloe and baby powder, making me want to invite her back to bed for round four, but I can't. Rounds one through three are still fresh in my mind, and it could take months for my humiliation to fade. "What the hell am I going to do with you?"

Rebecca touches my cheek, her gaze resting on mine. "Don't freak out on me, okay?"

"Too late."

"Was I that bad?"

"On the contrary." I take another long swallow of coffee. The tears welling in my eyes won't go away. "I'm so fucking confused."

Rebecca takes my cup and sits it on the nightstand. "It's okay to be confused." She wraps her arms around my shoulders, and we sit still for a moment. Then she says, "I'm going to go now. Seems like you need some time alone. I'm sorry if I rushed things."

"It's not your fault. It's mine."

"Let's not talk about fault. I had a wonderful time, and I'd do it all over again. I hope you feel the same."

When I don't reply, hurt registers on her face, but she smiles and pats my hand before heading for the door.

I throw back the blanket and start to get up, but Rebecca waves me away. "You lie still. I can let myself out."

I should protest, but I don't.

She pauses in the doorway. "Will you call me?"

I nod, not knowing if I ever will work up the nerve to see her again.

* * *

The echo of the walled room rings in my ears. That's good, familiar, something I've done for years. Nothing unusual here, nothing to worry about, nothing to regret. The racquet feels like it always does, light but powerful in my hand, under control. Forehand, backhand. Forehand, backhand.

I whack the small blue ball hard against the front wall, watching it slam into the surface and bounce back to me. That's the thing about racquetball—no matter how hard you hit the ball, it always comes back. No matter how good or poor your shot, the ball will never end up more than a few feet away. And with four solid walls, no one can see when you make stupid plays or flail about like a three-hundred-pound ballerina. No one knows how inept you are.

A knock sounds on the back door, and Tonya crouches through. "Hey. How long have you been here?"

"A few minutes." I toss her the ball and step toward the back of the court. "You serve."

"Don't I get to warm up?" She twists the racquet strap around her wrist and gives me a once-over. "What's up with you? You look funny."

I shrug and turn away. "I thought you were going to warm up."

"Oh, my God. You got laid, didn't you?"

"Shut up."

"No way. I've got to hear this." She takes one step toward me. The slap of her court shoe bounces around the room.

"What makes you think you know everything?"

"I don't know everything, but I do know you, and you got laid. When? Where? Who? Rebecca?" Her excitement bubbles into an out-and-out laugh.

"Drop it."

"Details, girl, I want details."

"Shut up and serve."

"So tell me about it. Was she as good as she looks?"

The night rushes back to me—Rebecca's skin, her breath, her scent. Muscles twitch in my groin. My heart trips on its last beat, and deep red creeps up my cheeks. I stammer something about being a lady and refuse to discuss it.

Tonya's lips twist into a devilish smirk. I know that pornographic thoughts are flashing behind her eyes like a raunchy DVD playing in slow motion. She's savoring the image of every kiss, every nibble, every thrust.

Finally, she says, "Bet she was good, but then again, you haven't done it in so long I guess anything with a pulse would be good."

I whirl on her. "I said serve the fucking ball!"

"Damn, don't be so defensive. I'm happy for you, that's all."

I turn away before my tears spill. "Are we going to play, or what?"

Tonya grabs my shoulder and spins me around. Her expression sobers. "What the hell is wrong with you? That woman is a hottie. She's a score to be proud of—I sure would be."

"Well, I'm not proud." Part of me wants to get it out, to talk to her about my feelings, but Tonya won't understand. People like her never do.

"It's not like you picked up some skank at a bar. You landed a good one. Enjoy it." She pats my shoulder like I've hit the winning basket at the buzzer. A game, that's all any of this is to her.

My frustration flares, but I clench my teeth. "Serve."

Tonya bites her lip, her expression shifting from curiosity to concern. "What gives, Claire?"

This time the tears won't stop, and I'm sobbing by the time she wraps her arms around me. We sit down on the hardwood floor, and she watches me as I try to regain some sense of dignity.

"Talk to me, baby."

"I feel like a heel, that's all," I whine between sobs. "I broke every promise I made."

"Promises? What promises?"

"I promised... I swore." I drop my head. Tonya's stare is too intense. "I told her I'd never be with anyone else. No matter how long it took, I'd wait. I put my hand on the Bible and swore."

"You're kidding, right? You were stressed out. You'd have said anything to keep her. You'd have done anything, but nothing worked, did it? You can't hold yourself to those promises, and I can guarantee that no one else does."

Now I'm getting angry, maybe because she's right or maybe because I'll never admit it. "Sport-fucking may be okay for you, but I happen to have some morals. Women are more than bedpost notches. Promises mean something to me."

Tonya jumps up and glares at me. "What the hell is your problem? Every time I try to get you to face facts, you turn it into some kind of moral judgment on me. You know what your problem is? You're a chicken shit. You're so damn scared of getting hurt again that you'll use any excuse to keep from getting close to anyone."

"I wouldn't talk if I were you." I'm on my feet, screaming. "You're so goddamned afraid, you won't even go out with the same person longer than a month."

Tonya stiffens. "There's one little difference, old buddy. I'm happy with my life. I like the way things are for me. You, on the other hand, are fucking determined to be miserable."

"What do you know about misery?" I want to reel the words in, but it's too late.

Her eyes narrow, and she grits her teeth. "Watch it, Claire. I've let you get by with a lot for the past few years, but you're about to cross the line."

She's right, I am about to venture into forbidden territory, but I don't care. I'm angry with myself, with Lora, with Rebecca. I need a fight, and I'll take any I can get. "How come you get a line that can't be crossed, and I don't? How come I have to forget my past, and you don't?"

"I have forgotten."

"Bullshit."

"Whatever." Tonya picks up the ball and throws it at me. "Serve, damn it, before I get mad."

"Hell, no. You started this, and I'm going to finish it." I drop my racquet. It clanks against the floor.

Tonya holds her hands up and gives me a time-to-cool-it look. "Okay, okay. Let's not get all stressed out here. I know it's the first time you've been with anyone else, and I guess that's a little freaky for you. All I'm trying to say is that it's okay to fuck someone else."

"Then let me fuck you."

She smiles that wicked little grin she saves for potential conquests. "Thanks for the offer, but you know that's not my thing. I'm a giver, not a taker."

"Why won't you let me touch you, Fly? Why doesn't anyone ever touch you? Is it because you can't take your own advice? Can't you let go of your own past?" God, I'm smug. If I were her, I'd knock the piss out of me.

The grin is gone, and by the look on her face, she wants to do more than hit me. She wants to kill me, but she manages to keep her tone flat. "Claire, I know what you're doing. You're mad at yourself and you're taking it out on me, but this is going too far."

I expect her to charge, to let me have it with both barrels, but she just stands there. I hang my head, ashamed. "I'm sorry, Fly."

She doesn't seem to hear and keeps talking in the same even tone. "I was a whore on the streets when I was ten years old. I turned every trick in Atlanta to keep my parents pumped full of heroin and booze. Those men did things to me that shouldn't be done."

She blinks and tilts her head. "Now all I want to do is give pleasure instead of having it ripped out of me. Is that so wrong?"

"No, honey, it's not wrong." I go to her and wrap my arms around her waist. It was stupid to compare our pasts. My suffering is that of an adult, a grown woman with the power to make choices. My decisions turned out to be wrong, but they are mine, and only I am to blame. It's a miracle Tonya's even alive. Asking her to conform to my way of thinking is like asking a sparrow to swim.

Tonya stifles her tears and strokes my back. "I know how lucky I am. If they hadn't found me when they did, I'd either be dead or a crack freak like my sisters. But someone did save me, and my new parents gave me a good home, a place to feel safe. The scars will never go away, though. They're part of me."

"I had no right... I'm so sorry."

"No, I'm the one who's sorry, buddy. I didn't realize the pressure I've been putting on you. The past is all we have that's really ours, good or bad. I hate seeing you so miserable, that's all. But do what's right for you, and I'll stand by you." She gives me a squeeze.

Her words make perfect sense. Why fight it? My past is mine, and it changed me. I'm not the same person I was and never will be. I have to stick to what's right for me and stop listening to those who keep telling me that my life is supposed to be something else.

Even me.

CHAPTER 37

Was I insane? Who was I trying to kid anyway, believing I could sit by and let Lora carry on with some other woman behind my back? No one deserved that. I certainly didn't. I'd been beating the streets for fifteen years, working till I nearly dropped, and for what? For Lora, of course.

After all my sacrifices, I'd been reduced to a foolish little person, pretending not to know better, hobbling through my daily routine wearing blinders. But my shroud of self-delusion could only hide so much, and after weeks of denial, I had to accept the truth.

The seemingly unrelated fragments had been coming together. More credit card receipts from different restaurants around town, the phone number still tucked away in Lora's jewelry box, and the late Monday and Thursday evenings, after which her mood would go from despondent to elated. But she hadn't been taking late appointments as she'd claimed. I'd checked.

I'd found her cell phone bill hidden in her lingerie drawer, the jewelry box number appearing more often toward the end of the monthly statement. Each time I looked at those seven digits, a sliver of trust chipped away.

My latest discovery had brought me to the boiling point. I sat at my desk, hands clenched into white-knuckled fists, heart racing. My mascara had long been ruined by tears. I glanced from Lora's picture to the clock on the wall. Ten a.m. She'd be in sessions till after two. Very little time, when you consider the turn my life was about to take.

I picked up the tri-fold brochure I'd found in Lora's briefcase and scanned it again, hoping to find some redeeming evidence.

The Elms. A romantic resort tucked away in the breathtaking North Carolina Mountains. No question, the place was a paradise. The rustic A-frame built of pine logs and surrounded by evergreens invited couples to lounge by the heated indoor pool, dine in the five-star restaurant, or hibernate in well-appointed rooms.

The brochure was filled with photographs of handsome men and their gorgeous women friends, all wearing toothpaste-commercial smiles. Before my eyes, the models turned into Lora and her faceless lover, arm in arm on a hiking trail, swatting tennis balls on a pristine clay court, or sharing intimate conversation over flutes of champagne. I gagged.

The toll-free reservation number was circled in black ink, and two dates were scrawled across a photograph of the inn's honeymoon suite. Under the dates was a reservation confirmation number. In less than three weeks, she would be sharing a weekend getaway with her mystery woman.

I choked down the bile rising in my throat. Let them go on their little tryst. Let them make love in the canopy bed and whisper senseless rubbish to each other. Let them go to hell, but damned if she'd come home to find me waiting in blissful ignorance. Damned if I'd be her fool for one more day.

* * *

I left the office early that day, the last day of my life. Pulling out of my parking space, I opted for the long way home. No sense rushing, Lora wouldn't be there for hours. It was Thursday, the day for her little bi-weekly rendezvous with the almighty, swimming-in-cash Z.

Storm clouds lingered near the peaks of the western mountains—an apocalyptic omen. I stopped at the red light at the corner of State and Commerce. The radio was tuned to a country music station, and a woman's sultry voice moaned a heart-wrenching song about divorce. I felt like a drug addict coming off a week-long high, all trembly and confused, needing a fix. But there was no fix for my addiction. I had no choice but to crash and burn.

The light turned green. I punched the gas and the Lexus's tires squealed as I switched off the radio.

What was I going to say? That it was over? That I'd been playing the fool for weeks and wouldn't do it any longer? That she'd betrayed everything we'd worked for? That all the time we'd spent together was a joke? A string of clichés that I thought would never apply to me raced through my mind. In a wink, they all applied, and I felt like a Melissa Etheridge song about to be written. But the last verse was a mystery, the final crescendo about to be played out before a thunderous halt to the music. And then what? Dead silence?

What if she refused to leave? How could I handle it if she begged my forgiveness and promised to break off her affair? Could I accept her explanation if she said it meant nothing and was only the result of the stress she'd been under? Or what if she said she'd wanted to find out what it was like to be with someone else? Did I love her enough to forgive?

Yes, I did.

But I didn't expect it to play out that way. She'd probably apologize, say it wasn't my fault, and pack an overnight bag. In a few weeks, we'd be going through the house, dividing the loot. We'd pick through sentimental junk, decide who paid for what, and back a U-Haul up to the front door. Lora would take the dining room furniture. I'd get the computer. Other things, possessions with too many memories, or things we'd forgotten we had, would be sold off. In short, our relationship of eighteen years would be reduced to an expensive yard sale.

When I arrived home, I went to the bedroom and changed clothes. As I buttoned my Levis, I glanced toward the clover at our bedside. I snatched up the frame and glared at it. It still looked new, fresh, and alive after all the years. Tears welled in my eyes—damned if she'd get the clover. It was mine. After Lora was gone, it would remind me to never believe anyone again when they said they loved me.

When love carried conditions, it wasn't real anyway. Just like my parents. They loved me as long as they didn't think about my sex life. My brother loved me as long as he didn't have to put too much effort into it, make too many long-distance phone calls, or send too many Christmas cards.

What had Lora's requirements been? Had she loved me as long as no one interesting was around, as long as no one had as much cash as I did? Or maybe she'd loved me till her love ran out. Maybe our final years together had been nothing but the result of her leftover compassion for me. Perhaps she'd done the best she could, staying all that time, supporting my crazy notions, watching me chase pipe dreams.

I plopped down on the bed and stared at the clover. It knew the truth, but wasn't telling.

The clock caught my eye. 4:30. In another half hour, Lora and her new lover would be together while I sat home, waiting.

Not this time. I grabbed the phone and dialed. Lord knew I'd seen the number enough to have it memorized. One ring—my jaws clenched. Two rings—my left hand curled into a fist. Three rings.

"Hello?" She sounded older, maybe mid-fifties. Her voice was strong and deep, a mix of power and detachment. I froze.

"Hello? Is anyone there?"

I cleared my throat. "Is Lora Tyler there, please?"

A pause. "Why, no. She isn't. Who's calling, please?" Our polite formality was ridiculous. She was sleeping with my wife, for God's sake, and here I was, giving her the please-and-thank-you routine when what I wanted to do was reach through the line and grab that sleazy whore by the throat.

"Who's calling, please?" she repeated, sounding a little trapped but maintaining her composure.

"This is Claire Blevins. Perhaps you've heard of me?"

Another pause, longer than before. "Yes."

"Then you know why I'm calling. Please ask Lora to come home as soon as possible. We have a few things to discuss before this charade goes any farther. There'll be all the time in the world for you later."

The woman's voice went softer, almost apologetic. "She doesn't want to hurt you. She thinks it's for your own good. I tried to convince her to tell you weeks ago."

Fire rose in my gut. How dare this woman speak to me this way? How dare she pity me? I swallowed hard and in a level tone said, "I'll be the judge of what's for my own good, thank you. Please give her the message."

As I hung up, I heard her say, "Of course."

That ought to give her something to gnaw on, I thought. For once, I was in control. I'd made my move, and now it was Lora's turn to counter. I dropped the framed clover onto the bed and jumped up. I had to work off some energy if I expected to keep cool for the final showdown.

I was still pacing when the phone rang. What timing. It had been less than ten minutes since I'd landed my first punch by calling Lora's lover. "Hello?"

"Claire, what the hell is going on?" Lora's tone bordered on hysterical, just the way I wanted it.

"Funny, I was about to ask you the same question."

Silence.

"Well?"

"Not over the phone. I'll be home in fifteen minutes."

Lora was crying and for some odd reason, I longed to comfort her, to wrap my arms around her and tell her everything would be okay. That we'd both made mistakes and we'd work it out, just the two of us, like we always had. But I'd suffered for weeks, wondering what she was up to, finding one clue after another. The pain had fed on itself, growing into a monster bent on retribution, and my momentary spark of compassion drowned in a welling desire for vengeance. I hung up without saying goodbye.

I marched straight to her jewelry box. What an absurd place to hide her lover's phone number. It was like she'd wanted me to catch her. Hmm. Wonder what her psychology manuals would say about that. I snatched the scrap of paper from its hiding place and wadded it up in my fist. The second punch. The knockout should be easy after that.

Twelve minutes later, I heard Lora come in through the kitchen door. She stopped in the den, looking ragged and pale, and shrugged out of her jacket. When she met my gaze, the sympathy in her eyes curdled my blood. Who the hell did she think she was? Did she think I couldn't handle it? Well, I could and I was about to show her how well.

I charged, hurling the wadded scrap of paper at her. It bounced off her chest, her hands flailing after it as it dropped to the floor. Lora seemed to be in a daze. She watched Jitterbug scamper toward the note and sniff it.

"Did you really think you could keep this from me?" I screamed, pointing toward the paper on the floor.

She stooped and picked it up, straightened it out, and glanced at the writing before wadding it up again and stuffing it into her skirt pocket. "How was I so careless?" she muttered.

"I don't know. How *were* you so careless?"

She stumbled to the sofa and sat down. Lora's eyes scanned the room as her thoughts found words. "You shouldn't find out this way. It's not right. It's not time."

"I think it's high time, past time really." I stood firm, arms crossed, but inside my true voice cried out, come on baby, tell me I'm wrong. Lie to me and I'll believe you. Please, honey, say it's not true.

She shook her head.

"How long has this been going on?"

She faced me, but didn't meet my eyes. "I've been seeing her for about six weeks."

CHAPTER 38

I rock back in my chair and look at the clock—it's nearly noon. I've been dodging Choppy's for three days, citing meetings and a full calendar when Rebecca asks why. Truth is, I'm afraid to see her. Despite the crippling guilt stabbing at me from all sides, Saturday night's affair is etched into my mind, a hypnotic watercolor of swirling shades. Rebecca's touch haunts my dreams, her eyes fill my waking hours, and her whispers echo within my ears. I've got to stop this.

My one redeeming grace is that part of me is still chaste, thanks to my pesky period, but now my hormones have leveled and I'm free. The only thing standing between Rebecca and my body is my ever-weakening resolve, and if I see her, that could melt as easily as springtime snow.

But it's time to stand up and do the right thing. I'm tough. I can sit down with her, explain that I just can't get involved, that she's a wonderful person and deserves someone who can give her more. Maybe we can even still be friends.

Mary, the office manager, breezes in and drops a folder on my desk. She stops dead, her Elizabeth Taylor eyes boring into mine. "What's wrong with you?" So much for the Liz Taylor image—by the sound of her voice, Mary had razor blades for breakfast.

"Wrong? Nothing's wrong."

"Horse manure." She plants her hands on her hips, a defiant posture I've come to detest over the years.

"Is this the proposal for Triad Bank?" I snatch the manila folder from the corner of my desk.

"Don't ignore me." Her breasts jiggle in time with her tapping foot. "You've always been so focused, Claire. I know you've had a rough patch, but lately you've been downright strange. One day you're happy as a lark, and the next you look like you've lost your best friend."

"Maybe I'm manic-depressive, or whatever they call it these days. Bipolar?" I open the folder and pretend to read.

"Hogwash. If there's anything wrong with you that a good kick in the hindquarters wouldn't cure, I'll eat my hat."

"You're not wearing a hat."

"Don't tempt me. I am wearing size nine heels, and I'm not afraid to use them." She raises a clenched fist and waves it near my face. If she makes good on her threat, the diamond on her ring finger might leave a mark.

"No one ever accused you of minding your own business, did they?"

"Not when I see someone acting as odd as you. I've kept my big trap shut for a long time, but I know what's going on with you." Mary tucks her skirt beneath her as she perches on the edge of the visitor's chair. She reminds me of myself as a kid. I'd ask Mom for a quarter, and she'd say I couldn't have one, but I'd stand there till she got tired of looking at me and gave in.

"You can't know, Mary. You think it's easy for me because I'm different."

She huffs and rolls her eyes. "Don't go playing that queer card on me. I don't buy it. Love is love, no matter who's involved. And make no mistake, Miss Prissy, I know all too well what it's like to be with someone one day and wake up alone the next. I wasn't much older than you are when my first husband left." She stops and shakes her head, lips pressed into a tight red line, eyes far away. "That's water under the bridge, but the point is..."

I put down my pen and give Mary a hard stare. "Look, I'm sorry if I underestimated your open-mindedness, and I appreciate your concern. I've gotten a little off track, that's all, but I'm back on now and everything's fine."

"You take the cake, you know that? Once you set your mind to something, you're as stubborn a person as I've ever come across." Mary leans toward me. "That track you're so proud of being on just may be a dead end. Think about that." She doesn't look at me again as she rises and leaves.

Dead end, live end, who cares? It's my track and I'm staying on it. If you're lucky, you get one great love in your life, and I've had mine. Anything else would be a lie. Yes, I've stumbled, been tempted to play at a fake relationship, but that's all over. I'll clean up the mess I've made with Rebecca and forget all this ever happened.

* * *

I steer into Choppy's parking lot and have trouble finding a space. Good, Rebecca will be busy. I park under a budding elm tree near the street and check my makeup in the rearview mirror. As I stroll toward the building, the sunshine is warm on my face, but a gentle breeze reminds me that we could still have some cool nights ahead. My heart sags at the thought—cool nights spent alone in a big house with a cocker spaniel and a horror movie. On the bright side, I'll be saving a bundle on lunch tabs.

Inside the restaurant, I wait to be seated. The balding man in front of me is wearing too much aftershave, and I sneeze four times before he leaves. When the hostess leads me to a booth near the bar, I sit down and bury my head in the menu.

"Hello, stranger." Rebecca slides into the seat across from me. That didn't take long.

I put my menu aside. Big mistake. She's smiling, her eyes holding mine, that infernal dimple begging me to kiss it.

My knees go weak, and I struggle to keep my voice level. "Looks like you've got a good crowd today."

"Not too bad for a Wednesday." Rebecca glances around before looking back at me. She leans in. "I've missed you."

I look around the bar as if I'm expecting someone. "Work has been crazy this week. Three of my local sales reps have huge projects on my desk, and one of my installation foremen is out with a broken arm."

"How are things aside from work?"

"About the same. Jitterbug is due for shots next week, and I need to make an appointment with the vet. Jared and Elizabeth are taking a vacation, and the kids are going to stay with me this weekend. I'm not looking forward to that. They can be a real handful. Tonya says to tell you hello. How are things with you?" I'm talking so fast the words are running together, making little sense.

"Nothing special. Work, work, work. You know how it is."

A harried waitress I haven't seen before scoots up to the table and brushes a shock of blonde hair from her eyes. "Hi, welcome to Choppy's. I'm Diane, and I'll be taking care of you today. What can I get for you?"

Rebecca gives her an approving smile and looks at me. "Diet Sprite and a garden salad with ranch dressing?"

"Yes, that'll be fine." I fold the menu and give it to the waitress who scurries to the next table.

I arrange my silverware. "I hear we're supposed to have nice weather this weekend, temperature may hit the seventies on Saturday."

"That's what I heard, too."

She's scanning me. I hate it when she does that. It's like she can see right into me.

Rebecca nudges my foot with hers. "I was hoping we could get together again soon."

I look at her again and my determination slips a notch. I roll my shoulders and stretch my neck, but the muscles get tighter. "Uh, yeah, we'll get together sometime soon."

Rebecca peeks at her watch. "Listen, I've got some paperwork upstairs that I need to take care of. Want to go up with me for a minute? We can take your lunch with us."

After a long pause, I say, "Okay, but only for a minute. I've got to get back to the office."

I follow Rebecca to the bar where she tells the waitress we'll pick up my order in the kitchen.

This isn't going as planned. I was supposed to let her know I cared about her as a friend, but instead, I'm thinking about attacking her as soon as her apartment door closes. I imagine her scent filling me, her lean body against me, her lips on mine.

No, this isn't going well at all.

CHAPTER 39

I didn't hear the bathroom door slam behind me, or the lock click into place; didn't feel my knees hit the tile floor, or the contents of my stomach splash into the toilet. But I heard the banging on the door and her ambiguous words pounding in my head.

I sat on the floor, my back against the wall. The tile was cool under my hands. Emotions bounced around my head. I told myself it wasn't true, tried to convince my intellect that it was all a bad dream. Despite my suspicions, despite all the signs, I'd held out a shred of hope. Lora would never betray me, never let someone else's hands touch her, someone else's lips kiss her. I'd wanted to be wrong, prayed to be wrong, but it was true. Lora had admitted seeing someone else.

Horrid visions flashed in my mind. An unknown shadow groped her naked body, and Lora writhed with pleasure beneath it. The visions became clearer until my senses were overwhelmed by the imagined sound of her breathing, the aroma of her sex, the vision of her nails tracing tiny lines down someone else's back.

Vomit surged again, and I scrambled back to my knees and retched into the toilet. Acid burned my throat. I couldn't breathe. I sat there five, maybe ten minutes, staring at the bathtub, my worst fear smothering me.

Lora was still banging on the door. "Claire, what the hell are you doing? Are you all right? Let me in."

I didn't answer, didn't move. My head roared with questions that had no real answers. Why did she stop loving me? What did I do so wrong? How had I mistreated her? Frantic, I searched my memory for some evil deed, something rotten enough to force her into someone else's arms.

Everything around me looked fuzzy—gleaming brass faucets, monogrammed hand towels, beveled mirror. Was this what my life had come down to, an unfocused photograph of the perfect suburban bathroom? Is that what I'd worked so hard for, spent so many nights on the road for, to end up cowering on the floor, broken and alone?

My pain surged into a hurricane of anger, rage braced to lash out at anything. I jumped to my feet, lungs heaving. In the mirror, I caught my reflection, but it wasn't me. It was an animal, wounded, furious, and poised to attack. It was that animal who raised her fist and slammed it against the mirror. When the mirror shattered, a shard of glass struck my fist, slicing a long, jagged cut between my knuckles and along the back of my hand. I stood there, looking at my torn flesh, watching red ooze spill out.

"Claire, goddamn it, if you don't unlock this door, I swear I'm going to break it down!"

I struggled to speak, barely able to voice my rage, "Break it down, you bitch. You and your whore, break it right on down. You can take this whole goddamned house and shove it up your asses, brick by fucking brick."

Then a strange sense of nothingness came over me. Something in my brain dulled my awareness, shut down the delirium, and left me standing there, watching my blood drain down the sink.

A distant pounding assaulted my ears, metal against metal. Once, twice, and again. Then a rustling noise, creaking, splintering wood.

The door flew open and Lora rushed in. Her eyes fell on my bloody hand. "Oh, my God. What did you do?"

She tossed the claw hammer aside and reached for me, but I recoiled, slinging crimson spatters onto the floor. "Don't touch me. Don't you dare touch me."

"Look at me." She grabbed my shoulders and turned me toward her. I couldn't meet her eyes. She snatched a towel from the bar beside the sink and wrapped it around my hand. "Jesus. I was afraid of something like this."

She pressed hard on the cut for several seconds, then unwound the towel and inspected the damage. As she turned on the faucet, I noticed her hands. God, I loved her hands—strong but gentle. Where was I going to find hands like hers?

"You're going to need stitches." Lora didn't look at me as she wet the towel and rewrapped it around my hand.

I just stared at her. My lover, a stranger.

Lora pressed the towel tight. Her touch made the hair on my arms stand up. She took my chin and made me look into her eyes. "Claire, listen to me. Are you listening?"

I nodded.

"You're a survivor. You're going to get through this." Tears streamed down her cheeks.

I shook my head. "No."

"Yes." Her voice trembled. She swallowed, blinked hard, and swallowed again. "I'm going to take you to the hospital and get you stitched up. We'll talk about it when we get home."

"No."

"We have to talk about it. There's no going back now." She took my free hand; her skin was like ice. "Don't worry, I've worked out all the details. I've tried to make this as easy as possible on you."

"Easy? You think this is easy?" I had no more tears. My face felt like it would burst.

"You're right, it won't be easy." She wrapped her arms around me. I leaned into her and held her tight.

"Baby, please don't leave me. Whatever I've done, I'll make it right, I promise. I can't live without you." My knees buckled and we sat on the floor together. Lora held me, rocking, whispering, and telling me it would be all right.

I wanted to believe her.

CHAPTER 40

I follow Rebecca through Choppy's kitchen. A cook wearing a hairnet and stained apron is quartering tomatoes with a serrated knife. She glances at us, then returns to her work.

Rebecca picks up my salad and drink from the prep line and covers the plate with plastic wrap. She backs out the security door into the brisk outside air. As she climbs the stairs ahead of me, her hips sway close to my face. An itch shoots through my privates. The need to be with her is overwhelming, suffocating.

When we reach the top of the stairs, she turns to me. "Don't look at the mess. I was running late this morning and didn't have time to make the bed." She hands me the salad and drink, fishes her keys from her pocket, and unlocks the door.

I follow her in and look around, expecting the place to be trashed, but aside from the crumpled bedclothes, the apartment looks fine. There's a blue coffee cup in the sink and a pair of sweat socks in front of the sofa. Wonder what she'd say about my house if she saw it after one of my weekend pity parties.

Rebecca drops her keys on the kitchen counter and heads for the filing cabinet that I never fixed for her.

"I'll take another look at the filing cabinet if you want me to." I put my salad and drink on the counter and glance nervously out the window. The clear sky reminds me of last Saturday, when we went horseback riding. It's a natural progression when my thoughts meander to Saturday night and I remember the feel of her arm draped around my waist as she slept. She looked so serene, a lingering afterglow flushing her cheeks, an air of satisfaction surrounding her.

I haven't changed the sheets since our rendezvous. I realize that every night since, I've snuggled up to her pillow. I shudder despite the apartment's stuffiness.

Rebecca digs through some files, her back to me. "Don't worry about this hunk of junk. I'm going to replace it. Got any suggestions?"

"I might be able to set you up with a new unit." I take a step toward her. The fixation is supposed to be under control. For the past few days, I've done everything to tamp out my desire, but now that we're alone, it's back with a vengeance. It drives me toward her and weakens my conviction to end this before it's too late.

When I'm within two feet of her, she turns and smiles, jabbing another spear into my armor. "I'll trust you," she says as she whizzes past. I follow her back to the kitchen. She opens the manila folder and spreads its contents on the table. "I know I've got a copy of that bill somewhere."

Somehow I expected to be fighting her off, explaining how I can't carry our relationship farther, how she's a great person and anyone would be lucky to have her. Instead, I'm half-chasing her around the studio with no idea what might happen if I catch her.

I stuff my fists into my jacket pockets and shift my weight from one foot to the other. My shoes feel too tight. "Rebecca, I think we need to talk."

She freezes but doesn't look up. "About what?"

"The other night, when we... when..."

She finally looks at me from the corner of her eye. "When we made love?"

"We didn't make love. We fucked." Okay, that was a low blow, but I let it stand.

Hurt skips across her face, but she doesn't flinch. I can barely hear her voice when she says, "Call it what you want to, Claire, but I'm a big girl and I know the difference. I think you do, too."

"I just meant... well..." I clear my throat and try to remember the speech I rehearsed this morning in front of the bathroom mirror. "It's not you. It's me. I'm not in a position to get involved. I never will be."

Rebecca gazes at the stack of papers, blinks, and looks back at my eyes. "If that's the truth, the real honest-to-God truth, then I have no choice but to accept it."

"You think I'm lying?" A flash of anger rises within me—that's better.

"I think you're kidding yourself."

There's nothing confrontational in her posture or tone, but I go on the defense. "I kidded myself for a lot of years, but now, if there's one thing I do know, it's how to face facts. I learned it the hard way."

She removes a single sheet from the stack, closes the folder, and steps past me.

I follow her with my eyes. "Just out of curiosity, why do you think I'm kidding myself?"

She crams the folder back into the filing cabinet. "I shouldn't have said that. Forget about it. If you say you face facts, then you do."

"No, I want to know."

"Look. I'm sorry if I misunderstood what we've been doing for the past few weeks. Obviously you don't want the same thing I do, so let's just keep it friendly, okay? We had some fun together. I don't want to end up regretting it."

"Come on. You think you know me, so let me have it."

"Why are you trying to pick a fight? I heard what you said. I don't like it, but I respect it, okay?"

"But you don't understand, do you?"

Rebecca takes a few steps toward the kitchen before stopping. She shoots bullets at me with her eyes. "Are you going to explain yourself?"

When I don't reply, she says, "I thought not."

"Why do you say I'm kidding myself?"

"Since you're so determined, I'll tell you. I think you're so hung up on your ex that you'll never give anyone else a chance. You want to fight with me so you don't have to deal with the fact that you might have feelings for me. You'd rather not even try than risk getting hurt again."

"You've got it all figured out, haven't you?"

"No, there's one thing I don't have figured out. Why in hell are you so attached to someone who obviously doesn't want to be with you? If she's so great and you two were so in love, then why aren't you snuggled up like bugs in a rug?"

Something inside me starts to boil. I shouldn't be standing here listening to this crap. She doesn't know anything, and she sure doesn't know me. I turn toward the door.

"Wait, Claire, don't leave like this." She catches my arm. "I don't want to fight. I honestly don't understand what's going on, but I do care for you, probably more than you think."

I spin on her, ready to lash out, but the kindness in her eyes overwhelms me. I pull her close and hug her tight. "I'm sorry, Rebecca. I should never have let this get so far. I knew from the beginning it could never be anything, but you're just so smart and kind, and..."

"Sexy. Don't forget sexy."

"Oh, God, I could never forget that." With an awkward laugh, I step back and hold her at arm's length. "You're something else."

"And I'm going to make some lucky woman very happy, right?"

"That's not exactly what I was going to say."

"Close enough. I don't know what it is about you, but I seem to know what's going on in your mind. I don't understand it, I just know it." Her eyes are wet. "I don't think you want to break it off. But for some reason, you're going to." She watches my expression, and when I don't reply, she says, "Damn. I knew it."

"I'm sorry, but I just can't be with anyone else." The confusion in Rebecca's swirling green eyes deepens. There's only one way to make her understand, but the demons are still alive, still jabbing at me after all this time. Can I show them to Rebecca? Can I let her see the person I really am?

"Talk to me. I'll try to understand."

"It's complicated. In my head, it makes perfect sense, but when I try to say it out loud..."

"Give me a chance. Let me try to see it your way. If you never want to see me again, I'll respect your decision. But at least tell me why. I mean the real why, not this other crap you've been feeding me about not being in a position to do this."

She's right, I owe her this much. I take a deep breath and steel myself. "Her name is Lora."

CHAPTER 41

The sky had gone cloudy, so when Lora punched the remote on the visor and the door rose with a moan, the garage remained dim. The beige towel around my cut hand was ruined. The bloodstain looked like an inkblot in one of Lora's psychology textbooks. Come to think of it, the pattern did resemble Mrs. Dally, my third-grade teacher, with its big fat center and wild hairy spikes shooting out from all sides.

Lora looked out the rear window as she backed the Camry out of the garage. Then she glanced at my hand. "Hold it up."

Keeping the towel in place with my left hand, I hugged my right hand to my chest. I didn't feel the same urgency to get to the hospital that she seemed to. Sure, there was a lot of blood, but the cut didn't seem deep. I could wiggle my fingers, and it didn't hurt that much, just felt like a bee sting.

We whizzed out of the driveway and onto Valley View Drive. When we reached the first corner, Lora made a rolling stop and revved the engine as she turned left onto Lakebridge.

I was in a fog, trying to make sense of the day. I'd found the brochure from the lodge, decided to confront Lora, and gotten myself all worked up for the fight of my life. I was going to be cool and in control, but when she'd admitted to seeing the other woman, I'd gotten hysterical and made an ass of myself by breaking a perfectly good bathroom mirror and slicing open my hand in one fell swoop.

"Just tell me why," I said.

She shook her head. "There is no why. These things just happen."

"That's a sucky answer. Quit being a fucking analyst for five minutes, will you? Just tell me how it happened."

"How?" She glanced at me from the corner of her eye. "I don't know for sure. It's complicated."

She started in on one of her drawn-out explanations about how the brain works, but I cut her off. "Okay, skip the details. Just tell me this. Is she better than me?"

"Who? Better how?" Lora gunned the engine.

"I want to know if she's a better lover than me."

Lora snapped her head around and looked at me. "A better lover? What the hell are you talking about?"

"I figure this *Z* must be one spectacular fuck. Or maybe I just got boring after all this time." Bitterness lingered on my tongue. I shrugged and looked out the window so she wouldn't see the tears in my eyes.

Lora slammed on the brakes and steered the car to the shoulder. "You think I'm sleeping with Zola?"

"So that's her name? Zola? She sounds old. What is she, about sixty?"

"She's seventy, for Christ's sake, and she's my therapist." Lora grabbed my shoulder and pulled me around to face her. "I wouldn't fuck Zola Hart, or anyone else for that matter."

"Zola Hart?" The Z, the drawn heart. Was it just shorthand for her therapist's name? Had I been wrong all this time? I was stunned, caught between wanting to believe her and dismissing her lies. "But the phone number, the late nights, and that receipt from Damron's... I know you weren't with June that night."

Lora closed her eyes and rubbed her temples. "You're right, I wasn't with June. I invited Zola out for drinks, and we talked. That's all, I swear."

"The receipt wasn't for your credit card. So you invited her out, and she paid?"

"That's right. She's very wealthy—her husband sold some kind of software design to Microsoft for a bundle. She never lets anyone else pay for anything, and she just takes on special cases in her spare time. That night at Damron's was when I asked Zola if she'd take me on as a client."

"But all the other... I found receipts..." I stammered, trying to make her explanation fit, wiggling the new scrap of information in and out of the puzzle I thought I'd already solved.

"Baby, I know I've been acting weird, but I've had a lot of things to take care of. I swear, I've never cheated on you."

She shifted into park and leaned across the armrest. We fell into each other's arms, kissing, crying, laughing, repeating the words we'd said hundreds of times. "I love you, honey. Never be anyone but you. Only you. Please forgive me."

I don't remember who said what, but it didn't matter. For the first time in weeks, I knew Lora was telling the truth. I had been wrong, she wasn't having an affair, but it still didn't add up. She had no reason to keep therapy appointments a secret. It was routine for mental health workers to undergo therapy. If listening to other people's problems all day wouldn't drive you nuts, what would?

But hard as I tried, I couldn't get the puzzle to come together. She was upset about something, and it had nothing to do with my distrust or insecurity.

I pulled away and stared at her. "Look, I know there's more to this. What is it?"

"I thought you knew. Zola said you'd figured it out." Lora put her hand on my leg. A tear trickled down her cheek. "God, I didn't want it to be this way. I wanted us to have a nice weekend at the lodge." She looked at my hand. "It's still bleeding. We'd better go on."

Lora pulled back onto the road and swerved to miss a squirrel, nearly losing control of the car. "Remember that inner-ear infection I had about two months ago that I couldn't seem to shake?"

A strange tingling started up my legs. "Sure. You had to go through three rounds of antibiotics."

"It wasn't an ear infection." She signaled right and skidded onto Bingham Road. "How's your hand?"

"Forget my hand and slow down. If it wasn't an ear infection, what was it?"

"Dr. Powell ordered a series of brain scans, just to be safe." Lora's lower lip trembled, and she bit down hard on it.

"Brain scans? You mean an MRI? A CAT scan? You never told me that."

"I didn't want you to worry."

"Worry? I'm worried now. What the hell is going on?" I could barely speak around the lump in my throat.

She didn't look at me. "We've got a little problem."

"How little?" My stomach tightened.

"About the size of a grape." She tapped the right side of her head.

I couldn't bring myself to envision anything other than a soft, sweet fruit. A grape wasn't threatening. Grapes were good, tiny surprises that rolled past my tongue alongside slivered almonds in my mother's chicken salad.

More tears flowed down her cheeks. "It's inoperable."

Lora's words drifted past me, falling impotently around my ankles. I wrapped the towel tighter around my hand. "I think the bleeding is slowing down."

"Claire, did you hear me?"

"Probably won't take more than six or seven stitches."

"I have a brain tumor."

"Guess I won't be playing racquetball for a while."

"It's growing."

"Hope it doesn't leave a scar."

"They can't stop it."

"I hope Jared's working. Elizabeth says he can sew you up better than a tailor."

"Claire, listen to me!" Lora's voice boomed and bounced off the steel roof. "I'm dying."

"Don't be silly. You're not dying. Dr. Powell is so old he can't read an X-ray. First thing tomorrow, we'll go to someone who knows what he's doing and get this thing cleared up."

"I've been to three doctors, and they all say the same thing. Depending on how fast it grows, I could have up to a year. Chemo might help slow it down, but it would buy me a few months at best."

"Bullshit. You can't trust the quacks around here. We'll go to Duke or Vanderbilt. Those people know what they're doing. Yeah, that's what we'll do. We'll drive over to North Carolina tomorrow and see the doctors at Duke. They'll get this cleared up, you'll see. It's all a big mistake, probably a glitch in the machinery. They have much better equipment at Duke, too."

A light rain started to fall, and Lora switched on the windshield wipers. "The best doctor at Duke has already reviewed my case and agrees with the prognosis."

"The people at Duke are idiots! We need to go to Vanderbilt. Yeah, that's it. We'll drive down to Nashville, and after they tell us everything's okay, we'll take in the Grand Ole Opry. That'll be fun, won't it? Maybe we'll see somebody famous."

I looked out the window. We were headed into the industrial part of town, an area dominated by dirty two- and three-story buildings and smokestacks that belched who knew what into the sky. The light rain had lifted a gummy residue from the street, and passing cars threw it against the windshield in tiny, smearing specks.

Lora's voice was low, resigned. "I'm not going to take chemo. I don't want to linger on, be a burden to you."

I laughed and sang, "She ain't heavy. She's my lover." The situation was ridiculous, absurd. Lora was thirty-six years old, for God's sake. She had another fifty years in her.

She smiled, then frowned. "The pain isn't bad yet, but it will be. Dr. Powell said he'd give me a prescription for morphine when the time comes. If that doesn't work, he's got stronger options."

Lora kept talking, but I didn't hear. I just gazed at her, scanning the line of her profile. I used to tell her that she looked like Sophia Loren, but she really didn't. Lora's beauty was softer, more delicate.

I concentrated on her lips, those full, kissable lips that took me to ecstasy for the first time so many years before and could still lead me there over and over again.

Lora took my hand and interlocked our fingers. "Claire? Are you listening? Claire, snap out of it."

Somehow I managed to face her. Those eyes. God, those eyes. And that smile, now turned into a worried frown. I squeezed her hand. "I love you."

She was still looking at me, through me like she always could. She knew what I couldn't say, understood the feelings inside me that went beyond expression. Lora was the only one who'd ever known me, the real me, the scared kid who had fallen in love with her best friend on a rainy afternoon in October. All that love couldn't just vanish, not after all we'd shared, not after all we'd discovered together. It certainly couldn't be destroyed by something no bigger than a grape. It just couldn't.

Lora smiled at me. "I wouldn't change a thing, baby. You've made my life worth living."

I smiled back.

Then I cried.

Lora lived for seven months and sixteen days.

I died right then and there.

CHAPTER 42

"Lora didn't leave me. She's dead."

I've never said the words out loud before, and they hang in the air, each letter a dagger that stabs at my eyes. I blink back tears.

Here I am, sitting at Rebecca's kitchen table, telling her my sob story, while my lover is lying under six feet of hard-packed earth in a grave I haven't visited since the funeral. The funeral. What a joke. Mrs. Tyler wouldn't look at me. Can't blame her, I couldn't look in the mirror for weeks. If I had, I would have seen a pitiful shell of a woman with no more concern for her appearance than a bag lady. I probably sounded like one of those poor souls who roam the streets, talking to no one, laughing at nothing, crying at everything.

Rebecca sits across from me, arms folded, shoulders hunched. She dries her eyes. "I don't know what to say. I had no idea."

"I've never told anyone how I cut my hand, not even Fly or Elizabeth. As far as they know, I was cleaning the mirror when it broke. I never meant to tell you, but then I never meant to... anyway, you have a right to know."

"Why didn't you tell anyone the truth?"

"What was I going to tell them? That Lora was dying and she tried to protect me from it, but I went nuts and accused her of cheating on me? Some partner I turned out to be, huh?"

"You're being way too hard on yourself. You knew that Lora was hiding something, and cheating was the only thing that made sense at the time."

I take a napkin from the sunflower dispenser and mop my forehead. "She never talked about the day I cut my hand. She didn't bring it up once."

Rebecca sits quietly for a moment, then takes my hand. "Claire, you made a mistake, but it doesn't justify beating yourself up for the rest of your life."

"It's not just the mistrust. I wasted so much time trying to prove that I could give Lora as much as anyone could. I said I was doing it for

223

her, but that's not true. It was all to make me feel better about myself. My time was what Lora wanted. I should've been with her, taking her on those vacations she always dreamed about. I should've been there." I drop my head. "I begged her to forgive me, but she said there was nothing to forgive."

Rebecca touches my hand. "She was right. You did what you thought was best at the time."

"I'll never be convinced of that. She was the love of my life, and when she told me what she needed, I didn't listen. And in the end, I didn't trust her."

"This sounds corny, but maybe you need to look at the other side. You had something very special, something most people never find."

"I know I should be glad for the time we had, but I can't help feeling cheated."

"You were cheated."

"It's a moot point. I just wanted you to know."

She gives my hand an easy squeeze. "I wish you had told me sooner. I might have done things differently."

"You'd have pitied me, and I don't want that." I try to clear my throat, but the lump won't leave. "You see, Rebecca, when we were together, you weren't with me out of pity. I felt like you really wanted to be with me."

"I wouldn't have pitied you. Maybe I would have understood a little better what you've gone through. But now I know, and it doesn't change how I feel about you. I don't want to replace Lora, I never did. But I was hoping maybe there would be a space in your heart for me, too." She smiles. "I won't take up much room."

"That's the thing, Rebecca. You're the kind of woman who deserves a whole heart, all the space there is, and I don't have it to give. I tried to fool myself into believing this could be a casual thing, but it can't. I do care for you, and I want to love you, but there will never be anyone for me but Lora."

"What would Lora say about that? Would she want you to waste the rest of your life mourning her?"

"I never asked." That much is true. During Lora's last months we talked about a lot of things—life, death, love, fate—but I never let my future without her come up. Near the end, when she couldn't speak, I did all the talking, making grand promises, vowing my eternal fidelity. She heard me. I know she did.

I get up, and Rebecca follows me to the door. We stand in awkward silence for a second, then I say, "Come here."

Our embrace is tentative at first, but we soon relax and give each other a real hug. Her spicy perfume drifts into me, taking me back to my bedroom on Saturday night when her thighs closed around my ears, leaving me deaf and blind in the darkness, only her essence stimulating my senses. Rebecca is as overwhelming now as she was that night. I long to kiss her, but it wouldn't be right.

She puts her lips close to my ear. "If you want to call me, you can, okay?"

I nod, and as we part, she touches my cheek. I open the door and glance back. She's smiling.

A strange feeling creeps out of my subconscious. This is over, right? I'm going home, back to the way things were before Rebecca. Jitterbug and me. Elizabeth or Tonya over most every night, ragging me about one thing or another. Reggie worrying about sales, and Mary leaving the coffeepot empty.

That's my life, right?

* * *

I slip my hand under the faucet to check the temperature. Hot as hell—perfect. I shrug out of my robe and drop it to the floor. Steam bathes my skin as I shut off the tap and ease into the tub. Jitterbug sniffs my robe and shoots me a cockeyed glance before curling up on the bathmat.

Ever since I left Rebecca, something's been bothering me. A tiny mosquito darts around my head, barely in my field of vision. But when I turn to get a good look, it's gone.

I reach for my scotch and find it by the tub. One long pull, and the ice bumps against my lips. Four drinks and a hot bath. I'm finally warm inside and out.

I lean back and cover my eyes with a damp washcloth. The scotch is kicking in, and I start drifting away, flying to a place where nothing hurts and no one leaves.

"What the hell is your problem?"

I snatch the cloth from my eyes. Lora is in the tub with me. Her hair is in a loose bun with stray tendrils dangling around her bare shoulders. She's frowning.

"What are you doing here?" I'm strangely unfazed by the fact that she's been dead for three years.

"I thought it was time I straightened your ass out." She grins and blows bubbles toward me.

"Okay, if you say so." I watch her expression go from playful to serious.

"Why did you leave her?" Lora asks.

"Who?"

"Rebecca."

"How do you know about her?"

"I know everything. It's one of the perks of being deceased." Lora glances at Jitterbug. "God, she's grown."

I look at Lora, watch the way her lips curl around her words and the way her eyes wander over me. It's almost like she's really here. But I'm dreaming, right? It's one of those trite conversations we've had dozens of times since her death. My reply is old hat, the same thing I've been telling myself and everyone else. "Rebecca isn't you, Lora. You're the only person I'll ever love."

"You are so naive." She takes a long look around the room. This is not one of those shadowy hallucinations where she is a smoky apparition skulking in the fringes of my sedated brain. This is Lora, clear as day, being her real self, and knowing me down to the bone.

"Loyal, that's what I am." I try to sit up but can't. Even my arms are useless now.

She smiles. "You want to be with her."

"Do not."

"Liar."

I huff out a long breath and look away. Jitterbug is still lying on the bathmat, snoring like a moose, a calming reassurance that this isn't real. "I won't cheat on you."

"It's not cheating, hotshot. I'm dead, remember?"

"Oh yeah, I remember all right."

She shakes her head and another strand of dark hair escapes from the bun. Lora's never been like this before. In all my other dreams, she cursed me and blamed me for doubting her. I wonder how long it will take for this dream to degenerate into a nightmare.

"You're good now?" I ask.

"I'm better than good. I'm not suffering, and I still have you."

"Still have me?"

"That's my heaven, Claire. I get to be with you always. I watch you go to work every day, watch you come home at night. I've even seen you with Rebecca."

I blush. "I'm sorry."

"Why? You're happy when you're with her. You don't want to admit it, but it's true."

"No, it's not."

"I know everything, remember?" She props her arm on the edge of the tub. A smirk crosses her mouth.

"You thought you knew everything when you were alive. You were wrong sometimes then, too."

"Listen to me, Claire. All those years, you lived for the future. You lived for the days when we'd have a bigger house, or nicer cars." She stares hard at me. "Well, hotshot, this is the future. How do you like it?"

I manage to meet her eyes. "It sucks."

"Baby, all you've got is today. Don't waste it." Lora leans forward and hugs her knees to her chest. "I love you, and I know you love me. That'll never change. But you don't owe me anything. You can't spend the rest of your life doing penance for something that wasn't your fault. I don't want that for you. This isn't about jealousy, or trust, or who's had sex with whom. It's about love, real love. We'll be together again some day, but not for a long time." She pauses. I'm hanging on every word as she continues.

"Think about what you'd want for me if the situation were reversed. Would you want me to play the long-suffering martyr, or would you want me be happy?"

Everyone's told me to try to look at it that way, but coming from Lora, it makes more sense. Crazy? Probably, but that's the way it feels.

I look at her, into her eyes. They're as vibrant as they've ever been. "You know what I did with Rebecca?"

She nods.

"I think I might have feelings for her. Guess you know that, too."

"Yes, but I understand something that you don't. Your feelings for her don't diminish your love for me." Lora makes a buzzing sound through her teeth. She's that freaking mosquito who's been teasing me all afternoon.

"You're saying it's okay, that I can love two people at the same time?"

Lora laughs with a snort and waves a cautioning finger. "Only because I'm dead. If you'd pulled that crap while I was still alive, I'd have kicked your ass."

"I would've deserved it."

"I'm glad you met Rebecca. She's shaken you up a little, made you think about being happy again." Lora takes another peek at Jitterbug before gazing at me. Her eyes go serious, but a smile lingers on her lips. "I have to go now, but think about what I've said."

"Please stay for a while." I try to reach for her.

"I can't, but I'm never far away. Just remember what I told you. I love you. Now wake up before you drown."

My body convulses, every muscle flexing at once. My elbow bangs the side of the tub, and numbing pain torpedoes up my arm. Water sloshes onto the floor, and Jitterbug jumps up and barks. I look around.

Lora is gone.

CHAPTER 43

There are five stages of grief. At least that's what Lora's old psychology textbooks say. There may be folks out there who'll add a stage or two, maybe give them different names, but I'll stick with the five as I understand them.

The first stage is denial. I like this one. The bad thing never happened. You're in a plastic bubble where nothing hurts. When I'm in denial, I expect Lora to walk in and tell me it was only a nightmare, a cruel trick played by my imagination to show me how much I had to lose. She holds me till it's over, till my fear evaporates like a spring frost.

The second stage is anger. This one hurts. You're mad at everyone and everything. If a hinge squeaks, it pisses you off. You fly off the handle if your boss smiles at you, and God forbid someone should cut you off in traffic. This is where I pace around the empty house and curse myself for being fallible and her for not being immortal. But I mostly curse God for putting me in an unfair universe.

The third stage is bargaining. This one's gotten me into a lot of trouble. You'll make a deal with God, with the devil, or anyone else who might have a hand in reversing your fortune. You'll beg, you'll plead, you'll gouge your own eyes out to make things different. I promised my love, my fidelity, my total loyalty, and it didn't change a thing. But, by God, I vowed to stick to my promises, just in case.

The fourth is depression. What an ordeal. You're lost, powerless. You don't want to live anymore, and in a way you don't. You don't get out of bed, go to work, or see your friends. Things like hunger or thirst don't affect you. This is where I spent days in bed, barely ate for weeks, and prayed the most awful prayers—the ones where you beg to die and get the suffering over with.

The fifth stage is acceptance. You realize there's nothing you can do to change things, and although you still wish for it to be different, you get on with your life. Of all the stages, this one is the most difficult.

A dozen times over the last three years, I thought I'd made it to the fifth stage, but I hadn't. Not even today.

All this sounds simple enough, a kind of metamorphosis where you pass through each stage in sequence and eventually emerge as a beautiful butterfly, content and happy. It doesn't work that way. It's possible to skip stages, go through the same one several times, or get stuck in a spot indefinitely. You can spend months in depression only to revert once again to denial and start the whole process over. Or you can save up your anger till the end and walk into a crowded store with an AK-47.

And that damn fifth stage will throw you for a loop. You'll think you're sitting pretty, accepting everything and moving on, only to end up making more bargains, lashing out in anger, and denying the whole mess. It can take years to get to the fifth stage, and in between, it's a game of emotional hopscotch. Today you'll toss the stone and skip depression. Tomorrow, you'll skip denial or bargaining, but any way you play, it's an uphill course.

The fifth stage dangles before me now, and it seems closer than ever. I sit at my desk and pretend to work, but if anyone's paying attention, they'll see I'm shuffling papers and watching the clock.

I cross my legs one way and then the other, but can't get comfortable. Wearing jeans and sneakers makes it hard to feel businesslike, but a skirt and pumps aren't appropriate for my mission this morning.

One more glance at the clock; it's almost time. One last glance at Lora's photograph. At last I think I understand the little smirk on her face, the knowing smile that's eluded me for so long. But I have to be positive before going on.

The clock's hands tell me it's 8:30. Time to go.

I snatch my purse and jacket from the coat tree and hurry to Reggie's office. He's busy playing computer solitaire and cursing under his breath.

"Reg, got to go. Personal stuff. See you later." He waves and grumbles something about needing a red seven before I add, "The quote for Medical Imaging Group is on Mary's desk."

I breeze past Mary and shoot her a smile. "See you. Make sure Reggie looks over that quote before he gives it to Bob."

"Under control." She looks up. "Jeans? Where are you off to in such a hurry?"

"Maybe the rest of my life." My reply is cut short as the door closes behind me.

I don't need my jacket. The morning is a crisp blue that promises more spring weather, more red tulips and golden daffodils that bloom and sway in warm breezes, making way for summer. New beginnings, new awakenings. Is my life, frozen so long under winter's cruel grasp, about to emerge, fresh and green like the spring flowers?

I jump in the car and head off down Park Street. I pull into the parking lot of Zimmer's Florist. The blue and white cardboard sign in the window says they're open. I leave the car running, and as I push through the wooden door, I realize my radio is blaring—I'm a middle-aged woman acting like a teenager. Bully for me, hope this one lasts.

A bell jingles as the door closes. It smells like a funeral home, the too-sweet smell of the dead.

A dark, heavy-set man with watery eyes emerges from the back room. "Can I help you?"

"Yes, sir. I'd like two of the most beautiful long-stemmed red roses you have." I dig out my wallet.

He smiles. "Oh, you're very lucky today. There's a new shipment in this morning. Wonderful product, beautiful color, aroma of the angels." He sniffs the air and waves toward Heaven as he disappears into the storage area. He returns with two lovely bloodred roses on the verge of bloom.

"Perfect," I say.

"Would you like these wrapped together?" He pulls a single sheet of green floral paper from under the counter.

"Separately, please."

"Very good." With hands seeming too delicate for his thick body, he tucks a sprig of baby's breath alongside each flower and wraps them. "Will there be anything more for you today?"

"That's all." I give him the money and he wishes me a good day.

Back in the car, I wipe my palms on my jeans. I hope this is a good idea. Hope it doesn't backfire and send me on a one-way trip to oblivion. The next half hour will either cure me or kill me. I say a prayer as I turn onto County Line Road and see my destination looming in the distance.

I steer through the wrought iron gates, along the single-lane blacktop, toward the top of a green hill. I read the names: Adkins, Fleenor, Housewright, Wheeler. Some have been here for decades, others for days, but none will ever leave. Young and old, weak and strong. Such distinctions don't matter anymore. Those who've been left here don't care about the statue of Jesus at the top of the first rise, or the

Well of Redemption in the valley below. This place isn't really for them. It's for the living, for me.

Driving slower now, I guide the car left and pull to the side. A twinge hits me. It might be fear, or maybe remorse, but I pick up one of the paper-wrapped roses and open the door. That part goes smoothly enough. One foot out, then the other. Close the door.

Squinting in the morning sun, I'm disoriented. I've only been here once before, and that time was more like a bad dream. Soon enough, the stone comes into view. *Tyler*, and underneath, etched in the granite, *Blevins*. It's weird seeing your own name on a tombstone. I recall the way Mrs. Tyler balked.

"It's blasphemy," she said. "Let my daughter be normal in death."

But Lora anticipated her family's reaction and had her desires put in writing, set in stone, as surely as our names appear before me now.

My steps are heavy as I make my way up the slope to her grave, the place I'll one day share. Nothing will change that. I stand before the slab, and for some reason, I can't stop smiling. She's only a few feet away, and although we're separated by something more than distance, something indefinable, her heart beats in my chest. Her strength flows through my veins.

"Hey, baby." I place the rose at the base of the headstone. "Guess you've been wondering about me, where I've been, why I haven't come sooner."

I brush three brown leaves from her grave and sit on the grass beside her. The ground is damp and cold, and I shudder.

"Truth is, I haven't had the heart to come. Seems like being here would be giving up on you, giving up on us, and that's the last thing I ever wanted to do."

I hug my knees to my chest and take a deep breath. "I had a dream about you last night, at least I think it was a dream. You told me to get on with my life. Guess that's why I'm here. You see, ever since you left, I've been in this dungeon that I couldn't seem to get out of, but something's happened. I met someone I think I might be able to love. It's hard to explain. It can't be like it was with you. Hell, we grew up together, but I'm different now. I know things I didn't know then.

"I can still have a good life, right? I've been such an ass to Rebecca. She may not have me now, but that's not the point. With or without her, I have to move ahead and try to learn from the mistakes I made with you."

I reach down, pluck a blade of grass, and wrap it around my finger. "Moving ahead is going to be hard. I need to know for sure that it's okay with you. Somewhere in my heart, I believe you really came to me last night, that you were really there. Tell me for sure, Lora. Let me know it's true."

I glance down toward her grave and that's when I see it, standing there like a beacon among the scrubby grass. A four-leaf clover, as big and fresh as the one Lora found at our first apartment, the one that still sits at my bedside. My eyes fill with tears. Jesus, it is true. She was there. She came to give me her blessing.

I pluck the clover and hold it to my lips. "I knew it. I knew it." I laugh out loud and wipe the tears from my eyes. I trace the letters of her headstone with my fingers. "Thank you, honey. Thank you for choosing me, for sticking by me when I was foolish, and for loving me when I didn't deserve it. Most of all, thank you for being you."

Anyone watching would think I belong in the funny farm, but who cares? My lover reached to me from her grave, and from the depths of death, she gave me new life.

I leap to my feet. "I love you, Lora. I'll be back soon, but right now I've got another rose to deliver."

CHAPTER 44

Okay, so maybe all this with the dream and the clover at Lora's grave is a big coincidence, but it feels real, so I'm not going to overanalyze it. I'm going to grab for this chance while I can.

It's nearly 9:30. I tromp on the accelerator—maybe I can catch Rebecca before she goes to work.

The drive seems to take an hour, but I skid into Choppy's in less than fifteen minutes. I speed toward the back and park beside Rebecca's Mercedes, cut the engine and grab the second rose. Up the steps and to the apartment door. One down, one to go.

I knock hard, hiding the rose behind my back, and Rebecca opens the door a minute later. She's wearing a blue Adidas warm-up suit and jogging shoes, and looks surprised. "Hi. I didn't expect to see you this morning."

"What's this?" I ask, eyeing her casual dress.

"I decided to take the day off. Needed a little time to myself."

"Am I intruding? If this is a bad time, I can come back later."

"No, not at all." She stands aside and motions me in. "What's got you out this morning?"

I'm holding my head down shyly, peeking up at her, as I pull the rose from behind me. "Peace offering. Can we talk?"

"You didn't have to do that, but thank you." Rebecca takes the rose and sniffs its petals. "Like some coffee? It's fresh."

"Sure."

She pours us each a cup, and we sit down at the table. She props her chin in her hand and looks me over, a sparkle dancing in her eyes. "I'm glad to see you."

There goes that blush again. I feel like a schoolgirl. I take a sip of coffee. "Rebecca, I've been acting like an idiot ever since we met."

"You're not an idiot. No one can blame you for being a little off your game, considering what you've been through."

I clear my throat. "After Saturday night, I flipped out a little. Probably because it meant something to me, something I didn't expect.

You were right. We made love. We didn't fuck, like I said. That was rude."

"Yes, it was."

"I'm very sorry for saying that. I'm also sorry for the way I've treated you." I take her hand, and she doesn't pull away. "What I'm getting at is this. I'd like to keep seeing you. If you'll have me, that is."

Rebecca gives me a long stare, then looks away. "I've done some serious thinking, and I'm not sure I'm up for it. It's kind of like the time I was a kid, and my parents took me to Carowinds. I begged to ride the roller coaster, but Mom knew that my stomach was as weak as hers, so she didn't want me to. But I kept on till she let me, and sure enough, I threw up all over the place. I haven't even been on a Ferris wheel since." She smiles, then she sighs and tucks her hair behind her ears. "Claire, I do care, but I can't get on an emotional roller coaster with you. I wish I were strong enough, but I'm not."

My heart sinks. I knew this was a possibility, and I can't blame her for feeling that way. "Fair enough. I understand, and I don't blame you. But if you ever change your mind..."

"Let me finish." She presses her index finger against my lips and holds it there. "I'm thinking that we need to get a few things straight right now." Rebecca's eyes meet mine with a focus I've never seen before. "I know how much you loved Lora, but I can't compete with a ghost and shouldn't have to.

"I wouldn't ask you to forget her. I don't want you to. But I'm not her, and I never will be. I guess what I'm saying is, if you want me, and not a Lora substitute, then I'm willing to take a chance."

I kiss her finger before pulling it from my lips. "I don't expect you to be Lora. You're right, I'll never stop loving her, and I'll never forget. But it's never been a competition between the two of you. I don't care for you because you remind me of her, or because I want you to be her. I care for you *despite* my love for her."

Rebecca wrinkles her brow and frowns. "That makes an odd kind of sense, I think."

I laugh. "So you know what I mean?"

"Kind of." She taps her index finger on the tip of my nose. "I had a feeling you'd come around but not so soon. I didn't really expect to see you for at least two weeks."

"You know me too well already. How long will it take for you to read my mind?"

"I'm reading it right now."

"So what am I thinking?"

As she leans in to kiss my lips, Rebecca whispers, "I love you, too."

About the Author

Margaret A. Helms is a Virginia native, who lived in Chicago and Washington, D.C. before making her home in Tennessee. She has a B.A. in marketing from the East Tennessee State University, and spent several years working in the finance industry. Now she runs a wholesale produce business with Amy, her partner of 10 years. Margaret will be graduating from massage therapy school in March of 2007, and hopes to open her own practice soon after that.

Blue Feather Books is proud to offer this excerpt from Val Brown and MJ Walker's enchanting love story,

Connecting Hearts

Available from

Bluefeatherbooks
LIMITED

www.bluefeatherbooks.com

Denise could never have imagined just how the events of the past two months would change so rapidly. She had given up writing altogether, a higher purpose taking precedence over even the most cherished aspect of her life. Sara. Her aunt had declined at a rate much swifter then even the doctors had expected. During the first few weeks after Denise had widened the doorframe to Sara's bedroom the old woman had begun to lose all strength in her ability to walk. It wasn't long before the need for a wheelchair became a high priority.

It had been a hard transition to make; neither Denise nor her aunt were prepared for the loss of independence that it entailed. Not only had Sara's lower body strength departed, but her upper body's strength too. There were the occasional good days when Sara did manage to complete the odd task by herself, but for the most part it became impossible, and she declined a little more every day.

To say that Denise hadn't felt the strain would have been a lie. Even the poet would admit to herself that some nights when she had finally made her way to bed—if she hadn't fallen asleep on the sofa first—she would pass out as soon as her head hit the pillow. It wasn't just looking after Sara that took it out of Denise. There were many times while she would be dressing Sara or brushing her teeth that the old woman would just sit and cry. Not that Denise minded in the slightest; she was adamant about taking care of her aunt. She would do whatever she had to and whatever it took.

Denise had made many alterations to the house. She had converted the downstairs bathroom, installing a liftable seat into the shower to make it easier for Sara to still enjoy the luxury of taking a warm shower. She had constructed a higher frame for her bed to make lifting from the wheelchair to the bed and vice versa much more convenient.

Days alternated between good and bad. Between days when Sara would seem stable, to days when her emotions would overwhelm her, or her disease would advance further and she would lose a little more strength and independence. Denise did know that she needed somebody, and had gone through the motions of interviewing several nurses. But deep down inside something was missing. She felt none of these men or women would look after Sara the way she wanted. Denise also knew that as much as Sara had insisted that they hire a nurse, the old woman hated the idea of having a complete stranger look after her in ways that she was finding difficult enough allowing her niece to undertake some things.

Through it all Denise had managed to keep her resolve with the help of one person. Randa. Though thousands of miles away, the nurse had provided help and emotional support to Denise when she needed it most. The friendship had grown, and even Denise would acknowledge that. Never did she expect that she would be able to share aspects of her life with anybody the way she had done with this woman.

Sometimes when the day had been especially draining, Denise would retreat to her room and look at the picture of the woman who unknowingly gave Denise the emotional strength she needed to carry on when times were rough. Never had she felt the ability to be so open with another individual, and never had she thought she would come to care for somebody as much as she found herself doing with this woman. She enjoyed their correspondence, their contention on the superiority of British or American chocolate and their easy friendship.

As Christmas approached she had no doubt about the fact that she would send Randa a gift, and Sara had wanted to do so as well. Denise had told Sara about their constant chocolate debates, and so Sara had asked her niece to send the nurse a selection of her favourite chocolates. Denise, on the other hand, found the prospect of purchasing a gift slightly more difficult. She wanted to give Randa something that echoed her appreciation and sentiment towards the woman, but she found it hard to recognise exactly what that was. Fortunately, it didn't take long for her unconscious mind to make the decision; she just hoped Randa would remember exactly what this object was.

Denise had ventured into her bedroom and had crouched down under her bed to retrieve a small shoebox. Inside this box she kept the trinkets and memorabilia of her parents. Her father's silver hip flask, cuff links, and a single cigar that was a constant reminder of his aroma. Her mother's earrings, bottle of perfume that had long since spoiled, lace handkerchief embroidered with her initials and an antique bracelet.

It was the bracelet that Denise was looking for, a simple golden charm bracelet with one charm, a golden capsule that unscrewed to reveal a small scroll of paper. Upon this scroll, in very small print, was Shakespeare's "Sonnet Number 116." As a child, the charm and sonnet inside had fascinated Denise. She had explained to Randa that it was this poem that had sparked her desire for lyrical verse.

Hoping Randa would appreciate and comprehend the raison d'être behind the gift, Denise had placed it into a small red velvet-inlaid wooden box and had wrapped it in silver paper with a light-blue ribbon. She had mailed the package a day later.

Find this and other exciting Blue Feather Books
at

www.bluefeatherbooks.com

or ask for us at your local bookstore.

Blue Feather Books, Ltd.
P.O. Box 5867
Atlanta, GA 31107-5967

Tel/Fax: (678) 318-1426

Printed in the United States
218827BV00001B/31/A